"Will gold warm your bed at night?

"Will they tend you when you're ill, or weep for you when you die?"

Dumbstruck, Con struggled into his breeches, trying to think of something, *anything* he could say that might convince Enid to have him on his own terms.

For once it was her turn to have the final word.

"I think the world of you. I'd sooner have you for my husband than any lord or prince. If you thought half as highly of yourself as I think of you, you'd have nothing to prove to anyone."

Without giving him a chance to reply, she closed the door of the wash house, plunging it once again into stifling darkness.

"I have nothing to prove." Con tried to believe it, but the words rang false in his ears and the empty place inside him gaped wider than it ever had before....

DEBORAH HALE

BORDER BRIDE

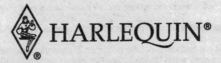

HARLEQUIN®

TORONTO • NEW YORK • LONDON
AMSTERDAM • PARIS • SYDNEY • HAMBURG
STOCKHOLM • ATHENS • TOKYO • MILAN • MADRID
PRAGUE • WARSAW • BUDAPEST • AUCKLAND

ISBN 0-373-29219-8

BORDER BRIDE

Copyright © 2002 by Deborah M. Hale

This edition published by arrangement with Harlequin Books S.A.

® and TM are trademarks of the publisher. Trademarks indicated with
® are registered in the United States Patent and Trademark Office, the
Canadian Trade Marks Office and in other countries.

Visit us at www.eHarlequin.com

Printed in U.S.A.

Please address questions and book requests to:
Harlequin Reader Service
U.S.: 3010 Walden Ave., P.O. Box 1325, Buffalo, NY 14269
Canadian: P.O. Box 609, Fort Erie, Ont. L2A 5X3

For my eldest son, Robert, the best birthday present
I ever received, who more than deserves a dedication
after eight books. Thanks for your patience, sweetheart!

Special thanks to Heidi Hamburg, who knew
just what kind of woman Con ap Ifan needed.

Chapter One

Have a care, now! a small voice whispered in Conwy ap Ifan's thoughts as he picked his way through the quiet, greening countryside of the ever-shifting border between England and Wales. *Watch your back. Stay on guard.*

He was a carefree, impulsive fellow by nature. It had taken him many years of mercenary service in the Holy Land and elsewhere to cultivate a sense of caution.

Con had the scars to prove it.

Perhaps he ought to heed that vigilant little voice, now. These borderlands, which Norman folk called The Welsh Marches, were far less serene than they might appear to the casual traveller on a fine spring day.

"Tush!" Con muttered to himself as he scrambled from stone to stone, fording a swift-flowing stream. Between planting and shearing, even Welshmen were too busy to make war at this time of year. And who'd take notice of a lone wanderer on foot, anyhow? Especially one with a bard's harp slung over his shoulder?

Once again Con congratulated himself on adopting such a clever disguise for this mission to his native land. In Wales, a bard could roam the country at will, with the door of every *maenol* open to him—always assured a seat of honor by the hearth, a good belly-filling meal, and a warm woolen *brychan* to roll himself in at bedtime.

When a bard plucked his harp and sang the heroic ballads that were his country's lifeblood, folk dropped their guard to listen. After the last notes died away, oft as not they'd tip another cup of ale or hard cider and grow talkative. Then Conwy ap Ifan, envoy and spy for Empress Maud, Lady of the English, would listen and weave another thread into his tapestry of intelligence about the Marches.

Not a spy! Con's sense of honor bridled. At least not in the usual sense of that word. He meant no harm to his countrymen, and never would he put the interests of a Norman monarch above those of a Welsh prince. However, if the ambitions of the border chiefs should harmonize with those of the Empress, it would make sweet music for all.

Sweetest for Con himself.

As he ambled along a well-trodden forest path, inhaling the rich, pungent scent of new life, Con recalled his Christmas audience with the Empress, and her special commission for him.

"My Lord DeCourtenay says you gave a good account of yourself when his forces recaptured Brantham Keep from Fulke DeBoissard. Thanks to the arrow you put through his elbow, that's one traitor who will never again hoist his sword against me. It takes a cool head and a true aim to turn your bow on a man who holds a knife to the throat of your dearest friend."

For all her imperial bearing, the lady had returned Con's admiring smile. Perhaps she'd been flattered that her arresting beauty still had the power to stir an attractive man some years her junior. Con had never been one to hide his appreciation of a pretty woman.

"Such a decisive fellow could be a great asset to me on

the Marches just now, sir. Particularly if he has an agreeable humor and a persuasive Welsh tongue in his head.''

Con had acknowledged the compliment and expressed his interest in hearing more.

The Empress chose her words with care. ''During these past years, while my cousin and I have contended for the throne, many Welsh border lords have seized the chance to take back lands conquered during the time of my sire and grandsire. It would be only fitting if my loyal southern Marches remained free of strife, while those manors which hold for Stephen of Blois suffered for their treachery.''

''Fitting indeed, your Grace,'' Con agreed.

As a Welshman, he had no sworn fealty to either the Empress or King Stephen, but his natural sympathy lay with Maud. For as long as he could recall, Con had always sided with the underdog in any fight.

The Empress swept a lingering look from the toes of Con's soft leather boots to the tangle of dark curls atop his head. She appeared to approve what she saw. ''A man who could tame some border lords on my behalf while inflaming others would be well rewarded for his labors.''

With a raised brow and a curious half smile, Con inquired what form that reward might take.

''I would be prepared to honor such an enterprising fellow with a knighthood.'' Maud's shrewd dark gaze probed his. ''Then I would equip him with suitable men and arms to return to the Holy Land. It would buy me favor with His Holiness the Pope as well as my husband's kinsman, the Prince of Edessa.''

Con had struggled to keep his face impassive, even while his heels yearned to break into a jig. By heaven, this woman could calculate a man's price to the groat. In a stroke she'd offered him the two greatest boons he had ever desired from life—advancement and adventure.

On this bright, green April day fairly bursting with promise, Con journeyed north, basking in the satisfaction of having fulfilled half his royal commission already. The more difficult half, to be sure, since it was a far easier task rousing Welshmen to war than persuading them to keep the peace.

During the long, dark months of winter, Con had made his way from cantrev to cantrev in the guise of a wandering bard. At each *maenol* he'd engaged in secret talks with the local border chief, counselling peace and consolidation of territory. Hinting at Angevine favor when Maud or her son, Henry, finally wrested the English throne from her cousin Stephen.

To a man, the chiefs of Deheubarth had heeded him.

Now with Empress Maud's promised reward beckoning, Con had come to Powys on the latter half of his errand, to stir up trouble for the Marcher lords of Salop. He judged himself at least another full day's journey away from Hen Coed, the stronghold of powerful border chieftain Macsen ap Gryffith.

When Con emerged from the eaves of the forest, he spied a thin plume of smoke rising from beyond the crest of the next hill. It must come from a dwelling of some kind. A dwelling where he could expect to receive warm hospitality on a cool spring night, along with the latest news from the surrounding country. All for the price of a song and a tale.

And if his usual luck held, he might find a comely lass among the household on whom he could exercise his ivory smile and extravagant flattery. Somehow, that prospect did not hold its usual appeal for Con.

Since coming to Wales, he'd found his appetite for feminine company unaccountably dulled. Could it be his age?

Though often mistaken for a good bit younger, he was a trifle past thirty.

Or was his fleeting interest in the women he met always tempered by bittersweet memories of *one* woman? Long-slumbering recollections roused since Con's boon companion, Rowan DeCourtenay, had found the one lady for whom he'd been destined.

Heading toward the smoke, Con shook his head and chuckled to himself. Queer that he should still burn for the one lass of whom he'd never made a conquest, when others he'd bedded had long since faded from his memory.

"Mother," sang nine-year-old Myfanwy as she skipped into the washhouse at Glyneira, "Idwal said to tell you there's a traveller come. Shall I fetch my harp and keep him company till supper? Or should I offer him water first?"

Enid looked up from her task of cleansing wool in the great iron cauldron. With the back of her hand, she nudged several fine tendrils of dark hair off her brow. They'd escaped her long braid, teased into curls by steam and sweat.

Traveller? Could Lord Macsen have come so soon?

Why did her belly suddenly feel full of wet wool at the thought of her chosen suitor arriving earlier than she'd expected him? Perhaps because Glyneira wasn't yet fit to receive such exalted company, she decided. For a dozen good sensible reasons, Enid wanted to wed the border chief. She couldn't afford to make an unfavorable impression.

"Of course you must offer him water straightaway, my pet. A big girl like you should know that by now." Enid couldn't help but smile at the child who looked so little like herself. Both Myfanwy and young Davy took after their late father, who'd had Mercian blood. "If our guest accepts, then we'll know he means to stay the night at least.''

The ceremonial offer of water to wash a traveller's tired feet was a tradition as old as the Welsh hills. If a guest refused, it meant he would not bide the night under his host's roof. If he accepted, then the hospitality of the house would be his for as long as he chose to stay. Enid cherished the comforting familiarity of such traditions.

Myfanwy bobbed her golden head, eager as eager. ''If the stranger says he'll take water, can I wash his feet?''

''Not this time.'' If Macsen had come to Glyneira, Enid wanted to make certain he was properly received—with her best ewer and basin, herb-sweetened water neither too hot nor too cold, and her softest cloths for drying. ''I'll see to it as soon as I tidy myself up. You can entertain him with your harping and singing, in the meantime. Go along now. Our guest will be pleased to hear you, I've no doubt, for you have a sweeter song than a linnet.''

As the child raced off, her mother called after her, ''Tell Auntie Gaynor I need her to come finish a job for me.''

The wool only wanted one more rinse. Enid knew she could trust her sister-in-law not to handle the fleece over-much and risk felting it.

Hiking up her skirts, she dashed the short distance from the wash shed to the back entrance of the house, startling an old goose that ruffled up its feathers and hissed at her.

''Keep a civil tongue, or I might pluck and roast you for our guest's supper,'' Enid warned the testy fowl.

The goose waddled off with its bill in the air.

The lady of the house managed to reach her own small chamber without being harassed further. After pulling off her coarse-woven work tunic, she rummaged in the chest at the foot of her bed, looking for an overgarment better suited to welcoming such an important guest.

A flash of green caught her eye. From the very bottom of the trunk Enid lifted a fine woolen kirtle, trimmed at the neck and wrists with close-stitched embroidery. Her breath caught in her throat as she held the garment in her hands.

During the years since she'd come to Glyneira, she had found one excuse after another to avoid wearing it, until she'd almost forgotten it existed. She had worn this fine garment on her wedding day, though it had been fashioned to impress a much grander bridegroom than Howell ap Rhodri.

It reminded Enid of all she'd risked once upon a time. And all she'd lost in the risking.

"Oh, don't be fanciful," she scolded herself as she slipped the garment over her head. "A kirtle's a kirtle and this is the best you own."

As she covered her hair with a fresh veil, a small boy barrelled into the chamber. A stubby-legged puppy scrambled through the rushes at the child's heels.

"Myfanwy said to tell you the man wants water." Blurting out his message, Master Davy looked ready to bolt out of the room as fast as he'd bolted in—until he caught a good look at his mother.

"What're you dressed so grand for, Mam?" Davy scooped up the puppy, who wriggled in his arms. "You look as fair as the queen of springtime. All you need is a crown of flowers in your hair like Myfanwy makes for hers."

"Queen of springtime, is it?" Enid blushed as she remembered a young fellow who'd once fashioned a garland of spring blossoms for her hair and offered equally extravagant praise to her looks. That fellow had danced all over her heart, then danced away...never to return.

"I mind you'll make a bard yet, Davy-lad." Enid ruffled

her son's honey-brown hair, determined *not* to let thoughts of Con ap Ifan spoil this moment. "But you make it sound as though your poor mother goes around like a slattern most of the time. Away with you now before that dog messes on the floor again."

As the boy ran off laughing, Enid noticed how tall he'd sprouted through the winter. It was a wonder he could still wriggle into his tunic, it had grown so tight. She'd have to look through her other trunk to see if there were any clothes Bryn had outgrown that might now fit Davy.

Thinking of her older son made Enid remember their guest. Of the many boons she stood to gain from wedding Lord Macsen, she most craved the chance to reunite her family. It'd been such a long time since Howell had sent the boy away for fosterage. She'd rather hoped Macsen might bring her son along on this visit.

A wistful pang gave way to questioning. It wasn't like Macsen ap Gryffith to travel alone, without a small but skilled escort of armed men. Did the border chief have reason to call on Glyneira in secret? Or could something be wrong?

From out of the chest Enid snatched a handsome basin and ewer of beaten copper along with linen drying cloths, all too fine for any but Glyneira's most honored guests. Making her way to the kitchen to fetch hot water, she schooled her steps to a brisk but decorous pace appropriate for a lady of the *maenol*. Her thoughts fluttered though, like doves in a cote when a fox prowled the ground below.

What if Macsen had changed his mind about the betrothal he'd hinted at when Howell lay dying? What if he'd never meant it in the first place—only wanted to calm her fears for the future? She'd managed well enough, had even come to enjoy being mistress of Glyneira in her own right instead of always deferring to a husband.

But the past winter had been an uncommonly quiet one. Such tranquility could not last on the borders. When strife erupted again, as surely it would, Enid wanted her children tucked up in the comparative safety of Hen Coed, buffered by a stout palisade with a canny warrior lord for a step-father.

Almost without her noticing it, the rhythm of her foot-steps quickened.

The nimble music of Myfanwy's harp greeted Enid as she entered the hall. For an instant the mellow glow of maternal pride radiated through her. Then she heard a second instrument join her daughter's, lower in pitch and more assured in touch. Myfanwy began to sing in her high, pure treble, while a masculine voice chimed in a pleasing harmony.

The voice had a most agreeable timbre in the mellow middle register, unlike the ominous resonant rumble of Macsen ap Gryffith's.

Enid crossed the cavernous hall with a halting gait, like a sleepwalker drawn by the Fair Folk. Something deep within her quivered to life at the sound of that all-but-forgotten voice. Or perhaps it shivered with foreboding.

She approached so quietly the two musicians did not pay her any mind at first. In the dim interior of the hall, Myfanwy's young face seemed to cast a radiance of its own, kindled by the admiring attention of their guest.

He was a handsome fellow. Not towering and brawny like Lord Macsen, but medium tall for a Welshman, his lithe frame fleshed with hard, lean sinew. The eastern sun had tanned his face since last Enid had beheld it, and any suggestion of boyish roundness had been pared away by the years.

Topped by a vigorous tangle of nut-brown curls, it was a well-shaped face in every way. Agile brows arched

above a pair of eyes that shimmered with lively charm.
Beneath the straight sloping nose with its potent flared nostrils, poised a tempting pair of lips. They were neither too
full nor too thin, but so ideal for kissing they made Enid's
own lips quiver just to look at them. Below that melting
mouth jutted a resolute chin, softened by the disarming
hint of a dimple. It was a face to break a woman's heart.

How many more had he broken since hers?

Clutching the basin with a remorseless grip to keep her
hands from trembling, Enid willed her voice not to catch
in her throat as she spoke loud enough to be heard above
the music.

"Well, well, Conwy ap Ifan, what are you doing in
Powys? The last I heard you'd hired out as a mercenary
to the Holy Land."

His voice fell silent and he glanced up at her with a
sudden questioning look. For a moment Enid's unhealed
heart wrenched in her bosom fearing he would not remember her.

Then his smile blazed forth. "Well, well yourself, Enid
versch Blethyn. What are you doing in Powys? The last *I*
heard, you were set to wed some princeling from Ynys
Mon."

Something about the set of his features or the tilt of his
head sliced through Enid like an arrow loosed at close
range from a powerful Welsh short bow.

Dear heaven! She must get Con ap Ifan away from
Glyneira before Macsen and his party arrived.

Chapter Two

A pity he couldn't linger here, Con found himself thinking as he cast an admiring eye over the *cariad* of his boyhood, since ripened into vivid, beguiling flower.

Enid's sudden appearance and sharp questions had taken him by surprise. Yet in another way they hadn't. Something about the child had put her mother firmly in his mind, though he'd scarcely been aware of it at the time. The sweet lilt of her young voice, perhaps, or some trick of her smile, for all else about the pair went by contraries.

The girl was fair and tall for her age and race, while her mother had the dark, fey delicacy of a true Welsh beauty. Full dark brows cast a bewitching contrast to her dainty elfin features. Her eyes were the dusky purple of blackthorn plums, and her hair—what Con could see of it and what he recalled—still black as a rook's wing. Skin like apple blossoms and lips the rich intoxicating hue of Malmsey wine.

Indeed, a kind of besotted dizziness came over Con as he drank in her twilight loveliness.

A trill of laughter from the child startled him halfways sober again. "Mam, do you mean to wash our guest's feet before the water gets cold?"

Enid gave a startled glance down at the ewer and basin in her hands as if they'd appeared there by magic.

"Aye." She took a step toward Con, then hesitated. "If you wish it, that is. I only heard secondhand that you'd accepted the offer of water."

"With pleasure." Con set his harp aside and pried off his boots, wondering if he'd only imagined the shadow that had dimmed her features. Had she hoped he'd change his mind about accepting the water? "After a day's brisk walk, your hospitality is most welcome. The young lady's music has already lightened the weariness of my spirit. Such a jewel is a mighty credit to you and her *tad*."

Enid had dropped to her knees on the rush-strewn floor, and begun to pour gently steaming water into the basin. At Con's tribute to her daughter, her slender form tensed.

"Myfanwy, *cariad*, will you go check how Auntie Gaynor is coming with the last rinse of the wool? That's a good girl."

When the child had made a subdued exit, Enid explained, "My daughter does mighty credit to her father's *memory*. She's much like him in many ways."

"I'm sorry." Con chided himself less for the compliment gone awry than for the envious curiosity that flamed in him. By the tone of Enid's answer, he might guess how much or how little she had loved Myfanwy's father.

It should not matter to him...but it did.

"Was it very long ago you lost your husband?" At the last instant he managed to stop himself from adding the Welsh endearment, *cariad*.

"In the fall." Enid pushed the basin toward him. Though her curt reply told him she didn't want to dwell on the matter, it gave no real clue about her feelings for the man. "There was some trouble with the Normans, so Howell joined the muster of Macsen ap Gryffith. He took sore wounds in the fighting. They brought him home where he lingered until the first snow.''

Con eased his feet into the warm water as he digested this intriguing scrap of news about Macsen ap Gryffith. If the border chief had lost men in an autumn skirmish with the Normans of Salop, he might not need much nudging to retaliate in the spring.

''What brings you to the borders?'' asked Enid, her head bent over the basin. ''Did you grow tired of plying your sword for hire to the Normans?''

Her question caught Con like an unexpected thrust after a cunning feint. For a moment his glib tongue froze in his mouth. If he told her he'd come on a mission from the very people who'd killed her husband, she'd likely turf his backside out the gate, traditions of Welsh hospitality be damned.

''You might say I'm taking a rest from it.'' No lie, that—not a bold-faced one, anyhow. ''I mean to go back to the Holy Land, though.''

As *Sir* Conwy of *Somewhere,* riding at the head of an armed company of his own men. The dream sang a most agreeable melody in Con's thoughts.

''In the meantime, barding lets me enjoy a bit of adventure without the danger. Mercenary or travelling bard, both make good jobs for a vagabond.''

''You've always had itchy heels, haven't you, Con?'' Enid mused aloud as she washed his feet. ''I suppose you'll be on your way from here tomorrow morning?''

The water was no more than tepid, but Enid's touch set flames licking up Con's legs to light a blaze in his loins. He could almost fancy it searing the itch of wanderlust from his flesh…but that was nonsense.

Though part of him longed to stay and visit, that tiny

voice of caution urged Con to go while he still had a choice.

"Tomorrow." He nodded. "Before Chester dogs arise, if the weather holds fair. I don't want to wear out my welcome."

A quivering tension seemed to ebb out of Enid as she dried his feet. For all her show of welcome, she clearly wanted to be rid of him. The realization vexed Con. He wasn't used to women craving his *absence*.

Enid raised her face to him then, and Con struggled to draw breath. In the depths of her eyes shimmered a vision of the playful sprite he remembered from their childhood—so close and physically accessible, yet as far beyond the reach of an orphan plowboy as the beckoning stars.

"I'm surprised to see you whole and hale after all these years. I feared you wouldn't last a month as a hired soldier."

She'd worried about him. The knowledge settled in Con's belly like a hot, filling meal after a long fast. He hadn't expected her to spare him a backward glance.

"White my world." That's what the Welsh said of a fellow who was lucky, and Con had been. "I've had the odd close shave, but always managed to wriggle out before the noose drew tight enough to throttle me. I'll entertain your household with some of my adventures tonight, around the fire."

He leaned forward, planting his elbows on his thighs. "That's enough talk of me, though. You never did say how you came to Powys from your father's *maenol* in Gwynedd. From time out of mind I heard nothing but that you were meant to wed Tryfan ap Huw, and go to be the lady of his grand estate on Ynys Mon."

Enid scrambled to her feet and snatched up the basin so

quickly that water sloshed over the rim to wet the reeds on the floor. "You ought to know better than most, Con, life has a way of turning out different than you expect."

Which was exactly how he liked it. How tiresome the world would be without those random detours, bends in the road, hills that invited a body to climb and see what wonders lay beyond.

But Enid had never thought so. More than anyone Con had ever known, she'd longed for peace and security. She'd craved a smooth, straight, predictable path through life, content to forgo the marvels if that was the price for keeping out of harm's way. What calamity had landed her here on the Marches where turmoil reigned?

Enid flinched from the memories Con's question provoked, in much the way she would have avoided biting on a sore tooth. Once in her life she'd taken a risk, hoping to gain the only thing she'd ever wanted more than a safe, ordered, conventional life. She'd rocked the coracle and it had capsized, almost drowning her. That ruinous venture had taught her a harsh but necessary lesson about leaving well enough alone.

The man who had cost her so dearly spoke up. "Did this turn in your life bring you happiness, Enid?"

How dare he ask such a thing, as if he had any business in her happiness after all these years? And how dare he pretend to be taken by surprise over the unexpected direction her life had taken? He'd been there when the road had forked, after all. Then he had wandered away, lured by the fairy-piped tune of adventure, leaving her to bear the consequences.

A sharp answer hovered on her tongue, but died unspoken.

If Con ap Ifan had forgotten what happened between them thirteen years ago, on the eve of his departure from her father's house, she did not wish to remind him—could not afford to remind him. For then he might guess what had become of her, and how it had all fallen out.

"It brought me my children." She measured her words with care, anxious not to disclose too much, nor rouse his curiosity further with blatant evasion. "They are the greatest source of pride and happiness in my life."

A grace she'd ill-deserved.

Con's face brightened, as if she'd told him what he wanted to hear. "No wonder you're proud of them. They're a fine pair, though I only saw the little fellow for a moment. Your last yellow chick, is he?"

"I beg your leave for a moment," she interrupted him, "to toss this water out."

Somehow she knew that after inquiring about the baby of the family, Con would next ask if she had any children older than Myfanwy and Davy. "I must see that supper's started, too. Will you take a drop of cider to refresh you until then?"

Con did not appear to notice that she hadn't answered his question. "Your duties must be many now that you're both master and mistress of the house."

He waved her away with a rueful grin. "I won't distract you from them. We'll talk over old times and catch up with each other during the evening meal. In the meantime, if there's aught I can do to make myself useful, bid me as you will. I can turn my hand to most anything."

"I wouldn't dream of putting a guest to work." She didn't want him snooping around the place, talking to folks about things he had no business knowing. "Take your ease and tune your harp until supper. It's been a long while since we've been entertained by a minstrel from away. You'll more than earn your bread and brychan tonight."

She bustled off to prepare for the meal. And to make

sure her children had plenty of little chores to keep them occupied and away from the hall until supper.

"He'll be gone in the morning," she muttered under her breath as she worked and directed others in their work. "He'll be gone in the morning. He'll be gone in the morning."

The repetition calmed her, like reciting the *Ave* or the *Paternoster*.

Yet along with the rush of relief that surged through her every time she pictured Con ap Ifan going on his way tomorrow morn without a backward glance, a bothersome ebb tide of regret tugged at Enid, too.

A small but bright fire burned in the middle of Glyneira's hall that evening, its smoke wafting up to the ceiling where it escaped through a hole in the roof. A sense of anticipation hung in the air, too, as Enid's household partook of their supper.

There were over two dozen gathered that evening, most distant kin of Enid's late husband. All eager to hear the wandering bard who, according to rumor, had fought in the Holy Land.

Enid sat at the high table with Howell's two sisters, Helydd and Gaynor. She had placed Con at the other end, between the local priest and Gaynor's husband, Idwal, who'd taken a blow on the head a few years before and never been quite the same since.

Though everyone at Glyneira had gotten used to Idwal's halting speech, outsiders often had trouble understanding him. Father Thomas was voluble enough to make up for what Idwal lacked in conversation, and then some. His uncle had gone to Jerusalem on the Great Crusade and returned to Wales years later to ply a brisk trade in holy relics. Enid trusted the good father to keep their guest talking on safe subjects.

Subjects that did not concern her or her family.

Once all were seated, the kitchen lasses bore in platters of chopped meat moistened with broth, and set one between every three diners, as was Welsh custom in honor of the Trinity. A young boy brought around thin broad cakes of fresh *lagana* bread on which diners could heap a portion of the meat dish for eating.

Gazing at their guest, Helydd leaned toward Enid and whispered, "My, he's a handsome one, isn't he? And so pleasant spoken. Is it true you knew him back in Gwynedd?"

Enid nodded as she worried down a bite of her supper. Though she'd eaten nothing since a dawn bite of bread and cheese, she felt no great appetite. "Con's mother was a distant kinswoman of my father. She died when the boy was very young, and nobody knew much about his father. Con used to coax the oxen for us until he got big enough to hire out as a soldier."

He had been the only other youngster around her father's prosperous *maenol* in the Vale of Conwy, for Enid's two brothers were several years their senior. Since neither of the children had mothers to keep a sharp eye on them, they'd run wild as a pair of fallow deer yearlings.

In spite of herself, Enid found her gaze straying to Con's animated features as he spoke with Father Thomas, watching with jealous interest for some reminder of the winsome boy she'd once loved so unwisely.

Sudden as a kingfisher, he glanced up and caught her eyes upon him. Though she scolded herself for her foolishness, Enid felt a scorching blush nettle her cheeks. She prayed the fire's swiftly shifting shadows would mask it.

The last thing she wanted was for Con ap Ifan to entertain a ridiculous notion she still harbored a fancy for him.

On second thought, there was *one* thing she wanted even less.

Con swilled another great mouthful of his cider and nodded in pretended interest at some long-winded tale of Father Thomas's. At the same time he tried to fathom the queer sense of dissatisfaction that gnawed at him.

What reason on earth did he have to be disaffected? He'd been met with scrupulous hospitality from the moment he'd crossed the threshold of Glyneira. He'd eaten his fill of plain but nourishing fare, and the cider here tasted far superior to that of the last place he'd stayed. The company appeared good-natured and eager to be entertained.

So what was goading him like a burr in his breeches? Con asked himself. Surely it wasn't childish pique at Enid for neglecting him? Or was it?

After all, they'd grown up almost like brother and sister for their first seventeen years, then hadn't lain eyes on each other for the past dozen odd. Was it too much to expect she might set aside her chores to spend a little time with him? Especially since he'd be off in the morning and might never see her again.

Clearly he'd hoodwinked himself into imagining she'd worried about him after they parted, thirteen years ago. If she'd cared for him half as much as he'd worshipped her once upon a time, she'd have shown him more than the dutiful interest of any hostess in the comfort a chance-come guest.

If he hadn't known better, he'd have suspected she was deliberately trying to avoid him, until she could send him on his way at the earliest opportunity. But what reason could Enid have for that?

"Were you ever to Jerusalem in your travels, Master Conwy?" The priest's question shook Con from his musings.

"Twice or thrice." He nodded and glanced from Father Thomas to Idwal, a big quiet fellow who followed their talk with a look of intense concentration. "Mostly I fought in the north, in the service of the Prince of Edessa."

The priest drained his flagon of cider, probably to grease his tongue for another rambling tale about his uncle.

Partly to forestall that, and partly because he hadn't been able to coax a straight answer out of Enid, Con said, "It can't have been an easy winter here since the master met his end."

Idwal's broad brow furrowed deeper, while the priest replied, "Not as bad as it might have been, perhaps."

"How so, Father?" When he sensed the priest was reluctant to say more, Con reassured him. "I only ask because Enid and I are old friends and distant kin. She might be too proud to beg my help on her own account, but if there is anything she or her children need, I'd find the means to assist them."

"You are a true Christian, sir!" Father Thomas clapped a beefy arm over Con's shoulders. "As you can see, this is no prince's *llys*, but folks aren't starving either. The lady Enid has always been a careful manager and Howell's sisters are both smart, industrious women. Though it was hard on them to watch Howell die slowly of his wounds, they had Our Lord's own comfort knowing they'd done everything needful to ease him."

Con replied with a thoughtful nod. The old priest had a point. What part of the hurt a body took from the loss of a loved one came from guilt over being unable to prevent or assuage the death?

"Everyone had time to grow used to the idea of Howell's going before he went," continued Father Thomas. "Not too much time, heaven be praised for mercy, but enough. Enough for him to make a good confession and die shriven. Who of us can ask for more?"

"You speak wisdom, Father."

The priest cracked a broad grin and nodded around the room where folk were leaning back from their meal, rubbing their teeth with green hazel twigs to clean them, and talking quietly amongst themselves. "I'm wise enough to know it's poor manners to keep the bard's stories all for my own amusement when the rest of the company is eager to hear."

He cast a look at Enid, who nodded. At that Father Thomas lurched to his feet and clapped his large fleshy hands for silence. "Attend you, now! We have the very great honor this evening of a proper bard among us. Conwy ap Ifan is kin to our lady Enid and a native of Gwynedd. He passed the winter months in the southern cantrevs and spring has lured him north to Powys. In his time, he's ventured far abroad, travelling through the kingdoms of the Franks and as far away as the Holy Land. But I will sit down and hold my tongue now, so you may hear the rest from his own lips. The hall is yours, Master Con."

The company cheered as Con hoisted his harp and left his seat at the high table to move nearer the fire.

"I thank you for that eloquent welcome, Father Thomas." He pulled his fingertips over the harp strings in a quick run. "It's true I have wandered far abroad in my travels, but it only taught me the wisdom of the old saying 'God made Wales first, then, with the beauty he had left-over, he fashioned the rest of the world.'"

If that didn't dispose the crowd in his favor, nothing would. Yet as he spoke the words, Con knew they were more than hollow flattery. These past weeks, as he'd reacquainted himself with the land he'd forsaken in his youth, it seemed as though a skilled but invisible hand plucked at the cords of his heart, making warm, resonant music such as he could only echo with his harp.

"Here's a tune I often sang to myself in far-off places when I grew lonely for home." Con plucked out the bittersweet melody he'd played so often. "*Llywn Onn.*" "The Ash Grove."

"The grand Ash Grove Palace was home to a chieftain, who ruled as the lord of a handsome domain."

Around him folks swayed to the music and began to hum haunting harmonies.

As he went on to sing of the chieftain's beautiful daughter who had many rich suitors, no amount of will could keep Con's gaze from flocking to Enid.

"She only had eyes for a pure-hearted peasant, which kindled the rage in her proud father's chest..."

That hadn't been the way of it, of course. Enid had been too dutiful a daughter and too practical a creature ever to brave her father's displeasure by choosing a lowly plowboy over the nephew of a prince.

"I'd rather die here at my true love's side than live long in grief in the lonely Ash Grove."

As the song wound to its beautiful, poignant conclusion, was it his foolish fancy, or some capricious trick of the firelight...? Or did a mist of tears turn Enid's eyes into a pair of glittering dark amethysts?

What of it, good sense demanded, if a woman who'd been recently widowed got a little teary over a plaintive song? Only a fool would think "The Ash Grove" meant to her what it had long meant to him.

Besides, it was too early in the evening for sad songs. Time to lighten the mood.

"Here's one for the children." Con swept his gaze around the room, winking at each one in turn. "I hope they can help me sing it, for I always make a fearful muddle of the colors."

"Where is the goat? It's time for milking." He cocked a hand to his ear and the young ones sang back to him, "Off among the craggy rocks the old goat is wandering. Goat white, white, white with her lip white, lip white, lip white…"

By the time they called the black, red and blue goats, everyone was laughing and clapping. Con followed with several more light ditties about robins and larks and the return of springtime. Then he recited the familiar story-poem about the children of Llyr being magically transformed into swans.

As he oiled his throat with a few more drops of cider and tuned his harp for more music, Con noticed Enid trying to usher her protesting children off to bed.

"Let them stay a while longer, why don't you?" He added his own entreaty to theirs. "Remember when we were their age and the bard from Llyn came to your father's hall? How vexed we were over being chased off to bed."

Enid shot him a glare of purple menace that told him she remembered all too well. He'd had a grand idea they should crawl onto the roof and listen to the music that wafted up the chimney. It had all gone without a hitch until Enid had fallen asleep and rolled off the roof, knocking out a tooth and breaking her arm. He'd been able to scramble away and pretend innocence. Since Enid had vowed by all the Welsh saints that she'd been alone in her mischief, he'd escaped the skinning he probably deserved.

How many other wild schemes of his had she paid the price for over the years?

Before Con could ponder that question, Enid scoured up a grudging smile for her children. "Very well, then, you may bide a little longer. Only a wee while, though, mind? And only because the pitch of this roof is steeper than my father's. You'd break your young necks, like as not."

Myfanwy and Davy exchanged sidelong glances and mystified shrugs. Con understood, though. He winked at Enid and was rewarded with a reluctant twist of her lips.

"I'll keep it brief," he assured her.

"You do that." If Enid meant to sound stern, she didn't quite succeed. "It isn't only the children who need their rest. Others have a full day's work ahead of them tomorrow, and you have a long walk to wherever you're headed."

Wherever he was headed? To Hen Coed and Macsen ap Gryffith. Another step closer to that knighthood and his triumphant return to the Holy Land. Why did that prize not glitter as brightly as it had just a few hours ago?

Never one to dwell on unpleasant thoughts, Con pushed the question out of his mind.

"Here's a song I learned in Antioch," he told his audience, launching into an eerie wail of a melody.

That prompted the Glyneira people to ask him all sorts of questions about his time in the Holy Land. Without too much poetic embellishment, Con managed to hold them spellbound with tales of his adventures—the wonders, the opulence, the intrigue. When a wide yawn stretched his mouth, he realized he'd been talking far longer than the "wee while" he'd promised Enid.

He ventured a sheepish glance her way, only to find her looking as enthralled by his tales as the rest.

"I mind it's past time to put the harp on the roof," he

said, meaning they should bring the festivities to an end. "Here's a quiet tune to lull you all to sleep?"

As he played, folks fetched their brychans and found good spots among the reeds to stretch out for the night. Enid motioned her children away to their private chamber. Con wondered if this was the last glimpse he'd have of her before he headed off to Hen Coed at the cut of dawn.

After the last notes of the lullaby had faded into the night, some of the company responded with muted applause. Others murmured their approval of the night's entertainment. Father Thomas bid Con an effusive farewell before wending his way home.

"Fine music," declared Idwal, nodding his head slowly.

"Indeed it was," agreed Gaynor, holding tight to her husband's arm. "What a pity you have to be on your way so soon, Con ap Ifan. How grand it would be if you could stay and entertain at the wedding."

Con flashed a regretful smile at Gaynor's younger sister Helydd. "I wish I could oblige you. But the man who takes so fair a bride won't need any songs or poetry from the likes of me to crown his joy of the day."

After an instant's bewilderment, the lady blushed. "Oh, I'm not to be the bride, Master Con. Once Enid and his lordship are married, I hope they can find me a—"

"Enid?" Con squeaked like a half-grown boy. Then Helydd's other words sank in. "His lordship?"

"Aye." Gaynor beamed with pride. "Macsen ap Gryffith, himself. He's due to arrive in a few days' time. Enid pretends it isn't all settled, but we know better. I haven't a doubt in the world but there'll be a wedding ere his lordship departs Glyneira again."

Well, well. Con bid Idwal and the women good-night, then rolled up in the thick, coarse-woven brychan he'd been given.

Why venture off to meet Lord Macsen if the border chief was coming here? Glyneira might be the perfect place for them to confer, more distant than Hen Coed from the prying eyes of King Stephen's vassals at Falconbridge and Revelstone.

Con settled into sleep with a contented sigh. Now he and Enid would have plenty of time to warm over their old friendship—before she wed the border chief.

Somehow *that* thought threatened Con's peaceful dreams.

Chapter Three

Though Enid slept in later than usual the next morning, she was not sorry for it. The hounds of Chester had long since risen, no doubt. Con ap Ifan might be miles from Glyneira by now, depending on which direction his roving inclination took him. And she'd been spared the polite necessity of seeing him off and wishing him godspeed.

Yet some bitter herb had crept into her sweet brew of relief at Con's going.

"Think no more of him," she chided herself as she buried the handsome green kirtle at the bottom of her trunk once more, then pulled on another, better suited for all the work she must do to prepare for Lord Macsen's arrival.

Con's surprise coming yesterday had made her realize the border chief might appear any day. She wanted the *maenol* in good order to welcome him.

Despite their late night, her children had not slept past their normal rising time. Myfanwy must be out feeding the fowl, while Davy would be off conning lessons with Father Thomas.

With no company and the prospect of a good day's work ahead of her, Enid dispensed with a veil. Instead she combed out her long dark hair and plaited it back into a thick braid, with only a passing speculation as to how many white threads it had sprouted as a result of Con's unexpected advent.

As she dressed her hair, Enid mulled over the preparations needed for Macsen's arrival. They must butcher a few geese and perhaps a suckling pig so the meat could hang. She'd send Idwal with the hounds to bring in some fresh game. The hall must be swept out and fresh rushes strewn with sweetening herbs.

Once all those tasks were seen to, she would turn her attention back to such of the wool clip as she'd chosen to keep for their own use. The rest of the shorn fleeces awaited a visit from the merchant in early summer. Now that the wool had been washed, it would need to boil with dye plants, and mordant to fix the colors.

Did she have enough woad on hand to dye a batch blue for a new cloak for Bryn? Enid mulled the question over on her way to the wash shed. As she rounded the corner of the house, her mind already planning the pattern of weave, she collided with...

"Con ap Ifan! By Dewi Sant, what are you still doing here? I thought you meant to be on your way early."

If he minded her uncivil greeting, Con gave no sign. "Call it the caprice of a bard."

With those airy words and the casual hoist of one shoulder, he razed Enid's carefully constructed plans to the ground.

"You and I never truly got a chance to talk over old times," he added by way of explanation. "Though you got your ears filled with all the news of my doings, I scarcely know a jot about you. Why, I had no inkling you were set to wed your first husband's lord. As private as a mole, you are, woman. Most ladies I know would boast of such an honor even before they offered a guest water."

"How did you come to hear of that?" The abrupt question had hardly left her lips before she guessed the answer.

"Your sister-in-law told me last night." Con confirmed Enid's certain suspicion. "After you'd taken the children off to bed. Gaynor said it was a pity I couldn't stay to entertain the wedding guests. On reflection I agreed it would be a terrible shame. So I made up my mind to accept your hospitality a few days more."

Suddenly aware of how close he hovered over her, Enid took an unsteady step away. "Gaynor's a good soul, but she gets ahead of herself betimes. There's nothing settled between Lord Macsen and me by way of wedding."

A teasing light twinkled in Con's blue eyes, like the swift dance of water over a stony mountain riverbed. "You do expect him to come soon, though? And you have hopes of him?"

"What business is it of yours if I do, Con ap Ifan?" Enid wasn't sure what vexed her more—his dangerous decision to linger at Glyneira, or the fear that each day he spent here would make it that much harder to part with him again.

"I only clapped eyes on you yesterday for the first time in a dozen years. You're burnt brown as a Saracen and you fought long in the service of the Normans."

The more she spoke, the hotter her indignation kindled. "You said yourself, you mean to go away again as soon as you may, leaving who knows what kind of a pig's breakfast behind you. You've got no call to meddle in my plans or even to know what they might be."

Con flinched back from her vigorous rebuke as he might have from a man brandishing a sword. "What's got into you, woman? I thought we'd parted as friends. Besides keeping your young ones awake late last night, I haven't done you any harm since I've come under your roof. Why must you scold me so, and do your best to chivvy me away? Am I not welcome in Glyneira? You did offer me water…"

And that bound her, damn his hide! Having paid so dear a price for her youthful rebellion, Enid could no longer imagine transgressing against the laws of tradition that obligated her.

"I thought you were someone else." She doubted the excuse would sway him.

"Macsen ap Gryffith?"

She resented the sharp edge in Con's voice when he spoke the border chief's name. "As it happens, yes."

"Are you saying you wouldn't have offered me your hospitality had you known who I was?" If she'd kicked Davy's puppy, the boy and the dog together could not have treated her to such a look of innocent, injured reproach.

"Yes…I mean…no" she sputtered "…that is…" If she wasn't careful, she might pitch herself into Con's arms or gather him into hers.

"Have I risen too high to suit you, Enid versch Blethyn?" Con's posture stiffened and the yearning azure of his eyes froze to dark ice. "Is that it?"

He was the one imposing on her hospitality, rooting into all sorts of matters he had no call to concern himself about. The gall of the fellow to answer her back, proud as a prince!

"I'm sure I don't know what kind of air you're mincing."

"Do you not? Then I'll be plainer, shall I?" Con's chiseled chin jutted. "When I was a poor plowboy in your father's house and you the intended bride of a great lord, it amused you to befriend me. Even flirt a bit to exercise your wiles for your future husband."

If Enid had soaked her cheeks for a week in bloodroot,

she could not have dyed them any redder than they must be at that moment. Con thought she'd been toying with him, when instead she'd been over her head and ears in love.

"Now that you've come down a bit in the world," said Con, "while I've come up, it doesn't suit you, does it, your ladyship?"

"I never heard such idle talk…"

"Let me tell you one thing, then, Blethyn's daughter, I've warmed the beds of plenty women richer and higher-born than you since I left Wales. And they seemed to like it well enough." With that, Con spun on his heel and stalked off.

Enid stood rooted to the packed earth of the courtyard, trembling with a mixture of fury and dismay. She feared the bubbling cauldron might also contain a tiny but potent measure of that well-aged poison…desire.

He was right in what he'd said, Con knew it better than he knew the gospel. He stormed the length of the timber-walled compound, not certain where he was headed.

When they'd been boy and girl together under her father's roof, ripe to bursting with all sorts of forbidden inclinations, Enid had fanned his calf-love into a blaze that had consumed him day and night. Especially at night.

How often had he woken in his loft bed above the oxen's stalls, rampant and slick with sweat over a dream of that elusive girl naked in his arms?

As much as he'd been lured into mercenary service by the call of adventure and advancement, Con had also fled headlong from the demons of lust that had gnawed at his young flesh. And the bitter certainty that he had no chance in the world of winning Enid versch Blethyn.

Con barely noticed his steps slowing.

If she'd been haughty and scornful of him, it would have been so much easier to bear. For then he'd have craved only her ripening beauty, and any other girl would have made a tolerable proxy. But Enid had never once hinted at the difference in their stations and expectations. Then again, she hadn't needed to. He'd been aware enough of the gulf between them for both.

As far back as Con could remember, she'd always spoken and behaved as though he was every inch the equal of the princeling her father meant her to wed. To the most menial member of Blethyn ap Owain's household, struggling to cultivate a sense of worth, Enid's manner toward him had been sweet balm.

"Fie!" Con kicked a tussock of weeds that had forced their stubborn way out of the courtyard's hard dirt. "You're thinking yourself in circles, fool! Was she only toying with you back then? Or did you imagine her soft looks because you craved them so badly?"

A deep halting voice issued from the stables, "You must...talk slower...if you mean me to answer."

Enid's brother-in-law emerged into the courtyard with a dung fork in one hand. A big fellow was Idwal, with ruddy-brown hair and a nose that looked like it had been broken at least once. That and his size might have given him an air of grim menace, but for his guileless blue eyes and ready grin.

"I need no answer, friend." As Con's mouth stretched wide, he could feel his annoyance with Enid slipping. He grabbed onto it and tried to hold tight. "I was only thinking with my tongue, as ever."

"Oh." Idwal nodded as if he understood, but his jagged features contorted slightly in a look of puzzlement.

It passed in a flash, chased off his face by a broad smile. "Fine music you made...last night." He broke into a chorus of "Goat white, goat white, goat white," then stopped abruptly. "Will you play again tonight and tell more stories?"

That was the question of the day, wasn't it? Con thought. Would he let Enid's coldness drive him out of Glyneira, to blunder into Macsen ap Gryffith on his way to Hen Coed, or chance missing the border chief altogether?

His time in the East had taught Con not to waste effort chasing quarry that might come to him if he exercised a little patience.

"I've a mind to stay a few days more. Would you like that?"

"Oh, yes!" The vigor with which Idwal's head bobbed up and down warmed Con. In the fellow's uncomplicated welcome, he found an antidote to Enid's baffling shifts of manner.

"I may even hang about until Lord Macsen comes." Con mused aloud. "He might think it an honor that Glyneira has a bard on hand to entertain him."

Idwal considered and appeared to see the sense in that, even if his clever sister-in-law couldn't.

Con himself was still firmly on the fence. This would be an ideal opportunity for his talks with Lord Macsen. All he had to do was wait around for the plum to drop into his lap. On the other side of the balance, his pride rankled at the notion of staying where he wasn't welcome.

From as far back as Con could remember, he'd been blessed, or cursed, with the ability to see both head and tail of a coin at once. For the most part it had been an advantage, helping him make peace between his fellow warriors when they fell out among themselves. It had come in handy on his mission for the Empress, too, letting him see events through the eyes of the chiefs he was trying to pacify. By anticipating their arguments, he'd been able to marshal all the reasons to counter them.

Perhaps he'd been too hasty with Enid—blinded by his own tetchy pride and the old ulcerous wound of his hopeless boyhood longing for her.

"There's only one wee problem in all this, Idwal." Con blew out a breath, not certain if he was more exasperated with Enid...or with himself. "I think the lady of Glyneira would just as lief be clear of me."

Idwal mulled the idea over and over, like an old hound worrying a tough bone.

"No," he ventured at last. "That's just...her way. She's not a...merry lass like my Gaynor. There's a...sad place in her. A sore spot she fears folks may...poke at...if she lets them too close like."

He grew more and more agitated with each word, until at last he broke off, slamming the tines of his dung fork against the dirt in frustration. "I must sound...a fool. I'm that bad...with talk now. Words is all riddles to me."

"Don't you fret, Idwal." A qualm of shame gripped Con's belly. What was his imagined slight compared to this man's struggle to make himself understood? Or whatever troubles Enid might carry on her slender shoulders? "You talk better sense than lots I've heard. It can't have been easy for any of you at Glyneira since Howell was killed."

Idwal calmed. "Not bad...for me. I do as I've done...all along. Muck out the animals. Watch the gate. Hunt some. Enid has the...running of the place. Wants to keep it...going...till the lad's of age."

It would be many years until Master Davy was old enough to lift the responsibility from his mother. No wonder Enid had looked for a strong, canny husband to share some of the burden. And no wonder she shrank from the prospect of a troublesome guest underfoot while she was trying to prepare for her suitor's coming. Considering some of the mischief he'd gotten up to during their childhood, Enid had good cause to believe he might be more bother than he was worth.

Then and there, Con swore he'd be no fuss to her. He would work his heart out in the next few days to prove his worth.

"Have you another fork, Idwal?" he asked, striding toward the stable. "Two can muck out a barn twice as fast as one. Then we can go scare up some game for the feasting when Lord Macsen comes."

She must have gotten rid of him after all, Enid decided as the day wore on with not a sign of Con ap Ifan around the *maenol* compound.

Not that she'd been looking for him, of course.

As she went through the familiar steps of wool dying, Enid swept her thoughts clean of the dreadful fancies that had plagued her. When Macsen ap Gryffith and his party arrived at Glyneira, Con would not be here to meet them.

Con would not set eyes on Macsen's fosterling, her twelve-year-old son, Bryn, and see the truth he might have guessed sooner, if he hadn't willfully blinded himself to it.

That her late husband had not been the boy's father.

The flutter of panic in Enid's chest eased, but an ache of regret took its place. She would probably never again set eyes on the only man she'd ever loved for she had driven him from her door with harsh words.

She'd had no choice, Enid reminded herself. Con had lain waste to her life once already. She had so much more to lose now than she'd had then.

Her plan to bind her family closer together, safe as

downy chicks under motherly wings, would all be for naught. Even if Macsen would still marry her once he found out the secret she'd hidden for so long, she'd be sure to lose Bryn.

The boy was so much like Con—daring to the point of foolhardiness, eager to venture forth into the big dangerous world beyond Powys. If Bryn discovered he had a Crusader for a father, the boy would stick to Con like a burr.

And Con? He'd be just irresponsible enough to permit it, like as not. Imagining fatherhood a great lark without sparing a thought for the responsibilities.

For the first time, Enid understood something of her father's actions when she'd informed him she could not wed the man he had chosen for her because she'd surrendered her virginity to a young plowboy turned mercenary. At the time she'd thought her father harsh and hateful.

Part of him might have wanted to punish her for challenging his authority and thwarting his plans of a grand alliance, but another part had likely just wanted to protect her in the way she now longed to protect her own children.

"Mam!" As if summoned by her thoughts, Davy came tearing into the wash shed. "Mam, come see. Idwal and the bard have brought meat and fish!"

O Arswyd! For a moment Enid struggled to catch her breath. She should have known it would not be so easy to rid herself of Con ap Ifan. As a boy, he'd deafened his ears to scoldings until all but the most severe physical punishment rolled off his back. His temper might have flared a little when they'd spoken that morning, but Con had never been one to nurse a grudge. His quickness to make up a quarrel had baffled and infuriated her by turns when they'd been young.

How would she ever get rid of a man who refused to take offense and leave? Unless she defied the most sacred traditions of her people by chasing off her unwanted guest at the point of a sword?

"Come, Mam!" Impatient with her delay, Davy grabbed Enid by the sleeve and tugged her into the court-yard.

For a moment, she could barely see Con through the crowd that had gathered around him and Idwal. As Davy towed her toward them, though, the flock of admirers parted.

Idwal toted a mess of fat brown trout, while Con held aloft a pair of good-sized hares by the hind legs. Catching sight of Enid, he waggled the rabbit carcasses and flashed her a smile of such infectious appeal that the corners of her lips twitched in spite of her.

"Now, no talk of guests sitting idle and being enter-tained while the rest of the household is scurrying to make preparations," Con insisted. "Clever fellow that he is, Id-wal found the means to satisfy both. I enjoyed a fine day's hunting, and we've brought back a fair catch to stock the larder."

The look of beaming pride on her brother-in-law's broad features made Enid bite back the sharp words that tingled on the tip of her tongue. What could she say that wouldn't knock poor Idwal flatter than a cake of *lagana?*

Did Con understand just how dirty he was fighting?

"A few more days like this," quipped the bard-turned-hunter, "and you'll be able to gorge Macsen ap Gryffith until he's as round as the old Earl of Chester!"

In what she hoped would pass for a bantering tone, Enid replied, "Lord Macsen won't thank us if he grows too heavy for his horse to bear him. Still, we should be able to furnish a good table with such a fine catch."

She glanced around at those who'd gathered. "Don't forget, we have other preparations to make for our expected guests from Hen Coed, and our regular spring tasks besides."

As the small crowd dispersed back to their chores, Gaynor took the hares from Con. "Let me go hang these, won't you? My, they're fine and heavy. Bring the fish along, Idwal, that's a good fellow."

The children ran off after their aunt and uncle, leaving Enid and Con standing alone outside the wash shed.

A ridiculous wave of bashfulness suddenly swamped the mistress of Glyneira. Swallowing several times in quick succession, she nodded toward the low building behind her. "Can we talk for a moment, Con? In here, where we won't risk being overheard by anyone who cocks an ear."

He followed her into the shadowy interior, lit only by what sunrays spilled through the open door and by the small fire that crackled under the dye cauldron. Beneath the faint reek of smoke and the sharp aroma of the dye plants hung the smell of wool.

Enid spun around to face Con...too quickly. He blundered into her and for a heart-pounding instant they gripped each other to keep from falling. The innocent fumble of Con's hands on her fully clothed body made Enid burn for him as she never had for her lawful husband, God rest him.

"I'm sorry, I didn't mean—"

"No, Enid. *I'm* sorry." Con's hand trailed down her arm to offer her fingers a fleeting squeeze before letting go. "Sorry for bumping into you just now, and sorry for making such an ass of myself this morning. Of course it's no business of mine who you wed or when."

And nothing could persuade him to *make* it his business. Enid dismissed that twinge of regret the way she would have swatted off an insistent fly.

"As it happens," Con said, "I have a bit of business to

discuss with Macsen ap Gryffith. And Glyneira would be a better spot to meet with him than Hen Coed, for a number of reasons. You'd be granting me a great favor if you let me stay. In the meantime, I'll put myself at your service to do whatever needs doing around here. Be it to prepare for your company or to get your spring crop sown. I'm not the mischief I used to be as a lad. I swear, you'll never know I'm around.''

Don't make promises you can't keep, Con ap Ifan. Enid nearly choked to prevent that thought from coming out in words. She would know he was around. Her body would tingle with the knowledge from daybreak until dusk every day. Through the dark, empty hours of the night, that tingling would intensify to an unbearable itch.

But how could she deny his request without blurting out the secrets she dared not reveal?

Just as when they were young, he'd woven a circle of words around her—all the reasons and sound arguments his facile mind could spin so easily. He even seemed able to anticipate her objections and counter them before she got them out of her mouth.

All she had was her tenacity and patience. Sometimes, if she clung to her opinion stubbornly enough, she would wear him out. But not often. More frequently, he would dizzy her until she lost her grip and tumbled into his sticky web.

Perhaps he suspected her present silence was an effort to dig in her heels against him, rather than a desperate scramble to rally a reply.

Grabbing the tip of the long braid that hung over her shoulder, he tickled her cheek with it, the way he'd often teased her in their younger years. ''Come, now, Enid. I don't mean you any harm.''

Of course he wouldn't *mean* it. He would cause her

harm, though, if he stayed. She tried to hold on to that painful certainty, even as her head spun and she tilted toward Con.

Somehow, their lips found each other.

On several special occasions Enid had tasted mead, sweet and intoxicating. Con's kiss was better. It seemed to transform her blood into honey, flowing in a thick, languid pulse. In her breasts and her loins it distilled into something hot and tipsy.

Before she could melt into a puddle of seething need on the floor beneath him, Con wrenched himself away from her, muttering some guttural Saxon-sounding oath.

"I beg your pardon, Enid." His easy poise shaken for once, Con staggered back toward the door. "I didn't mean to do that! I don't know what came over me."

As he fled, Enid struggled to bring her rebellious feelings back under control.

Though that kiss had hoisted her high only to cast her back down again, she did not regret it. For she had glimpsed the key to ridding Glyneira of Conwy ap Ifan.

Nothing would spur him to run so far and so fast as if she made believe she wanted to keep him here with her.

Forever.

Chapter Four

Have a care now! Con's tiny voice of caution fairly bellowed as he reeled his way out of the washhouse. Enid's kiss resonated on his lips like a perfect golden note plucked on an enchanted harp of the Fair Folk.

How could he have stolen that kiss?

True, he tended to speak before he thought and act before he spoke. Over the years he'd learned to exercise some prudence, though. Particularly when there was much at risk...as there was now.

Kissing the lady of the *maenol*, uninvited, might constitute offense enough for her to withdraw the hospitality of her house. And how agreeable an ear was Macsen ap Gryffith likely to lend the man who'd been taking liberties with his intended bride? If Con cherished any hope of success in his mission, he realized he'd better tread warily around Glyneira from now on.

Around the mistress of the place most warily of all.

He heaved an unbidden sigh, part rueful...part wistful. For one sweet fleeting moment, when Enid had stepped into his embrace and fit there with a sense of perfect *rightness*, nothing else had mattered to him. Not ambition, not wanderlust, not even his own life.

Fie! Con shuddered to think of another person having such power over him.

Before he could ponder the threat, Enid's children barrelled past him—young Davy hotfoot in pursuit of his sister, both of them squealing with infectious laughter.

"Where are the pair of you bound?" he called after them.

Myfanwy skidded to a halt. "Auntie Gaynor sent us to gather kindling."

"Want to come?" Davy collided with his sister, who gave him a playful shove. The boy entreated Con with a wide smile no less bright for the loss of one or two milk teeth.

"Why not?" He might do worse than keep out of their mother's sight until supper.

The girl grabbed one of Con's hands and the boy the other. Together they towed him toward the *maenol* gate. Their eager grip on him and their unfeigned relish of his company provoked a curious warmth in Con, as though someone had wrapped a snug but invisible *brychan* around his shoulders.

"Auntie has plenty of kindling." Myfanwy glanced up at Con, her blue eyes twinkling. "She only wanted to get Davy out of the kitchen before he scalded his hand trying to fish a scrap of meat from the stew pot."

Con laughed as he squeezed the boy's hand. "Hungry, are you?"

Master Davy gave a vigorous nod. "Big folks can go without eating till nightfall, but my belly won't hold as much as theirs to last me."

"And you still have your growth to make." Con hoisted the little fellow off the ground as the three of them ambled through the gate. "Tell that to your Auntie Gaynor the next time smells from her stew pot set your mouth watering. Or offer to test a spoonful to make sure it's properly seasoned.''

He remembered all his own wiles for coaxing an early bite during his hungry boyhood years. Having no position in the household, he'd learned young how to get what he wanted by making himself agreeable. The skill had stood him in good stead as he'd matured and his appetites had…changed.

"Properly seasoned!" crowed Davy. "That's a good one. I'll try it tomorrow."

"Only don't let your mother catch you." Con pulled a face for Myfanwy's benefit. "Or she may guess where you picked up the trick. Then she won't be any too pleased with either of us."

"I don't think she was any too pleased with you from the minute you came, Master Con," teased the girl. "What spite has she got against you? When you were young, did you used to tag along and pester her the way Davy does me?"

The question tripped Con up. "I reckon I might have caused her a spot of bother in my time." Was that how Enid had remembered him—as a troublesome tag-along?

They reached a copse of beech trees that bordered a large field within sight of the *maenol*. Though both children knew the chore was only an excuse to get them out from underfoot, Davy and Myfanwy quickly set to work, competing to see who could collect the biggest load of twigs. Con joined in their game, scrambling to assist whoever fell behind.

Would he ever know this kind of simple fun with children of his own? Con wondered as he dropped a fistful of twigs onto Davy's pile. Fatherhood was a matter he'd never spared much thought before.

With good reason, he reminded himself. A child would

tie him to one woman, possibly even to one place. That prospect held little appeal for a wanderer of his ilk. It wasn't all selfishness that made him shrink from the notion of having a family, either. Con knew his own shortcomings too well to fool himself into thinking he'd make a good father.

It was one thing to gambol about with Enid's youngsters, more like a fellow playmate than anything. He wouldn't want to bear the ongoing responsibility for keeping them fed, clothed, sheltered and protected from harm. Yet, for the first time in his life, Con acknowledged the possibility that his solitary existence might be lacking something important.

They had amassed two fine piles of kindling when their uncle called from the gate, "Time to…eat."

"Coming, Idwal," chorused the children.

Davy lifted his heap of twigs only to have half of them fall to the ground again. His lower lip thrust out.

"Here." Con unfastened his cloak and spread it on the ground. "Make a great bundle and I'll carry it back for you."

Pleased with the idea, the children shifted both piles onto Con's cloak, than ran off ahead as he hoisted the light but bulky burden over his shoulder. He got halfway to the open gate when some ponderous movement out in the field caught his eye. A stocky youth manoeuvred a plow, pulled by two yoke of oxen. The beasts strained fitfully as the lad now and then poked the rumps of the hindmost pair with a stick.

"Boy!" Con shouted. "Did you not hear Idwal? It's time to eat."

The lad shook his head. "I want to finish this furrow before night falls, if I can only make these shiftless brutes pull as they ought. At the rate they've been going, this field won't be fit to sow until midsummer.''

Con had forborne to criticize. He recalled all too well what it was like to have everyone picking on him and finding fault. But hearing something like a plea in this plowboy's gruff young voice, he set down his load of sticks and vaulted over a low stile into the half-tilled field.

"Let's see if between the two of us we can't get this furrow plowed before supper's all eaten." Con rubbed the oxen's brows between their long horns and crooned a few words of nonsense to them.

He held out his hand to the boy. "Give over that stick of yours, will you? Let me see if I can't put it to better use."

Beckoning with the slender rod until he drew the beasts eyes, Con began to walk backward, calling them to follow in the singsong litany he'd learned as a boy. "Hai, you oxen! Come, then, come. Plow you this last furrow, there's the fine brawny fellows. Then we'll set you free to drink and graze and rest."

Straining into their yolks, the oxen followed him, as the astonished plowboy clung to the heavy share they pulled. A foolish flame of satisfaction flickered in Con's heart that he hadn't lost this homely skill he'd once despised.

When they reached the end of the furrow, he patted the beasts on their sweaty hindquarters and accepted the boy's profuse thanks. Then he carried the children's kindling into the *maenol* and deposited the great load of twigs in the bin beside the kitchen door. Finally he made his way to the hall, and tried to join the company unnoticed.

It didn't work.

He had barely set foot over the threshold when Enid left her place at the high table and bore down on him. Con braced himself for a scolding at best, eviction at worst.

"Conwy ap Ifan, where have you been skulking?" She slipped one slender but capable hand into the crook of his elbow, drawing him toward the table. "Idwal and I have been waiting on you. Though *I'm* not so hungry, he has a sharp appetite from all the hunting and fishing the pair of you did today."

Struck as dumb as any ox, Con let himself be led to the slightly raised platform. To his further amazement, Enid slid onto the bench beside her brother-in-law and pulled Con down next to her. Con peered the length of the table, surprised to see that Father Thomas had been relegated to the company of Gaynor and Helydd at the far end.

"Will you play and sing for us again, tonight?" Enid passed Con his round of *lagana* while Idwal heaped his own with meat. "Everyone enjoyed it so, last eve."

"I...suppose." Con heard his words struggle out in a halting manner, more like Idwal's speech than his own glib prattle. "If you...like."

What had gotten into the woman? If she'd greeted him with such warmth when he'd first arrived at Glyneira, Con would not have been surprised. But after last night's frosty reception, this morning's quarrel, and that abrupt kiss in the washhouse, Enid's sudden change in manner left him puzzled and suspicious.

"Don't look at me like I'm apt to bite you, old friend." Enid longed to hug herself with glee—her plan was beginning to work already. If Con looked skittish now, imagine how fast he'd flee when she pretended to mistake some scrap of hollow flattery for a marriage proposal. "You and I got off on the wrong foot yesterday and I beg your pardon, for the fault was all mine."

She had bungled things badly, Enid owned to herself. For a start, she should never have kept Con at arm's length, seating him at the far end of the table, then spiriting the children away to bed and never returning to the hall for a word of good-night. If she meant to keep Con from finding out anything she didn't want him to know, she must stick close to him, telling him only those things she deemed safe for him to hear, acting as a buffer against slips like the one Gaynor had made last night.

As she reached to scoop a bit of meat onto her bread, Enid let the back of her hand swipe against Con's. When the touch set a giddy sensation wafting within her, she reminded herself it was only a ruse to drive him away.

"I was that surprised to see you again after so many years, it took me aback. I hope you'll forgive me for being so ungracious, and let us start over."

Con choked on a hasty bite of his bread, but gave a vigorous nod as he coughed to clear his throat.

"I knew you would." Under the table, she pressed her knee against his, enjoying Con's unease at the same time she felt uneasy over her enjoyment of the sensation. "You never did hold a grudge."

No, he hadn't been constant even in that. Was it any wonder he'd found his way from one woman's bed to another? Perhaps it was a mercy from heaven that Con hadn't stayed at her father's house and been made to wed her, rather than running off to play at war and freeboot around the Holy Land. Sooner or later he'd surely have strayed, and broken her heart worse than his going had.

Howell hadn't been without his faults, God rest his soul. But at least he'd never been unfaithful to her.

"So you're content to have me stay awhile at Glyneira?" Con shifted her a sidelong glance as he helped himself to more meat.

"How could I expel a guest who's claimed the hospitality of my house?" How, indeed? "You're welcome to remain with us for as long as you wish, Con."

Then she muttered as if she did not mean him to overhear. "Maybe even longer."

Perhaps Con didn't hear…or perhaps he didn't understand. For the first time since he'd stepped into the hall, the watchful tightness in him seemed to slacken. "I'll keep out of your way, I promise. And I'll do all I can to help you ready the place for the more honored guests you're expecting."

"You and Idwal have already made a grand start at stocking the larder."

Idwal had been following their talk with silent attention as he ate. Now he ventured a comment. "Con is a fine…shot."

"But you knew where to find the game, my friend." Con shrugged off the praise. "And how best to harry it into range of my bow. The pair of us make a well-matched team."

Though he chewed on his food and made no reply, a proud, self-conscious smile spread across Idwal's broad face. When Con lowered his hand onto the bench, Enid fumbled for it and gave his fingers a quick squeeze that had nothing to do with her plan for ousting him from Glyneira.

"Do you mind the time you took me hunting up in the Gwynedd hills and got us lost?" she asked Con.

Hot and sweaty from walking, they'd stripped off their clothes and cavorted in a stream like a pair of otter pups. When Con had swiped her bare flesh in play, the sensation had felt different than any time he'd touched her before. From that day, her girlish fondness for him had taken on an ever sharper edge of womanly desire.

"Lost? Not a bit of it. I knew where we were well enough." Con took a long thirsty swig from his cup of cider. "It was all those hills and trees between us and home that caused the trouble."

She could laugh over it with him now, marveling that the years had not tarnished his easy confidence. At the time, she'd feared they might wander the wooded hills until they starved. Worse yet, she'd worried over how her father would rage when, and if, they found their way back.

Fortunately they'd stumbled across a narrow brook, followed it to a larger one, and followed that until it emptied into the River Conwy some distance downstream from her father's estate. There had been scoldings and punishment when they got home after sunset, none of which had dimmed Con's enthusiasm for their next adventure.

That night before he'd gone whistling off to his bed in the hayloft, he'd tickled her on one cheek with the tip of her braid as a feint to let him swoop in with a kiss on the other. "All's well that ends well, eh, Mistress Worrywart? Think what fun you'd miss if you didn't have me around to make life exciting for you."

She might have told him that she didn't crave excitement the way he did, but what would've been the use? Con had needed a steady diet of thrills the way most folk required meat and drink, air and sleep. He'd never been able to fathom how anyone might feel otherwise.

"I'll skin that brace of conies we bagged to line your winter hood." Recalling Con's parting words to her on that eventful night, Enid's belly churned.

She'd treasured that hood lined with soft rabbit fur—one material gift from a lad who'd had so little to give, apart from the elusive magic of his company.

Here he sat beside her again after all these years, a man grown, one lean hip pressed snug against hers, eyes glittering with infectious merriment which time had not dimmed. That old bothersome magic stirred again just beneath the surface of Enid's skin, prompting her feet to dance, her voice to sing and her heart to skip in a fast wild jig.

A coal burst in the hearth just then, with a loud crack and a shower of sparks. Almost like a warning that she might be playing with fire.

Enid gave a guilty start at the noise and pressed her hand to her bosom.

Casting her a wry look, Con chuckled. "You're strung too tight, woman. I imagine it's a great responsibility to be master and mistress both of Glyneira. You need to take your ease now and again. It's not good for a body to work and worry all the time. Physicians in the East say it'll put the humors out of balance, then you'll be more apt to fall ill."

From Enid's other side, Idwal spoke up. Was it only her fancy, or had her brother-in-law grown more talkative in the short time since their guest had come? "You should…take her fishing…Con."

"That wasn't quite what I meant." Con stuffed his mouth with meat and bread, as if the familiar act of eating suddenly required his full concentration.

"I think it's a fine idea," Enid said. "I can hardly remember the last time I was out in a coracle. Don't they say a change is almost as good as a rest?"

The little round boats favored by the Welsh might be the perfect vehicle for her flirtation with Con. Out on the river they'd be well away from any curious eyes and ears. The whole experience might bring back pleasant memories from their youth when they'd paddled about on the upper reaches of the River Conwy in Gwynedd.

Besides, Glyneira needed to lay in a greater supply of fish against the arrival of Lord Macsen and his party. And while they were out there, close and alone, Enid would cast her net for Con ap Ifan.

When the time came to leave his place at the table and take up his harp, Con couldn't decide whether he was sorry...or relieved.

What had gotten into Enid? Her explanation sounded sensible enough—that she'd been too surprised by his sudden arrival to greet him as graciously as she ought. Somehow, he couldn't bring himself to swallow it whole.

The Enid he'd known would never change course in so drastic a fashion, especially in the blink of an eye, like this. She'd never been given to impulsive action, like he was. And once she'd made up her mind, she clung to it with calm tenacity that no amount of reasoning or arguing could sway. Often enough, Con had thought the elfin slip of a girl more stubborn than any massive ox he'd ever coaxed to plow a furrow.

Picking up his harp, Con spent a few moments tuning it. Then, with his eyes fixed on Enid, he began to play and sing.

"Blackbird, oh, blackbird with your dark silken wings. Blackbird with your beak of gold and your silver tongue. Fly for me to a distant shore and ask there how my beloved does."

Whenever Con ap Ifan had crooned this ballad during his long voluntary exile from the land of his birth, Enid's face had always been the one to rise in his mind.

This spring evening, as he plucked his harp by her fire and drank in her slender, dark beauty with a thirsty heart, the words of the second verse took on a more urgent meaning for him.

"One, two, three things are past my skill. One, two, three things I cannot master. How to count all the stars in heaven on a winter night. How to polish the silver face of the moon. How to fathom the mind of my beloved.''

He'd known Enid longer than he'd known any other woman, yet she remained an enigma to him. Perhaps that was part of the spell that had held him in her power for so many years. The woman was a challenge and a mystery wrapped within an enchantment.

As the last note of the song died away, Enid's face paled to the cast of winter moonlight while her eyes darkened to the bottomless black of the night sky between the stars.

Why?

Perhaps if he could puzzle out the riddle of her, aided by his hard-won knowledge of the world and his pleasantly acquired understanding of women, he could free his heart from her gossamer hold. But did he dare run the risk that she would snare him so tight, he might never want to escape?

Chapter Five

Perhaps her plan wasn't such a wise one, after all, Enid mused the next morning as she hurried through her usual duties, and prepared to set off fishing with Con. Her last scheme involving him had gone so disastrously wrong. Rather than forcing Con to stay and her father to let them wed, that one night in Con's arms had cost her what little freedom she'd possessed.

Last night, when he'd stood by her fire and crooned "Blackbird, oh, blackbird," his gaze had never once left her face, growing more fervent whenever he sang the word *beloved.*

What was there about blue eyes that made them look so sincere? Could it be the color of the sky on a clear day, or water undisturbed that let one see far and deep?

To how many other women had Con sung those words in the past thirteen years, while she had been nursing a wounded heart, raising their son, and trying to salvage a life for herself and her children out of a marriage she hadn't wanted? How many other women had he caressed with his candid blue gaze, convincing them and perhaps himself, that the passing attraction he felt for them was love?

She could not afford to be fooled into believing he cared for her. No matter how blue his eyes, how engaging his smile, or how sweet his kisses.

Intuition warned her that this strategy to get rid of Con might turn on her, like a high-strung horse in battle or an untested coracle over swift water. By spending time with him again, trying to lure him into some rash words of commitment, she ran the risk of stirring up her old feelings for Con.

Behind her, Enid heard a familiar jaunty whistle. One that made her breath quicken and her mouth go dry, hard as she willed them not to.

"Are you ready, then, Enid?" Con called. "I feel as though I've already put in a full day's work dancing before your plow. I could do with a few hours out on the water to cool me down."

The sound of his voice made Enid feel the need to cool down as well. A faint flush prickled in her cheeks and the verge of her hairline grew damp. She told herself not to be so foolish. She was a widow, past her thirtieth year, after all. A mother of three children, not some green girl without the sense to know how much bother a man could be.

This man more than most.

Spinning around to face him, she warned herself not to heed the glimmer in his eyes.

"There's always plenty to do around a place this size," she replied in a tart, teasing tone. "Most of all in the spring. But I can spare a few hours to fish with you.

"Come." She held out her hand to Con. "I'll show you where we keep our coracles."

A qualm of doubt passed across his face, but fled as quickly as it came. He reached out to clasp the hand she offered, with the humid grip of a man who'd put in a good morning's work.

"They make the coracles a little different here than they do in Gwynedd," she said as they scrambled down the bank to a wide stream that flowed east to join with the River Teme. "It's to do with the frame, mostly. They handle much the same, I'm told. It's been that long a while since I netted fish with coracles, I hope I can remember how."

Con gave her fingers a squeeze. "You mustn't suppose I've had the chance to practice off in the Holy Land all these years. Never you worry. There are some things a body remembers long after the mind believes it's forgotten. You only need to make a start and not think too hard about what you're doing, then it'll all come back to you."

He couldn't have tailored an opening for her much better than that. To ignore it would be disdaining a heaven-sent opportunity. Enid thrust aside all her misgivings about this plan.

"You mean like that kiss you gave me yesterday in the washhouse?" She stopped and turned, so Con would have to slam into her. "Did our bodies remember what our minds had tried to forget?"

She failed to reckon with his swift warrior's reflexes. Con checked his step in midstride, bringing him within a finger's breadth of her, yet not touching except for the hand she clasped.

"That…could be." Con's Adam's apple bobbed in his throat as he thrust his free hand through the tangle of brown curls which spilled over his brow. "I told you I didn't do it on purpose. I told you I was sorry and that I'd not let it happen again. Can we not just drop the matter? Pretend it never happened?"

"Did I ask for your apology?" Enid lofted an encouraging glance at him as she rubbed the pad of her thumb over the base of Con's. "Did I demand your assurance it wouldn't be repeated?"

Her questions appeared to unbalance him as her abrupt stop had failed to do.

"Well now, I don't know that you did in so many words. But surely…with Lord Macsen coming, and the two of you…"

Enid lowered her voice. "He hasn't arrived *yet*. Nothing's been settled."

Before Con could summon an answer, she tugged him on down the hill to where three of the light, bowl-like boats rested upside down on the shore. They had frames of ash wood over which reeds had been woven, then made waterproof with a coating of linen soaked in pitch. An admirable little craft, a coracle could navigate the shallowest water, then be hoisted over onto a boatman's shoulder for an easy walk between streams.

There was only one fly in the ointment. Coracles demanded a good deal of skill from whoever wielded the paddle. A novice boatman could easily find himself whirling round and round, carried off on a wild ride by the current.

Just as her old passion for Con might do to her if she wasn't careful, Enid realized with a spasm of alarm. Ah, but she had a good sturdy paddle to help her retain control. One end was the desperate necessity to keep Con away from her son, the other was the painful recollection of what her girlish fancy for him had cost her. The skill to ply that paddle came from the hard-won understanding of how wrong they were for one another in so many ways.

Letting go of Con's hand, she turned over the smallest of the three coracles and shifted it to the water's edge.

"Pass me a paddle, will you?" She took her place on

the low-slung seat. "Then stand ready to dive in and res-
cue me if I tip over."

"You'll manage fine." Con winked. "Don't fret so
much. Just be easy and enjoy the adventure."

"Fine for you to sa-aaay." Enid squealed when he gave
her coracle a gentle nudge into the stream.

For a moment she felt as though she had three left hands
all fumbling the paddle. The boat began a dizzy spin. Then
Enid stopped thinking so hard about what she must do.
Instead she let her hands move as they wished. One end
of her paddle dipped into the water, caught, and stopped
the coracle turning.

By the time Con was ready to cast off from shore, she
had begun to feel the almost-forgotten rhythm drumming
in her sinews once again—a quick responsive dance, with
the river as her powerful partner.

She was able to spare just enough of her attention to
call out, "Mind you bring the net, Con, or we won't be
taking many fish this afternoon."

He bowed with an exaggerated flourish, "As you command, Lady of Glyneira. I am your humble servant."

Enid used her paddle like a huge spoon, to fling a splash
of water his way. "Don't be mocking me, Conwy ap Ifan.
You haven't a humble bone in your whole body and you
never did!"

During that instant she let her attention wander, the coracle got away from her again, twirling her downstream
before she managed to bring it back under control. All the
while Con stood on the bank laughing at her awkward
efforts to handle the fractious little craft.

It was Enid's turn to laugh when he pushed off into the
water and promptly began to spin in circles. Muttering a
stream of curses in some outlandish tongue, Con fought

with the coracle until he nearly tipped himself into the water.

"A fine way to take your ease, this," Enid called to him, her voice laced with genial mockery.

"Get away with you!" As the current drove Con's boat close to hers, he grabbed at the edge and pushed it into another spin. "This was Idwal's idea, not mine, I'll thank you to remember."

Enid squealed with mirth as she battled to remaster her dancing coracle. Con laughed, too, though whether at her or himself, she wasn't sure.

His laughter sounded so good in her ears, perhaps it didn't matter what had prompted it.

Out on the river that sun-dappled spring afternoon, the years Con had been apart from Enid drifted off downstream one by one. With each jest, each volley of laughter, and each meeting of their eyes, a powerful current of remembrance carried them closer to the old days when they'd been inseparable companions.

"We can't frolic about here until sunset and come home with an empty net," Enid protested when they'd finally regained some of their old knack for managing the coracles.

"Why not?" Con asked. "I say it'll be time well spent supposing we don't so much as *see* a fish."

"You would." Enid pulled a wry face, soon tempered by a fond smile. "One of us must be practical though."

"You would," Con countered with a grin of pure devilment.

That sparked a gleeful battle to see who could soak the other worst, accompanied by shrieks, whoops, and fits of laughter that left them limp and gasping for breath. By the time they noticed their surroundings again, they had floated some distance downstream.

Canopied by wide-reaching branches of tall trees on both banks, the stream broadened and deepened along this stretch of water, slowing the current. Gazing around him with newly appreciative eyes, Con admired the rich, varied pattern of greens.

"In all my travels, I've never seen a spot more lovely than this." He hadn't meant to give voice to the thought.

As long as he could remember, Con had cherished the notion that distant places must be better than his humble home. Without a doubt, he'd seen many marvels in his travels. But their exotic beauty had not touched his heart as did this lush expanse of border wood. Nor had any bejewelled Byzantine courtesan stirred him as did this diminutive Welsh widow in her coarse-woven work gown.

Now Enid gazed around her, too. "I take it for granted most of the time. Or think it's only because this is *home* that I find it so wondrous. Thank you for making me look at it with fresh eyes, Con." A shiver went through her slender frame.

A gentle breeze raised Con's skin in gooseflesh, too. "Damn me for a fool, drenching you like that! We'd better dry ourselves off before we try catching any fish or all we're likely to catch is a bad chill."

For a moment Enid looked as though she meant to argue the point. Instead she replied, "It mightn't be much use trying to cast our net just now, anyway. After our carrying on, the poor fish have probably all swam off to Hereford, frightened for their lives."

As she paddled toward a grassy outcropping of riverbank, she called to Con over her shoulder, "You needn't bear all the blame for getting our clothes damp. I was every bit as quick to splash as you, and a better aim. I expect you're twice as wet as I am.''

How could he resist such a challenge?

"Never!" He struck the water with his paddle, sending one last great spray raining down on Enid.

"Bounder!" She scrambled ashore, her movements nimble as a girl's, hauling her coracle up onto the bank. When his craft came within reach, she grasped the lip and toppled it, sending Con flailing into the water.

He came up sputtering, "I'll make you sorry for that."

After heaving his coracle onto the bank and retrieving his paddle before it floated away to England, Con wallowed ashore and raced off chasing Enid, who already had a good lead on him.

She'd kilted up her skirts so as not to trip herself, perhaps not realizing that the provocative glimpse of her bare legs spurred Con to run faster in pursuit.

His nostrils flared wide, drawing in air to feed the fire inside him. His pulse pounded a swift beat in his ears. It outstripped even the muted thud of his fleet footfall on the soft earth carpeted with last year's leaves and new growth of ferns and moss. His body roused with the wild instinct of a stag scenting a doe.

Leaping over a fallen tree trunk, Enid spared a quick glance behind to find Con gaining on her. Dusky eyes flashed mock terror and genuine mischief.

As she crossed a sun-drenched patch of thick moss, Con tackled her from behind. His diving grab brought them both down onto the springy turf in a reckless tangle of limbs, panting with laughter...and perhaps something more?

With each deep draft of air Con gulped, the capricious odor of spring assailed him—sweet new growth rising from the pungent decay of the old. He caught the scent of a woman, too. Wet wool, wet hair, the subtle musk of sweat...and desire?

Beneath the coarse fabric of Enid's kirtle, the soft flesh of her breasts heaved against Con's chest. Her bare leg slipped between his. Her thigh rubbed against the lap of his breeches, sending a surge of pure animal lust coursing through him.

He groped for her leg, shoving her gown higher as his lips sought hers. The way his body throbbed to lose himself in her, it felt as though he'd spent the past thirteen years in a cloister rather than well and frequently bedded by a succession of eager women.

Or perhaps those years and those women were nothing more than the dreams of an ambitious youth. Perhaps he was still only a boy of seventeen, green as spring grass and aching fit to burst for the ripening maiden who tantalized his every thought. *Cariad Enid Du.* Dear dark Enid.

His mouth closed over hers—demanding, yet pleading, too, in its way. Her kiss put him in mind of hard cider. Half tart, half sweet, wholly intoxicating. As her arms encircled his neck and her fingers plowed passionate furrows through his unruly hair, Con had reason to be glad of his sodden clothes.

At least they might prevent his fevered flesh from bursting into flame.

If she let Con keep on like this, the heat of her body was apt to make her clothes dry from the inside out! Enid wriggled beneath him, wishing Con had been this eager on the night they'd begotten their son, rather than ale-addled and content to let her have her way with him.

Their son! Enid's tardy self-control caught up with her at last. Her aim had been to lure Con into a verbal commitment, not a physical one. She didn't dare let him sow another babe in her belly, ruining her hopes for wedding Macsen ap Gryffith.

Fighting her lips free of his, she fought her own desire at least as much as his.

"Do you always work this fast to satisfy yourself when you come to a new place, Con ap Ifan?" Frustration sharpened Enid's voice as she pushed her skirts down to cover her bare thighs. "How quickly you forgot your vow not to kiss me again."

Con jerked back from her, his face betraying more surprise and dismay than when she'd upset his coracle into the stream. "You...you said you'd never demanded that promise."

"Nor did I, but you gave it all the same." The puzzled, hurt look in his eyes reproached Enid almost as much as her own conscience. By nature she preferred fair and open dealing, not this sticky tangle of lies and schemes.

"It's well enough for you to stroll into Glyneira from who-knows-where, lift my skirt as the fancy takes you, then wander off again. I have my future to think of, and my children's." At least that much was true.

Con peeled himself off of her. Putting a little distance between them, he crouched at the edge of the moss bed, leaning against a stout tree stump. "You know I didn't mean it like that, Enid."

His features bore a truculent look she remembered from their younger years, when he'd been scolded or punished unjustly. How often had she taken sole blame for one of their misadventures to keep Con from getting that look?

"How am I supposed to know?" She pressed her attack, despising herself for it, though she knew it must be done for her children's sake. "After you boasted of all your conquests? How am I different from any of them?"

"I didn't love them!" The words burst out of Con with

such force, Enid sensed he would've tried to contain them if he could have.

For an instant she hesitated. Reason prompted her to press the attack and send Con ap Ifan packing. His reckless admission had caught her unwary. She'd expected this campaign of hers to take longer. Perhaps she had better not spring the trap prematurely.

"And you fancy you love *me?*" Retching up a bitter chuckle, she shook her head in disbelief. Once upon a time she might have swooned to hear Con come close to declaring such feelings. Thirteen years in purgatory had taught her to distrust the dubious promise of heaven while fearing the certain threat of hell.

A sheepish crimson tinted the bronzed flesh over Con's high, jutting cheekbones. He dodged the searching gaze she shot him, perhaps afraid of what his unguarded eyes might reveal.

"You and I, we had something special between us, once," he said. "We didn't dare act on it then. You know all the reasons as well as I do."

At least I had the courage to try! Enid clamped her lips together between her teeth to check the accusation she dared not voice. Suddenly she was grateful Con refused to look her in the eye. Otherwise he might have marked the foolish, futile tear she could not quell.

A tense, troubled silence stretched between them until Con shattered it. "Just because we couldn't own to the feeling between us, doesn't mean it wasn't there. Doesn't mean it went away."

With that he commenced to spin his web of words and reason around her. Did he truly mean what he said about the old bond between them, or was he just using it as bait to bed her? And if he had cared for her in the way he claimed, why had the reckless warrior gone tamely on his way while she, the cautious one, had risked all for him?

Little do you guess the trap I've laid for you, Con ap Ifan, Enid thought. *With every word, you blunder deeper and deeper into it. Once you get the bait well between your teeth, I'll spring it and make you run.*

She stroked her hand over the velvety moss, hoping she'd get at least one more chance to run her fingers through his hair before she had to bid him farewell forever.

"We were so young back then." Enid tucked up her knees and hugged her arms around them. "Neither of us knew anything of the world, or of other lads and lasses our age."

She'd met plenty of men in the meantime, most far better suited to her than this charming, restless vagabond. Why had none of them caught and held her heart the way he had?

A smile took her lips by surprise. "For a little while, just now, I wondered if the Fair Folk had played a trick on me by stealing the years away. I felt like a young girl again, with no responsibilities…no worries. Just the water, the sun, the trees and a handsome boy chasing after me. It was a rare gift and I thank you for it."

Con bobbed his head in a vigorous nod. "That's how it felt for me, too." Innocent mischief twinkled in his eyes. "Why can't we just go on that way—pretend we're sixteen and seventeen again, off on a day's larking?"

If only he knew how he tempted her…

"There's been a lot of water flow over the falls since those days, Con. Perhaps you can't understand since you answer to no one, with none to depend on you. I can't afford to think only of myself."

Was she warning him, or reminding herself? "My children and all the Glyneira folk need me."

Con shuddered—perhaps from the chill of his damp garments or possibly from the horror of being shackled by that kind of responsibility. "Then I suppose we ought to go see if there are any brave fish still lurking in the river after all our commotion."

"Not until we get you dried off." Enid stretched out her hand. "Give over that tunic and I'll hang it on a branch in the sun."

As Con shrugged out of the garment, she added, "Breeches, too, while you're about it."

"They'll dry on me well enough." He tossed the tunic to her.

"Please yourself." Resisting the impulse to gloat over Con's sudden attack of modesty, she stretched his overgarment across the splayed branches of a fallen sapling in a patch of sunlight. "I'm not sixteen anymore. I know what a man looks like with his clothes off. Come to think of it, I did then, too, since you and I swam like fish whenever we stole the chance."

She heard a rustle of underbrush behind her, but still let out a squeak of surprise when she felt Con's fingers tugging at the laces of her kirtle, and heard his voice so close to her ear.

"Have a jest at my expense, will you, *cariad?*" He pulled loose the ties that secured the back of her gown. "For all you weren't dumped into the water, your clothes are every bit as wet as mine. With all those folks relying on you, I'd hate to be the cause of you taking a chill."

Words of protest stuck in Enid's suddenly parched throat. With the protective cover of her woolen kirtle removed, she'd only have her thin, damp linen smock between her body and Con's impudent gaze. And if the tips of her breasts puckered, pushing brazenly out against the threadbare cloth, would Con blame it on a chill or would he guess the true reason?

That in spite of everything she still wanted him?

Heaven save him, he yearned for Enid worse now than he had when he was seventeen, with the first fire of manhood searing his young loins!

Con rolled over on the straw-strewn floor of Glyneira's hall and pulled his brychan around him in a futile quest to get some sleep. The harder he tried, the more it eluded him—rather like a certain bewitching woman of his acquaintance.

For a wonder, he and Enid had managed to bring home a good catch once they got around to casting their net between the two coracles. Perhaps their earlier antics on the river had drawn the curious fish to see what all the fuss was about.

Hard as he'd striven to keep his mind on the task, the vision of Enid's lithesome profile showing through her flimsy smock had hovered on the edge of his thoughts, ready to bedevil him. And how could he forget the touch of her soft thigh beneath his fingers, the movement of her body under his, the scent of her desire, or the flavor of her lips?

During the past thirteen years, he had seldom been obliged to suffer this nagging ache in his flesh. He'd forgotten how much he hated it.

Only a few weeks away from Gwynedd and anxious to staunch his homesickness for Enid, he'd let himself be seduced by a Saxon woman. She'd been buxom, fair and many years his senior, with nothing to remind him of his delicate raven-haired *cariad.* Since that first partner, there'd been a long succession of others. All more than willing, all relished at the time, all left well-satisfied with the exchange. None lasting, by mutual choice.

Where was a ready, undemanding woman now, when he so sorely needed one?

Enid's sister-in-law, Helydd, was a comely lass and she had shot more than one encouraging glance his way since he'd come to Glyneira. But a tumble in the hay with Helydd would only come at the cost of a wedding pledge. There wasn't a woman alive whose favors were worth the price of his cherished freedom to Con ap Ifan!

Not even...

Con rolled onto his back and tucked his hands behind his head.

No. It didn't bear thinking of.

For as long as he could remember, his ambition had been to see the wide world and make a place for himself in it. Though the knowledge that Enid must one day belong to another man had gnawed at his heart, he'd never entertained the possibility of wedding her himself. Only in part because her proud father would have slain him on the spot for such presumption.

Yet in some strange way, she did, and always would, belong to him.

The notion brought a smile to Con's face as he lay there, wrapped in the warm, sociable darkness, lulled by the comforting harmonies of grunts, snores, and the rustle of straw, all rendered to the rhythm of slow, regular breathing.

He had almost drifted off to sleep at last when another thought brought him bolt upright, his gut knotted and sweat beading his brow.

Perhaps *he* had always belonged to Enid, and always would.

Chapter Six

"Are you sure Macsen ap Gryffith is coming here?" Con asked Enid as he leaned against the broad trunk of an old oak with a mug of cool, refreshing cider in his hand. "I've been hanging about almost two weeks without a sign or a word of his approach."

"Of course he's coming!" Too late Enid realized she might have rid herself of Con if only she'd given him a false answer. "At least that was his intention when last I received word. Perhaps some matter has arisen to delay him or change his mind."

Something about Con's barbed tone and the intense, unwelcome feelings he'd set brewing inside her for the past fortnight made Enid speak sharply. "Did you suppose I only pretended to expect Lord Macsen in order to detain you here? You think highly of yourself, as ever, Con ap Ifan. If you aren't content to tarry, be on your way to Hen Coed at once, with my blessing!"

The prospect of his going sickened her worse than the miserable morning retches when she'd been with child. How she despised herself that weakness.

"Don't take on so. I'm more than content to stay, and grateful for your hospitality." Con offered her a glance of such winsome repentance it might have moved a stone saint.

But Enid was made of flesh that melted, and blood that burned. And she was far from a saint.

Con's words reminded her of what a shrill little voice in the back of her mind had been nagging about for the past several days. Lord Macsen would be here before much longer, and young Bryn with him, no doubt. The image of her son, so like his father's younger self, spurred her to roust Con from Glyneira without further delay.

Why had she not sprung her trap before this? Con had given her chances aplenty. Each time she had found some excuse to delay. It was not fair to punish him for her failing.

"You've more than earned your bread and brychan since you've come." She relented. "It would be enough if you only entertained us every evening with your music and stories. But you've stocked the larder with fish and game, all the while cheering Idwal happier than I've seen him in ages. You've kept Myfanwy and Davy out from underfoot, and the three of you have fetched in more kindling than we'll burn at Glyneira in a year. As for the plowing..."

She gazed over the wide expanse of meadow, its freshly turned earth a fertile red-brown. "I can't tell you how many springs Howell swore he would see that patch of fallow ground tilled and sown. But something always came up to prevent it. Trouble with the Normans mostly, foul vipers."

Con took a deep draft of the cider she'd brought him. Why didn't he look better pleased with the praise she heaped on him? Wiping his mouth with the back of his hand, he looked out at the partly plowed field. Avoiding her eyes...or so it seemed to Enid.

"I never was a sit-about. I'd rather keep busy, though I like a little variety in my chores. Idwal's a good fellow. I've enjoyed his company and the children's. And... yours."

That last word came out like a rotten tooth yanked by the blacksmith's tongs.

Was he offering her one last chance to make him run away? If so, did she have the will to take it before it was too late?

"I can't say I'm sorry Lord Macsen hasn't come sooner." She reached out and swiped her knuckles against Con's chin. "It's been a treat to have you around the place, and would be even if you had played the sit-about. I know it wasn't an easy life you had back when we were young, Con, but you and I had some fine times together. I'd almost forgotten how fine."

"I've never been able to forget."

Before she could pull her hand back, Con caught it in his, and pressed it to his lips. The acute carnal ache he felt for her hadn't abated, but something else overwhelmed it now and again. Something gentler but at the same time far more powerful.

"I beg your pardon if I made it sound as though I was anxious to get away," he said. "It's been a boon to me, spending time with you again...almost like the old days. Better, in some ways."

Enid nodded, the hint of a fond smile warming her dark, fey features. "We're not a pair of foolish children anymore. We've both seen something of the world. You more than me, but me as much as I want. And we don't need to answer to my father for any mischief we get up to."

"Do you see your father often?"

"Not since I left Gwynedd." For a moment Enid's voice tightened as though speaking of a painful subject.

Then she chuckled, convincing Con he must have imagined the other. "*Tad* was never one to travel far from home, any more than I. We hear news of him now and again, though. He's well. Prince Owain holds his *llys* there on the banks of the Conwy betimes, which flatters *Tad* no end. I expect he gives fiery, warlike counsel which the prince is wise enough to ignore."

Con felt the bottom drop out of his belly, as if a barely contained enemy force had suddenly despatched fresh troops against him.

"What's wrong with warlike counsel?" He let go of her hand so abruptly, Enid almost stumbled forward. "The Normans have been pushing into Wales ever since they subdued the Saxons. Chester and Salop have chewed up half of Powys. Now that they squabble among themselves, is not the time ripe to regain what we've lost?"

"At what price?" Enid sputtered. "You sound just like old Blethyn, for shame. My children lost a father to this feud with the Marcher Lords. You can't imagine what Idwal's lost, poor fellow. I don't want to lose my son—"

Such thoughts had been worrying at the edges of his mind. He didn't need Enid setting them after him in full bay. Downing one last deep draft, Con shoved the empty cider flagon back at her. "That's enough mincing air. I want to get the rest of this field plowed before I have to leave."

Why did he find it so hard to speak those last five words?

A dozen days he'd been at Glyneira, and already Con ap Ifan seemed like he belonged there.

A shiver went through Enid as she listened to him spin stories in the evening after their meal. Everyone else in the room hung on his words, from young Davy to Father

Thomas, as he described the battle for Brantham Keep and the ruse his friend Lord DeCourtenay had employed to gain entrance. A ruse concocted by his lordship's audacious bride.

"After we caught a party of DeBoissard's men hunting for Lady Cecily," Con told the Glyneira folk, "the lass bade us don their clothes and ride back to the keep in the middle of the night when the watchmen at the gate would not be wary."

Enid could hear the ring of admiration in Con's voice for this crafty, courageous woman, now the wife of his friend. Twin peas in a pod they sounded, this Cecily creature and Con ap Ifan. If any woman could tempt him to abandon his wandering ways, it would be such a one.

An enchantress who could make every day a fresh adventure. Or a warrior maiden who might just as lief heft her own sword and follow him on a Crusade.

Tossing back a deep draft of cider, Enid made a face. Had this brew gone a little sour?

More likely it was her own mood gone sour, she acknowledged with a sigh. Not that she *wanted* to domesticate Con—like the Normans did with their falcons. Nor did she have any desire to follow him into distant, dangerous lands, far from the comforting familiarity of home.

What she did want was to send him on his way before Lord Macsen arrived with young Bryn in tow. After that, she wanted to wed the border chief, who promised to give her everything she truly prized in life.

Except the heart-pounding passion that gripped her every time she saw, heard or thought of Con ap Ifan, her contrary heart protested.

Passion? Enid barely contained a snort of bitter laughter. What had passion ever brought her but trouble? It was a capricious emotion, as dangerous in its way as any far-off, foreign land.

Respect, fondness, affinity: those made a much safer foundation on which to build a marriage and a life. If only she had Con's skill at argument, she might convince her stubborn heart of it.

Enid forced herself to concentrate on what Con was saying, rather than on the way the firelight caressed his lean, striking features and burnished his rich brown curls.

"Then I drew back my bowstring, hardly daring to breathe. I knew if DeBoissard marked me, he'd put an end to Rowan before I could get a shot off."

A wonder he hadn't put an arrow through his friend's throat, rather than into his enemy's elbow. Enid's stomach churned just thinking about it. But that was Con for you—ever willing to risk the unthinkable, recklessly confident in his ability to prevail over impossible odds. Little wonder he frightened her every whit as much as he stirred her desire.

She could not afford to let him bide here much longer, carving out a place for himself at Glyneira that he would never stay to fill.

After he brought his story to a close with a flourish that had everyone cheering as though it had taken place before their very eyes, Con rubbed his throat. "I'll spare you my singing tonight. I'm as hoarse as a wooden nightingale."

Spying her chance, Enid seized it. "Are your legs too tired to dance, then? We have other musicians who can play a tune to accompany us."

She beckoned the head shepherd. "Nye, have you your pipe?" To the blacksmith she asked, "Your tabor, Math?"

The two men came forward with their instruments, sporting self-conscious grins as though they'd hoped for

just such an invitation. The others pushed tables and
benches back against the walls to clear a space for dancing.

Fixing on a bold smile she hoped would eclipse even
Con's precious Lady DeCourtenay, Enid approached him
with outstretched arms. "Shall we show these Powys folk
how quick the Gwynedd-born can step?"

Con's mouth stretched upward at the corners, all eager,
but a faint shadow that bespoke uncertainty darkened his
eyes. Had she offended him earlier when they'd argued
about how the Welsh should treat with the Normans?

Perhaps she had been too harsh. She didn't want the
men of Powys to sit back tamely while the outlanders gob-
bled up every acre from Offa's Dyke to the Caer Naervon.
Then again, as Father Thomas read from the Holy Scrip-
ture, there must be a time for war and a time for peace.
Useless, petty hostilities would only drain her people of
men and material they might need later when the Normans
stopped feuding amongst themselves and turned their com-
bined might westward.

With a suddenness that took her by surprise, Con
clutched Enid's hands, all the more willing for his first
hesitation. Knowing Con, perhaps it even added some per-
verse fillip to the venture. "You know me too well, lass.
I never could resist a challenge, or the chance to show off
a little."

He canted back, forcing Enid to do the same unless she
wanted to pitch into his arms. Then he began a swift side-
step, sending them whirling in wild circles.

Her heart tripped faster than Math's rolling beat on the
tabor, and a yelp left her throat, part terror, part exhilara-
tion. By the time they stopped, she had no choice but to
list against Con in an effort to keep from collapsing into
a dizzy heap on the floor.

As she clung to him, enjoying his closeness so much it

frightened her, she heard Gaynor say, "Powys will not yield pride of place to Gwynedd tamely, will it, Idwal?"

To Enid's befuddled eyes, it looked as though a pair of Gaynors and Idwals took the floor along with doubles of several others. By the time her head settled, the musicians had agreed on a tune and begun to play.

"Into the round with you, now!" Gaynor and Helydd pulled their sister-in-law away from Con and into the circle of women.

Some of the men pressed Con into service for their outer circle, which moved counter to the women's. So many steps, then the man opposite Enid grasped her by the waist and twirled her about. The couples linked arms and skipped a circuit before breaking up into male and female rings again.

On the second pass, Enid found herself opposite Con. His hands, strong from his archery yet gentle for his harp, almost spanned her waist. Even through her linen smock and woolen kirtle, she felt their warmth. A ripple of heat spread down from her waist until it lapped at her thighs.

Only a few times in her marriage had her lawful husband's touch roused her like this, always to end with some vague dissatisfaction worse than feeling nothing in the first place.

After the carol had reached its boisterous climax, Enid raised a hand to her brow. "That should shame me from boasting. I haven't the head for dancing I once had, especially on a full belly. If I don't get a breath of air, I may flay the goat."

She could picture herself crouched in the straw retching her poor guts out.

Clinging to Con, she begged, "Will you lend me your strong arm to step outside awhile? The last thing I'd need just now would be to turn my ankle or fall and twist my wrist.''

His muscles tensed. Enid could feel it through his clothes, and she wondered if he meant to refuse her.

Then Math and Nye struck up another tune and folks began dancing again. Under cover of all the exuberant noise, Con pressed his lips so close to Enid's ear, it was almost a kiss.

"Seeing as I'm to blame for making you dizzy," he murmured, "I'd better provide the remedy. A slow walk in fresh air sounds like the best tonic. Come along."

As he led her away from the hall, no one seemed to mark their going. Outside the spring night enfolded them in cool, soft intimacy. The new moon hung like the silver bow of some heavenly huntress in a deep black sky shot through with thousands of glimmering stars.

"We should have brought a brand to light our way," said Con. "Don't want to trip in the dark, do we?"

Enid chuckled. "It's not like you to be practical. Let's just sit on the stairs and bide here, so we don't go blundering over a sleeping hen or some such. I'm content we didn't bring a torch. It would have blinded us to the starlight."

As they settled on the steps, Con's fingers found their way to the nape of her neck in a delicate caress, quite chaste...yet powerfully intimate.

"It's not like *you* to be fanciful, Enid. For all that, you're right. Sometimes too garish a light obscures another that's more modest...but far and away more beautiful."

Was he talking about the Powys night sky, or something else? Enid wondered, wishing this starlit moment was a dream, so she could give in to it without reserve.

Softly, as if thinking aloud, Con added, "That same moon sheds her light on the Holy Land now. Wherever you go, she always watches you. Many a time when I longed for home, I'd look up at the moon's haunting face and think of her keeping vigil over you far away in Wales.''

"You longed for home?" Enid could scarcely imagine it. "I thought you'd count yourself well rid of the place.''

"Oh, I did…by times. Then other times I'd feel an empty place inside me and I'd rush to fill it with whatever came to hand—harping, gaming, drinking…''

"Wenching?" She hadn't meant to say it!

Con made no word of reply, but somehow she sensed him nodding in agreement.

She clamped her lips together, not trusting what might come out if she parted them. Silence settled between her and Con for a while, as the muted music drifted down from the hall to wrap around them in the darkness.

Telling herself it was part of her plan and nothing more, she let her head loll, until it came to rest on his waiting shoulder.

"Did they fill that empty place?" Strangely, she almost hoped he would say yes. Better that he'd found comfort in the arms of other women than going uncomforted all those years when the *hiraeth,* the homesickness, had taken him.

A great sigh heaved out of Con, a sound that put Enid in mind of distant breakers from the Irish Sea hurling themselves against the rocky coast of Llyn. "I fancied so at the time. Now I think I was cozening myself. There's a difference between taking up space and truly filling it.''

He inclined his head to rest against the crown of hers, grazing her hair with his cheek.

"One, two, three things are past my skill.'' He whispered the words of the old riddling song. "One, two, three things I cannot master. How to count all the stars in heaven on a winter night. How to polish the silver face of the moon. How to fathom the mind of my beloved.''

There was something she was supposed to say, now. It tugged at the skirts of her memory with small but insistent hands.

But how could her mind concentrate when her heart tumbled over and over, and her lips tingled with the need to kiss the only man she had ever loved?

Slowly, as if pulled by a spell of the Fair Folk he was trying to resist, Con angled himself toward her.

He'd heard it said there was witchery in moonlight. At that moment he did not doubt it. Something drew him and compelled him, something not of his own will. It drew him to engage Enid's full, soft lips when he knew he shouldn't.

It compelled him to speak dangerous words. "When I'm with you, there is no emptiness, *cariad.*"

Con trespassed that final brief space between them. Instead of her lips, he found her nose, so he kissed that, then he kissed her brow, her eyelids, her cheek, her chin. Likewise she kissed his face, whatever part his wandering brought within reach of her lips.

This was different than the primal urge that had sent him chasing after her in the forest, avid to quench the burning he sensed in her. And to quench his own fire in turn.

Now, even though he was roused as any proper man would be with a desirable woman so near, something else held sway over him. Something that warned him a mere physical joining with Enid would not fill him in the way he needed.

Perhaps her kiss held an answer to the mystery.

As Con paused, gathering his anticipation, the door behind them burst open and a small, furry, whimpering form barrelled down the wide, shallow steps.

Spouting a mild curse, Con jerked back from Enid, allowing the little creature to squirm between them.

"It's only Pwyll," called a small voice. "He needed to wee. Is that you, Mam? How's your head feeling? Myfanwy made me dance. Now my head's going round and round, too."

"Come sit with us then, Davy-boy, until it settles down." Enid budged away from Con, to make a space between them just wide enough for the child.

His small shadow dark against the flickering light that spilled through the half-open door, Davy descended the steps toward them.

"Auntie Helydd said I wasn't to disturb the pair of you." The boy squeezed into the gap between Con and his mother. "Pwyll and me didn't do that, did we?"

"Of course not," Enid ran a hand over her son's hair. "We're glad of your company, aren't we, Con?"

"True." Though he intended the word as a well-meant falsehood, the moment Con said it, he knew it was nothing of the kind.

Much as he had enjoyed his time alone with Enid and should have resented any intrusion, the child's presence brought him a tender, improbable sense of completeness.

The little dog did his business somewhere out in the courtyard, then scrambled back to his master. When Davy hoisted the wriggling pup onto his lap, Con reached over to pet it in an effort to calm the creature down. His hand brushed against the boy's…and Enid's as the three of them stroked Pwyll's furry coat.

Davy rested his head against Con's arm, almost as his mother had done. "You make everything merry, Con. I'm glad you came to Glyneira. Are you, Mam?"

Despite what had just taken place between them, Con braced himself for Enid's answer. While he didn't expect her to gainsay her son, he prepared for an awkward pause or a hint of something in her tone that would contradict her polite words.

"Yes, Davy." Her answer had the ring of a perfectly tuned harp string, one with a pure, dulcet tone. "I am glad Con came to visit with us. He's as welcome as the springtime."

He hadn't been at first, Con knew, but he was now. That was all that mattered.

Over the puppy's back, Enid's knuckles rubbed against Con's hand. He felt as though he'd received that interrupted kiss after all.

Davy breathed a contented sigh. "I want to be just like you when I grow up, Con—a bard and a soldier travelling all over the world, having all sorts of grand adventures."

Enid's hand froze, then jerked away.

"Get that foolishness out of your head this instant, Davyd ap Howell!" Her tone changed to a harsh, discordant jangle. "You have no notion of the danger that's out there. It's not all the grand frolic Con paints it to be with his tales."

"I didn't—" Con tried to object. He hadn't glorified the kind of life he'd led, had he? Hadn't made light of the risks involved or the frequent hardships?

And what if he had? Con bristled at Enid's unfair accusation. He *had* led an exciting, colorful life. If homesickness had chewed a hole in his belly by times, wasn't that a fair trade to escape the dull routine and petty matters of some Welsh backwater?

"I'll not have you filling my boy's head with this nonsense," Enid snapped. To Davy she said, "It's well past your bedtime, my lad. Little wonder you're spinning dreams while you're still awake. Go to, now. Take Pwyll and tuck him into his box for the night then away to bed with you.''

Apparently the boy knew better than to argue when his mother used that tone of voice. With a dutiful, ''Yes, Mam,'' he scrambled up the stairs.

Enid rose to follow.

Con wished he'd learned half the child's prudence, but he hadn't. Some petty demon in him would not back down from this woman's rebuke.

''Don't be too hard on Davy,'' he called after her. ''It's just a bit of boyish talk is all.''

She rounded on him. ''That's the very way *you* used to go on when we were young, Con. See what came of it?''

''What if he does decide to go off and become a soldier by and by? You can't wrap the boy in fleece all his life, and keep him tied to your skirts, Enid.''

''Can I not?'' she demanded in a harsh whisper, like a switch cleaving the air. ''You just watch me, Con ap Ifan! You don't know what it's like to care about someone better than your own life. So that you'd rather take any harm yourself than see it fall upon them. Precious little wonder you're empty.''

She turned from him and stalked off into the house.

If Enid had marched down the stairs and boxed his ears until they rang, Con would not have been more dazed.

Or worse grieved.

Chapter Seven

Enid woke the next morning with a heavy slab of grief pressing down on her chest until she could scarcely breathe.

Throwing a kirtle on over her smock, she resisted the urge to rouse the children from their beds. If Con had gone away, she didn't want to face their insistent questions or Davy's accusing looks.

What made her so wrought up at the notion of his going, anyhow? she chided herself. It was what she wanted. What she had been working to hasten.

Not working hard enough, though. When her chance had come last night, begging to be taken, she'd sat there in a daze, robbed of all reason by the sheer power of her re-awakened feelings for Con.

It had been balm to an old, corrupt wound, hearing how much he had longed for her. When he'd spoken of the void in his heart her absence had created, she'd understood all too well. For she had her own empty place which she'd striven to fill with her children, her duties as lady of the *maenol,* and the homely comfort of traditions.

Then Con had suddenly reappeared in her life. For all the havoc his coming had played with her plans and with her heart, it felt as though unseen hands had poured water into a jar packed with stones and sand. Though the jar might appear full, the soothing, cool water could still seep into every cranny.

What if she dumped all the sand and pebbles out of her life and simply filled it to the brim with…

No, that would be madness!

Con had unsettled her reason. He'd whisked her back to a time when she'd been free of responsibilities. That had a seductive appeal, but she was not a child anymore. And she could not go back to being one.

Nor did she want to.

The shackles that bound her to Glyneira were all ones she had forged herself and put on willingly. If they chafed her spirit by times or weighed her down when she was tired, that did not mean she wanted to cast them off forever.

With a fond glance at her younger children dozing in their truckle beds, Enid tiptoed out of the chamber, then descended to the scullery. There she found Gaynor carving up joints of game while Helydd salted and spiced them.

"I didn't mean to be such a slugabed this morning." Enid scarcely got the words out before a deep yawn overtook her.

Gaynor didn't look up from her work. "All that lively dancing can tire a body out."

Though her tone sounded mild, Enid knew Gaynor well enough to recognize when her sister-in-law meant more than she was saying.

Helydd hummed a little tune as she prepared the meat. "I suppose we'll have plenty of dancing in the evenings when Lord Macsen gets here."

"I expect so." Enid tried to ignore the flutter in her stomach.

It had been there even before Con's arrival, whenever she contemplated the notion of her remarriage. Lately it had grown more intense, no matter how often she repeated the familiar litany that wedding Macsen was what she wanted most in the world.

Gaynor glanced up. "Helydd, will you go fetch Idwal, like a good lass? He and Enid and I need to decide how many of the young swine we want him to butcher and when."

"Could you not go for him, Enid?" asked Helydd. "I'm right in the middle of this and my hands are all over salt and spices."

As Enid nodded and turned to leave the scullery, Gaynor said, "Just give your hands a wash, Helydd. It roughens the skin something dreadful if you handle the salt for too long. I'm sure Enid wouldn't mind taking a turn at it."

"Very well." Helydd shrugged, used to being bidden by her elder sister.

Enid took over Helydd's task without a word until the young woman had rinsed her hands and left the kitchen in search of Idwal.

"Out with it, Gaynor," Enid said at last. "What have you got a beetle in your head about this morning?"

Gaynor slammed the meat ax onto the chopping board with a force that made Enid jump back. "Never you fear, I won't hold my tongue. I want to know what you've been getting up to with this Con-fellow? Idwal and Helydd both have some daft notion he's courting you."

"Daft is right!" Enid kept her head bent over her work for fear Gaynor would spy the guilty color staining her cheeks. "Con's an old friend, nothing more. And between us two, I doubt he'll *ever* find a woman he'd be willing to wed. Or one who'd take him with his wandering ways."

"That's as may be," Gaynor grumbled. "You've gone

off alone with him more often than is seemly for a woman who means to wed someone else. Have you thought what Lord Macsen might say if he gets wind of it?''

Luckily for Gaynor she was the one wielding the meat ax rather than Enid. ''If it had been up to me, Con ap Ifan would have been gone the morning after he first came! I wasn't the one who urged him to stay and entertain at the wedding, was I?''

''God save us!'' gasped Gaynor. ''I didn't think of that. Me and my runaway tongue! I beg your pardon, Enid. I didn't mean to quarrel with you. If I have my heart set on you wedding Lord Macsen, it's only for your own good and for your wee lambs. I don't want to see it all thrown amiss by some careless flirting.''

''Nor me neither. You've no need to fret, though. I had sharp words with Con last night.'' The pungent odor of spices made Enid's eyes sting. ''I expect he's miles on his way by now, never to return.''

Gaynor shook her head. ''If he's bestirred himself farther than the courtyard, I'll be amazed. He told Idwal there were some repairs he wanted to make about the place. The last I heard the pair of them had plans to go hunting again tomorrow.''

Concentrating on her work as though her life depended on it, Enid did not trust herself to reply. If she spoke, Gaynor might hear the breathless relief in her voice and become doubly suspicious. Enid knew she shouldn't feel relieved—didn't want to feel relieved. But her stubborn heart would not be bidden.

He'd seen more defensible sheep biers!

Con shook his head grimly as he and Idwal inspected the timber wall surrounding the *maenol*. He knew it was madness to feel responsible for the safety of Glyneira, but he could not help himself.

"What happened there?" He pointed to yet another weak spot in the defenses.

"Mind the ice…this winter?" Idwal replied. "Big tree branches crashed down."

"That's one of the reasons the trees should be cut back from handy the walls." Con raked a hand through his sweat-damp hair. "Not much good having a wall, is it, if all your enemy has to do is climb an overhanging tree to let himself in?"

Idwal swiped a broad knuckle across his chin. "Well now…I see the…sense in that. We've been…lucky here. Never been attacked for years. Being so…small and out of the way. And with Hen Coed…between us and the Normans."

That might be about to change. Con swallowed the words before he could speak them, and almost gagged on their bitter taste.

If he was successful in his commission from the Empress, nudging Macsen ap Gryffith to make some raids across the border, the Norman Marcher lords might well retaliate in kind. In fact, if Con himself had the ordering of it, he'd be inclined to circle around the bastion of Hen Coed to strike at small, out-of-the-way, poorly defended Welsh estates.

Like this one.

Guilt smote him with the force of a rotting animal carcass hurled by a siege engine. Was all his ambition worth putting a vulnerable estate like Glyneira at risk?

"It never hurts to prepare for the worst," he muttered to Idwal. "What do you say we fell a few of those trees that stand too near, then use the timber to fix the weak spots in your walls?"

Idwal nodded. "Thanks to you…we're ahead in the plowing. We can spare the time. I'll have Math…hone the ax blades good and sharp."

Out of the corner of his eye, Con spotted Davy and Myfanwy dodging out through the gate. The girl carried a rush-woven basket on her arm.

Pulling his lips wide with two fingers, Con blew a piercing whistle. The children stopped and glanced back.

"Where are the pair of you going?" The sharpness of his tone took him by surprise.

"Off to gather acorns for the pigs," Myfanwy replied.

"Want to come?" Davy held out his hand.

"Idwal and I have some work to do. You won't be venturing too far abroad, will you?"

Davy flashed an impudent grin. "How far is *far?*"

The young whelp! Con felt his temper rising, goaded by an emotion akin to fear.

As Idwal lumbered toward Math's small forge, Con called after him. "I'm going off for a bit, but I'll be back by the time those axes are well whetted."

Idwal glanced at Con and the children, casting them a doting look touchingly at odds with his rough-hewn features. "Go on with the cubs. This job will keep."

Would it? Con wondered. For how long?

And what would it matter how secure a home he left behind for Enid and her children if they didn't stay safe behind its walls?

"Maybe we can do two jobs at once," he suggested when he caught up with Myfanwy and Davy. "I need to see which trees grow too close to the wall. Some will be oaks, that's certain."

Davy pulled a face. "But I wanted to go to the ridge, yonder."

"Is that so?" Con's stomach roiled. He and Enid had

wandered much farther afield from her father's house, but
that had been the peaceful Vale of Conwy in the heart of
Wales. This was embattled Powys. "If I promise to take
you there tomorrow, will you promise me never to stray
that far unless you have a grown-up with you?"

Myfanwy skipped along at his side. "Why must we do
that, Con? Davy and I know this country well—we'd never
get lost."

It wasn't *lost* he was worried about.

"Have you heard tell of the Normans?" he asked.

"I have! I have!" Davy jumped up and down. "They're
nine feet tall and they have teeth as sharp as a fox's. If
they catch Welsh children, they roast them and put them
in a pie for their supper!"

The boy related these grisly charges with such wide-
eyed relish, it was clear he recognized them for the tall
tales they were.

"Who told you that pack of nonsense?" As if Con
couldn't guess.

"Auntie Gaynor!" cried the children.

It was one thing to promote a healthy caution of their
enemies. Wild stories even a lad of Davy's tender years
wouldn't swallow were apt to make them more daring, not
less.

They found a large oak that had probably been a sapling
when Glyneira was first fortified. Over the years it had
grown tall and its branches had spread. An archer who
climbed it might find a solid perch from which to fire down
into the *maenol* courtyard.

As the children rooted about the ground beneath it for
acorns, Con tried his best to undo Gaynor's well-meant
blunder.

"I've lived more than a dozen years among the Normans, and never yet seen one roasting children—Welsh or

any other kind. As a race, they do stand taller than most Welshmen, but still far short of nine feet. As for teeth, they don't take pains to clean them like we do, so some of them have hardly any teeth at all, let alone fine sharp ones.''

The children looked a little disappointed by the unexciting truth.

"The Normans killed our *tad,*" said Myfanwy in a small voice. Perhaps it burnished his memory, pretending to believe it had taken evil giants to slay her father, rather than ordinary men with bad teeth.

"I didn't say they weren't dangerous." Con plucked an acorn from the ground and tossed it into Myfanwy's basket. "The Normans are crafty folk and they're land hungry. They might not pop you into a pie, but if they caught you away from home, they might take you back to their country and shut you up in a cell until your mam paid them a ransom."

A shudder went through him as he spoke of being imprisoned. That, rather than the possibility of death, had always been his greatest dread going into battle. It had given him the appearance of reckless courage by times.

Myfanwy and Davy looked at each other with what might have been the first flicker of true fear in their eyes. Much as he hated to have put it there, Con could not help believing fear of the Normans might be the beginning of prudence for these two.

Perhaps such talk reawakened his warrior's instincts. For when a twig snapped behind him, he spun about into a crouched defensive stance between the children and whomever had made the noise. Hardly aware of his own movements, he pulled his eating knife from the small scabbard belted around his waist.

Enid jumped back and let out a strangled shriek. One

hand went to her heart, as if she feared it would pound its way out of her chest.

Had she come to send him packing? Con wondered as he stammered an apology and sheathed his small blade. It mightn't have been her original intent, but after he'd drawn a weapon on her she'd be well justified to evict him.

A weight heavier than a millstone settled in Con's belly at the thought of such an exile.

Even after the first shock wore off, Enid's heart would not settle down to a steady beat.

Had she heard Con aright—cautioning her children to stick close to home? Impressing upon them the danger posed by the Normans in a way all her own warnings and even Gaynor's exaggerated monster tales had failed to do?

She wanted to throw her arms around his neck and kiss him soundly. And not just as a means to scare him away from Glyneira, either.

"Curse me for a fool! I hope I didn't frighten you half to death." Con fumbled so trying to sheath his knife, Enid feared he might lop off a finger. "All this talk about defenses and such has got me thinking like a warrior again."

"Or *not* thinking." Enid gulped in a deep breath, hoping it would calm her runaway heart. "I mind it might be like what you said about the coracles—your body acting without leave from your head." She managed a shaky smile.

He cast her a look of relief so endearing it set her knees weak. "Perhaps that's all it was."

He tossed her a wink with a grin for good measure, as though he hadn't a memory in the world of the terrible things she'd said to him last night. "We'll have to warn the Glyneira folk not to come up behind me sudden-like."

"Look, Mam, acorns for the pigs!" Davy came running with a handful to show her.

Enid did her best to look impressed. "It was kind of the squirrels to leave us a few."

"Come put yours in the basket, Davy," Myfanwy called. "Mam, can we go on to another tree? We've gathered all there are under this one."

"Go ahead." Enid slid a sidelong glance at Con. "Just don't get out of sight or earshot. Who knows but we might live closer to the English border someday. You'd do well to learn a little caution in the meantime."

The speed and the noise with which the children bolted off made Enid wonder how they'd manage at Hen Coed.

She and Con dawdled behind. At least with Myfanwy and Davy along, Gaynor mightn't be as apt to scold their mother about spending so much time in Con's company. And there'd be less fodder for gossip to reach Lord Macsen's ears.

Side by side Con and Enid walked, not touching, but close enough that she could feel his presence though she didn't glance his way. As the silence between them grew, she longed to break it. Her voice refused at first, but she kept trying until something came out.

"Thank you."

At the sound of her words, Con startled. "Thanks? For pulling a knife on you?"

Enid laughed, shattering the invisible wall that had stretched between them. "For finally putting a little fear of the Normans into those two."

"Oh, that. Been listening awhile, had you?" Con shrugged. "It may only last for a few days, but it's a start."

They walked a few more steps, then he spoke again. "I did a bit of thinking last night after you put Davy to bed. I'll be sorry if my tales make him more careless or apt to roam. Most soldiers as foolhardy as I am haven't been blessed with my luck, so I'm no fit example.''

Remembering every sharply honed word she'd thrust at him the previous night, Enid winced. ''I never should have said such awful things. You're a guest in my home and a bard. What else do Welsh harpers sing about besides glorious battle and tragic love? It would be as unfair as to blame you if Myfanwy took it into her head never to wed.''

''I would be sorry for that, indeed. I'd regret keeping some young Welshman from such a fine wife.'' Con stopped walking. They could see both children up ahead, gathering acorns and acting the fool a bit. ''I don't fault you wanting to keep Davy and Myfanwy safe. I'm sure I'd feel the same if I had young ones of my own.''

Given her choice, Enid would have preferred Con's knife in her belly than to hear those words from his lips, frayed to a ragged edge by a longing he might not even recognize.

Tell him! her conscience demanded. *He has a right to know.*

Keep silent! her mother's heart pleaded, *or you will lose Bryn to him.*

Was there no possible compromise?

''Enid?'' Con grasped her hand. ''What's wrong, *cariad*? You're as a pale as whey.''

The depth of concern that resonated in both his touch and his tone sent the color blazing back into her face and started a fragile bud of hope thrusting its stubborn roots into the parched terrain of her heart.

''I-it's nothing,'' she started to insist. Then seeing Con meant to let go of her, she added, ''Our talk just made me think of Howell and what happened to him, poor fellow.''

Forgive me, Howell! She sent a prayer winging heavenward to her dead husband. *For this falsehood and for so much else.*

Con not only continued to hold her hand, he grasped the other one in his, as well. "I'm sorry. You loved him a great deal, didn't you?"

After that last lie, the time had come to tell the truth. Not blurted out all at once, but advanced a piece at a time, the way she might cross a patch of thin ice on the river. Testing with one foot, letting more and more weight on it, all the while listening with bated breath for a warning crack that would send her scrambling back to the safety of the bank.

The paradise that might await her on the other side of that perilous divide would be worth all the terror of crossing it.

Enid swallowed a vast lump that clogged her throat and forced herself to look into Con's eyes. "Not at first, and never in the way you mean."

There! She saw it.

What exactly *it* was, Enid could not have explained. A silvery flicker in those lucid blue depths, perhaps? A subtle twitch in the corner of his mouth or a hardly noticeable catch in his breath?

Though the physical sign might be tenuous, its meaning was as clear to Enid as if Con had trumpeted it at the top of his lungs. And perhaps more easily believed since he took some pains to hide what he felt.

This mattered to him. *She* mattered to him. Not just to seduce as another passing conquest, or to hold as a distant ideal from the past, but here and now, for something more than her body.

And her children? Why should he try to teach them the kind of caution he'd always spurned? Why should he work so hard to shore up Glyneira's defenses and ensure a healthy harvest, unless they were beginning to matter to him as well? How much tighter might it bind Con to them when he discovered that he and Enid had a child together?

She'd let her old hurt blind her to what should have been plain—Con ap Ifan was not the same heedless, care-free lad who'd gone whistling away from Gwynedd without a backward glance. Again and again during the past days he'd tried to tell her that he *had* looked back, often and with deep longing.

The life of a hired soldier was no fit one for a man past his first flush of hardy youth. It must grow increasingly dangerous as strength began to wane and reflexes to slow. No wonder even the most restless peregrines finally succumbed to the long-denied urge to roost...and mate...and nest.

With his alert, searching senses, did Con plumb the depths of her thoughts as they stood there on the low green verge between the woods and the walls with hands clasped?

"What made you marry him, then, over the young princeling you were meant to wed?"

You, Conwy ap Ifan. My love for you sent me into this exile.

No, it was too soon to tell him. This time she must find the right moment, for all their sakes.

"It was not my doing, but my father's. The only choice I had in the matter was whether to pine away, or whether to make the best of what had befallen me."

The flesh on either side of Con's eyes and mouth tightened and his brows drew together. Somehow Enid knew her own face must look that way when one of her children ailed. "Did your husband treat you well?"

"He was faithful."

Enid saw Con flinch, and she was sorry. Still she must give poor Howell his due. She owed him that much.

"He was brave, though not foolhardy. He was a generous host and he took good care of his family. He loved this land and he died defending it."

"He sounds a fine man," Con agreed. Slowly he raised one hand to push a stray lock of hair off her brow. "But did he treasure you as he ought?"

The truth stuck in Enid's throat like a sharp little fish bone.

Con's hand drifted down the side of her face. "When I was far from home, it eased me to think of you living safe, prosperous and cherished on Ynys Mon. If I'd known the rights of it..."

Over his shoulder, a flash of movement caught Enid's eye—a lone rider approaching the gate of Glyneira. She recognized the long-limbed dark mount he rode, for this same messenger had come to summon the muster for Lord Macsen back in the fall. Later he'd brought tidings that Howell had been wounded. He could only be coming today to herald his master's arrival.

Macsen ap Gryffith would soon be here, and her son with him. Enid had run out of time.

Chapter Eight

"What is it, *cariad?*" A qualm of fear went through Con, more intense than any he'd ever felt on his own account. Enid had been acting strangely today...even for her. He'd seen high-strung horses less jumpy.

Speaking of horses, did he hear the soft thud of hooves behind him?

Before he could glance over his shoulder to check, Enid threw her arms around his neck and pulled his face toward her. Her lips made contact with his, slanted and parted, silently urging him to do the same.

Not that Con needed any urging to kiss the woman he'd adored so long and so hopelessly.

His arms locked around her and all the world seemed to dwindle away as Enid melted against him. His body roused, but he ignored that, too, as much as he was able. After all, he might never get another such chance, and he wanted to show her how he wished she'd been cherished during the years they'd been apart.

She fit into his arms as no other woman ever had. It felt as if she had first carved out the space and those coming after her had been forced to squeeze themselves into it...with scant success.

Long, deep and sweet, the kiss they shared was an intoxicating draft of rediscovery, mingled with well-aged tenderness, all spiced with a heady dash of hope. To Con ap Ifan, it seemed he had thirsted for such an elixir all his life.

"Mam! Come see!" The children's cries shattered the fragile bubble of intimacy that had encased Con and Enid.

She started back from him as though surprised by where she had found herself and wondering how she'd come to be there.

She spun about to answer the children. "What is it?"

"The apple trees have started to blossom," called Davy.

"The cherries, too," Myfanwy added.

Edging away from Con, Enid moved toward them. "I hope we'll have a fine harvest for cider making."

Con followed, though without any conscious intention of doing so. If he willed himself to hang back, he doubted his body would obey.

Beyond the south wall of the *maenol,* sheltered from the wind, squatted the fruit trees. Their rough, wrinkled bark and twisted branches gave them a look of little old women, but their unfolding blossoms, creamy white with a rosy blush, transformed them into beautiful maidens swaying in the spring breeze.

Enid hiked up her skirts as she hurried toward them. "Let me smell."

After inhaling deeply, she spun around as though the aroma had set her tipsy.

"Ah, there's no perfume in the world sweeter than apple and cherry blossoms." She mused aloud. "There's a wholesomeness about it, and a kind of innocence."

"Mind the bees," Con warned her. "You don't want to get stung."

This was a queer reversal for them, Con found himself

thinking. That Enid should plunge headlong after some rare pleasure, while he should see the lurking threat and counsel caution.

"Look at them all," breathed Myfanwy as she stared at the swarm. "There must be hundreds."

When the child fell silent, the hum of all those tiny beating wings swelled into a mellow, melodious drone. Just then Con could imagine nothing more pleasant than to rest on the soft grass beneath these trees and sate himself on the beauty of their sight, sound and scent.

Unless it might be to lie there with Enid in his arms, savoring the equally wonderful touch and taste of her.

Ever since he'd left Gwynedd, it felt as though he'd been in a tearing hurry. Whether in a fevered quest to experience every adventure and novelty the world had to offer, or running to escape old hurts and hopeless yearnings, Con wasn't sure.

Now, for the first time in years, possibly in his life, something urged him to stand still awhile. Perhaps in stillness, the good things he sought might come to *him*. In stillness he might savor experiences to their most flavorful depths, rather than just sipping the bland froth on top.

After a few moments watching the bees at their work, Enid turned to the children. "Let's fetch those acorns in, shall we? Auntie Helydd wants you to try on an old kirtle of hers, Myfanwy, to see if it will fit. And Davy, you must do something about that puppy. He wriggled into the pigsty again. It's a wonder the old sow didn't flatten him before Idwal plucked him out."

"Yes, Mam." Myfanwy twirled about, perhaps imagining how she might look in her *new* garment.

Davy raced away as fast as his young legs would carry him.

When Con inhaled one last whiff of fruit blossoms and

started after them, Enid motioned for him to stay. "I expect you'll want to inspect Glyneira's defenses without any young distractions."

He opened his mouth to tell her about Idwal and the axes, but before he could get the words out, Enid approached, speaking in a confidential murmur meant for his ears alone.

"Bide here until I come back. We need to talk, you and I. Alone."

Her usual earnest look had taken on a shadow of desperation. What could be wrong?

"Very well. I'll stay." Con shot her a glance that invited some explanation, but none came.

When Enid turned to follow the children without another word, he called after her. "Don't be too long. I have plenty of jobs waiting for me."

"They'll keep." Enid glanced back over her shoulder.

Struck anew by her delicate grace and dark loveliness, Con didn't bother to correct her. The jobs wouldn't keep, unless someone else offered to do them. As for himself, he'd soon be gone.

That notion tugged at him with a contrary mixture of regret and anticipation. The past week at Glyneira had been a welcome respite from his ceaseless wandering, but Con knew himself too well to believe he'd be content to remain here for weeks and months on end.

He spread himself out on the grass beneath the trees, his hands tucked behind his head. As he'd suspected, it didn't take him long to grow tired of just lying there, no matter how beautiful and restful the place. After a few moments he sat up again, watching for Enid's return.

Though he saw no sign of her, Con did get an idea how to occupy himself while he waited. Chuckling over an old sweet memory, he plucked a spray of apple blossoms and set to work.

Enid shooed the children into the *maenol* before her. She felt as though Fate had a sharp dagger pressed to her breast, forcing her to act.

Once she'd dispatched Myfanwy and Davy, she stopped by the stable where she found Idwal helping Lord Macsen's messenger tend to his mount.

"Lady Enid," the young man greeted her, "I come with tidings of my uncle's approach and a message that he repents his delay in coming."

"Glyneira is honored by his lordship's coming whenever he can spare us his company," Enid replied. "We know well he has many matters demanding his attention— matters that may serve our safety and prosperity. Besides, the wait has given us more time to prepare a fitting reception."

What would the border chief say if he arrived to find her promised to a wandering mercenary turned bard? Much as this week had proven to Enid about her lingering feelings for Con, she found herself suddenly besieged by an army of misgivings.

The last time she'd risked her future in a desperate bid to keep a departing Con with her, there'd been no one to bear the consequences but herself. Now she had so many people depending on her. They needed Lord Macsen's protection and his good will at least as much as she needed Con.

Out of the corner of her eye, she spied Helydd crossing the courtyard. Beckoning her sister-in-law toward the stable, Enid offered Lord Macsen's herald the most welcoming smile she could manage with so many doubts nagging at her.

"Though you did not arrive on foot, I hope you will accept an offer of water."

Catching sight of Helydd, the young man eagerly accepted Glyneira's hospitality.

"Good," replied Enid. "You may remember Helydd versch Rhodri from your past visits. She will see to your comfort."

"Aye." The young man gave a ready nod. "I remember well."

Guest and hostess exchanged a bashful but admiring glance.

"Come this way." Helydd beckoned their guest. "Did you have a good journey?"

"Very. This is a pleasant time of the year to be travelling."

As Helydd and the messenger turned to leave, Enid called out, "My son Bryn, does he ride with Lord Macsen's company?"

"He does." The young man smiled to himself, as if over some remembrance of the boy. "And mighty anxious to return home for a visit. He's talked of little else for a fortnight. I believe Lord Macsen may have finally taken to the road just to quiet the lad."

"I know how Bryn feels. I long to see him in equal measure." Joy and dread warred inside Enid as she watched Helydd lead their guest away to the house.

Anxious as she was for Bryn's coming, she had to admit it would ease her present predicament if he'd stayed behind at Hen Coed. Then she could have postponed her talk with Con. A talk whose outcome she could not foresee, nor was she quite certain how she wanted it to end.

She turned to Idwal, who was going about a few small chores in the stable. "Gaynor will get wind of all this soon enough. If she's looking for me, tell her I'll be back when I come. I have a matter that needs attending.''

Since her bidding scarcely needed a reply, Enid didn't expect more than a nod from Idwal.

But reply he did, with a single word that spoke volumes. ''Con?''

How much did his crippled thoughts grasp what swifter ones missed? To anyone else in Glyneira, Enid would have ignored the question, or told them to tend their own business.

Idwal deserved an answer.

''Con.'' She nodded. ''I need to know where I stand with him. Before the rest of our guests arrive.''

Idwal all but pushed her toward the gate. ''I…mind where you stand. Go on!''

Something about his eager assurance kindled an answering spark of hope in Enid. A trill of nervous laughter bubbled out of her as she slipped through the gate and headed for the orchard.

Some mysterious urge possessed her hands, making them fumble with the cord that secured her braided hair. Once it came untied, she shook her long dark tresses loose to dance in the breeze. The more to look like the girl Con ap Ifan had left behind in Gwynedd so long ago.

Something inside her fluttered, too. The way it had on that summer night when she'd stolen into Con's sleeping place in the hay mow and lain with him. At least today the sun shone bright and the man was not befuddled with drink.

Somehow both those things alarmed her even more.

Rounding the *maenol*, she walked toward the orchard. With one step her feet wanted to break into a blithe skip, if not a dead run. With the next she felt as if someone had lined the soles of her shoes with lead.

As she drew closer to the fruit trees, she did not see Con right away, and a gaping void formed in the pit of her belly. Then suddenly he stepped into view from behind one of the cherry trees aflower with breathtaking clusters of soft pink blossoms.

His eyes widened, as if better to drink in the sight of her. His wide handsome mouth curved in a smile of pure, delicious admiration. When he spoke, lavishing each word on her like a caress, she could not believe that he had ever addressed another woman so.

"By heaven, lass, they say fond longing gilds the memory, but I swear you're more fair even than I remembered you during all our years apart."

How could she deny it when he made her *feel* so beautiful?

She might have thrown herself into his arms then, if he had not held them behind him. His sun-bronzed warrior's face suddenly looked years younger and his eyes glowed with the bashful eagerness of a boy.

"I made something for you."

From behind his back he brought forth a cunningly fashioned circlet of apple and cherry blossoms. With a touch no heavier than the spring breeze, he nestled the floral crown in her hair.

For an instant, Enid wished she had a mirror of polished silver or even a still pool of dark water in which to admire her reflection. Then she caught a passing glimpse of herself in Con's eyes.

That was all she needed.

Con shifted his weight from one foot to the other. "I wish it could have been diamonds and rubies."

"Nonsense," she whispered. "Gems are cold and hard."

"They last forever."

"I'd sooner something rare and precious for an hour." What peculiar talk! If Enid hadn't known better, she'd have sworn Con's words were coming out of her mouth and hers from him.

"I did see the Empress of Constantinople once, fairly dripping in jewels." Con reached out to adjust Enid's chaplet of Welsh spring blossoms. Then his hand strayed down over her hair to graze her cheek. "She was not a hundredth part as fair as my Enid, the Queen of Springtime."

"Thank you for this." Gathering all her courage Enid added, "It makes me feel like a bride."

Con reeled back as though each of those softly uttered words had been a swift arrow aimed at his heart.

Why hadn't he thought of that before? It was the custom for brides to wear a wreath of flowers in their unbound hair. Sometimes the bridegroom wore one, too. Was this how Enid would look when she stood before Father Thomas to take her marriage vows with Macsen ap Gryffith?

Would Con have to stand with the rest of the company at the door of the little country chapel and hold his peace when the priest asked if there were any objections to the union? Would he have to pluck his harp and sing love songs at the bridal feast? And would he have to witness the disrobing of the bride and groom on their wedding night?

The prospect haunted him.

Enid caught his hand in hers and gave it a heartening little squeeze. "I'm glad we've had this time together, Con."

He found himself unable to frame an eloquent answer. "And I."

"You did love me, back in Gwynedd when we were

young, didn't you?'' Her dusky purple eyes held him, divining the truth with her intuition.

''You knew that, surely.''

She shook her head. With subtle brush strokes, wistfulness gilded her beauty. ''How could I have known when you never spoke? And then when you went away?''

''How could I speak?'' The old desperation mounted inside him like steam in a covered pot. ''A fatherless plowboy to the lord's daughter, and her promised to a princeling? I had *nothing* to offer you, Enid.''

He stabbed his finger toward the timbered wall that enclosed Glyneira. ''Not even a modest *maenol* on the borders. Besides, your father would have slain me on the spot for suggesting such a thing, just like the poor fool in 'The Ash Grove.'''

Her eyes told him she knew it was true. ''It nearly killed me to think of your going away.''

''Oh, *cariad,* you must see I could no more stay than I could speak. Even if I'd been content to hie oxen in the fields of some Welsh backwater, how could I have abided watching you wed to another man?''

How could he abide it now? The question slashed at Con's entrails.

An answering flicker of his own distress crossed Enid's delicate features. ''That morning after you first arrived at Glyneira, you claimed it *amused* me to befriend you back then. Accused me of using you to practice flirting.''

The recollection shamed him. ''I should have held my tongue.''

''Not if you believed it. But you mustn't believe it any more.'' Enid's dark eyes had never shone with such ardor, her voice had never rung with such conviction.

''You were the sun and the moon to me, then, Con ap Ifan. I never once thought of you being fatherless. Often as not I envied you for it. I didn't disdain you calling the oxen, either. It's as important a job as there is if folks are to eat. And there's almost a magic to it, the way those great beasts pull for you. Not because you poke them with a goad from behind, but because you call them and coax them to follow you.''

All his life, and especially since he'd left Gwynedd, Con had struggled to rise in the eyes of the world. Now the person whose good opinion mattered more to him than any other was saying she'd always held him in the highest esteem.

It knocked his balance awry…but in a good way.

''You have a magic in you, Con. It lights you up from inside and makes your manner blithe and easy. Who knows? Maybe your father was a prince of the Fair Folk.'' Enid took a step toward him, the fruit blossoms fresh and fragrant in her raven hair.

For reasons he could not fathom, Con backed away from her. ''You give me too much credit, lass. The highest I can hope is that I was bred by a wandering bard with a glib tongue and itchy feet.''

''That's all long in the past, anyhow.''

Again she approached him and again some wary instinct made Con retreat until he felt the rough bark of an apple tree pressing into his back.

Her voice dropped to a beseeching whisper that rolled like thunder in Con's ears. ''You said yourself, the feeling doesn't go away. You said I fill the empty places inside you.''

Enid swayed toward him, her lips held in an unmistakable invitation to kiss.

His own feeble voice of caution warned Con to resist. The moon-baying of roused passion drowned it out with ease.

Subsiding against the trunk of the apple tree, he planted his legs wide and gathered his comely wood nymph close until the soft folds of her clothes and the flesh of her belly pressed against his rigid desire. Then he kissed her in the way the amorous bees kissed the cherry blossoms—rubbing his body against hers and drinking in the sun-sweetened honey of her lips.

His hands roved over her, tugging her skirts higher and higher, mad with impatience at the wool and linen barriers to greater intimacy.

Enid responded with all the passion she must have worked so hard to curb during their youth. Had she, too, lain awake on sultry summer nights, aching to hold him in her arms?

Without words, her lips swore it had been so.

The delicate perfume of the fruit blossoms wrapped around them, mated with the golden warmth of the spring sun and the languid, sensual drone of the bees. Con ap Ifan had sported with many women in many different places, but none like this.

It felt akin to heaven on earth. His earth. Plowed by his hand, protected with his blood.

Enid drew back from their kiss, but such a little way that her breath whispered against Con's chin and the sensitive flesh of his neck. "Your feelings for me haven't gone away, have they, my *cariad?*"

"Gone? Nay." He chuckled at the notion, and at the blissful tickle of her tongue on his throat. "Swelled tenfold more like."

"And do I still fill the empty place inside you?"

"To overflowing." Just as he wanted to fill her, now, the way he'd so often dreamed of.

He hitched her skirts higher still, until his impatient hands could ply the provocative rounding of her bare rump. Given a few more moments, he might peel the kirtle and smock off her altogether until she wriggled in his arms perfectly naked, as befitted a wood nymph.

"Do you want me to marry Lord Macsen?"

"No!" She was *his*. Every caress of his hands on her bare skin claimed more of her. At that moment, his hot blood demanded he battle any other man who might wrest possession of Enid from him. "No, you mustn't."

She subsided against him with a sigh so rich in contentment it almost quieted the blaze of rage his passion had ignited.

"Then you'll wed me, instead, and stay at Glyneira always?"

The whispered words expressed less a question than a sweet certainty.

They went through Con like a blade of cold iron with a jagged edge.

Chapter Nine

Con had loved her, and still did more than ever. He would stay, and they would all be a family.

Enid dismissed a passing qualm about how they'd break the news to Lord Macsen, and how he would respond.

True, she had sensed a potent undercurrent of interest radiating from her late husband's lord every time he'd come to Glyneira. When their hands had chanced to brush while helping themselves to the evening meal, he had not flinched away, but stared into her eyes with a look that questioned and challenged. When she'd offered an opinion, he had listened to her with such intense attention it had made her stammer and set her heart pounding.

Nothing had ever been spoken of this disturbing awareness, nor had anything unseemly passed between them while Howell had lived. Now Enid fervently hoped she had misread Lord Macsen's intent. Otherwise relations between Glyneira and Hen Coed could become badly strained.

It didn't matter, though. Enid twined her arms about Con's neck and threaded her fingers through his hair. Even if it meant incurring the wrath of the powerful border chief, she'd be willing to risk it for Con. Just as she had once braved her father's fury.

Only this time Con would be with her, standing by her. Nothing else mattered.

For a few precious fleeting moments, Enid tasted heaven. When she felt Con's grip on her slacken and his body cease to strain against hers, she did her best to ignore it. When she sensed an unsettling air of aversion from him, she tried to dismiss it, as well.

Even her stubborn will could not hold the truth at bay forever.

"Now, Enid..." As Con reached back to disengage her arms from his neck, his voice took on a calming, almost wheedling tone—the way someone might speak when imparting bad news to a person prone to hysterics. "S-stay at Glyneira...forever? Us wed? You can't mean it."

Only twice before in her life had she peered into an uncertain future with such dread. First, on the morning after she'd surrendered her virginity to Con, when she'd searched the estate in vain for some sign of him. And again when her father had given her in marriage to Howell ap Rhodri, sending her into exile.

Back then, she'd clung to the foolish certainty that everything would have worked out if only Con had chosen to stay and stand beside her. With all her heart, she'd believed he could help her face whatever a threatening tomorrow might bring.

Now Con *was* the threat.

"Of course I mean it." Hurt and fear boiled within her, brewing up an overflowing cauldron of bitter wrath. "Why else would I say such a thing? And why do you make it sound as if I've proposed something impossible...or indecent? You've spent this whole fortnight pursuing me in some fashion or another—singing me love ballads by night, by day taking on all the duties of a husband and father around Glyneira.''

"Yes, but you must see—"

"No, Con ap Ifan, *you* must see! You've kissed me and handled me in ways only a husband has a right to. Can you deny that if I hadn't spoken of marriage you'd have me on my back in the grass with your man-part buried inside me?''

When Con hesitated, his mouth opening and closing in a palsy, she demanded. "Well, can you?''

"I'd be a fool and a liar to deny how much I want you, *cariad*—"

"How dare you call me that?''

Con kneaded his temples. "I dare because that's how I feel about you. It's how I think of you—how I've thought of you for as long as I can recall.''

Enid resisted the soft surge of pleasure that engulfed her heart at his words. If he didn't stop talking by contraries soon, she'd box his ears! "Then why in heaven's name can you not take me to wife? Is it my children? Can you not accept them to raise as your own?''

"You know that has nothing to do with it.'' His tone sharpened. "Myfanwy and Davy are a fine pair, but I don't have it in me to be a good father. Not even to a child of my own flesh.''

She whirled away from him, fearful her face or her eyes might betray something about the child of his own flesh. When she felt Con's hand light on her shoulder, she shook it off.

"This has naught to do with my feelings for you, Enid—the love and the desire. It has naught to do with the children, either. Only with me. I can't throw my future away for any woman…not even you.''

"What *future* awaits you that is so much better than a

warm home and the love of a family?'' Perhaps if it was
brilliant enough she could grasp and grant his reasoning—
not feel herself so lightly cast aside.

''Nothing less than a knighthood.'' There could be no
mistaking the fervor of ambition in his voice. ''I could
return to the Holy Land at the head of a force of my own
men. Not as a hired sword to the Frankish princes, but as
a nobleman in my own right.''

Knighthood? Nobleman? Those were Norman notions!

While Enid tried to make sense of it, Con kept talking,
his bluster running away with him. ''If you but knew how
long and how hard I've labored for this chance to prove
myself, you would not ask me to toss it away as if it
counted for nothing. This is a chance to make my dream
of a lifetime come true, Enid.''

His grand dreams! Just because they soared higher than
hers, with magnificent plumage, did they signify so much
more than her modest nestlings?

''By our Lord's death, you're a filthy spy for the English, aren't you?'' Rounding on him, Enid plucked the
blossom crown from her hair and hurled it at him.

It didn't hurl at all well.

With scarcely more substance than the fragile bonds that
connected her to Con ap Ifan, the delicate floral circlet
wafted toward him. The violence of Enid's heave broke it
apart into single orphaned blossoms that drifted to the
ground. How she wished it *had* been made of heavy gold
and hard gems that might strike him a blow half as painful
as the one he'd dealt her.

''That's what all this has been about!'' she cried. ''A mercenary pretending to be a bard, travelling along the border,
poking around our defenses. Using your wiles and the feeling
I once had for you to worm your way in among us.''

Her words appeared to accomplish what the blossom crown had failed to do. "That's not the way of it, Enid. I swear."

Con's handsome features darkened with that look of injured honor that Enid would once have done anything to avert. Now she hadn't a jot of sympathy for the treacherous bounder. She'd been a fool to fancy him anything like the openhearted, impish boy she'd once loved. Con ap Ifan had lived too long among the Normans and they had stolen his soul.

"I am on a mission for the Empress Maud," he confessed. "One that will help the folk of Powys and Deheubarth."

Though she couldn't listen to any more of his bold-faced lies, some weak, traitorous bent in Enid wondered how she would bear it if he stopped speaking and went away...and she never heard his voice again.

"And you wanted to use my *maenol* to advance this scheme with Macsen ap Gryffith?" Thank heaven she had kept the truth of Bryn's parentage from both the boy and his father. She would never want her son tainted with Con ap Ifan's betrayal of their people. "How could I have let you play me for such a besotted fool?"

"Stop being so bullheaded for once, and listen to reason," Con snapped. "Just because I can't wed you is no reason to wreck a fine opportunity for your lord and for the folk of Powys."

"For you and that empress creature, you mean." Her palm itched to strike him a blow he'd remember her by instead of her melting, vulnerable kisses. "I know better than to heed any more of your sly riddling talk."

The time had come to push her threat. "If you aren't gone from Glyneira by nightfall, I will take it as a sign you mean to wed me, after all. Then I will haul you up in front of Father Thomas to take vows…''

A look of horror flashed in his eyes that made her want to sink to the ground in tears. But damned if she would let some lapdog to a would-be Norman queen drive her to weep on his sorry account!

''…with Idwal's dung fork poked into your back if need be.''

Con stooped and plucked up one of the cherry blossoms at his feet. ''I'm sorry, Enid. You mean more to me than any woman ever has, but…''

His gaze faltered before the blistering reproach of hers. Skirting around her, he walked away, no doubt bound for the house to collect his harp and scrip.

Entirely against her will, Enid turned to watch him go. His usual brisk, jaunty gait had deserted him. If Con ap Ifan had been a dog, his tail would have been dragging in the grass. Enid barricaded her heart against any dangerous feelings of pity that might assail it.

''I mean more to you than any woman ever has,'' she whispered to herself as Con disappeared around the corner of the *maenol* wall. ''*But* not enough.''

Once before he'd left Enid. Left with no other choice, believing her well provided, never knowing how much she'd cared for him. Still regrets had gnawed at him over the years in spite of his determination to ward them off with the distraction of adventure and the lure of advancement.

Forcing one reluctant foot in front of the other, Con made his way to the *maenol* gate, across the courtyard and up the steps to the house.

This time he was leaving Enid in the full knowledge

that she needed him, and that she had always cared for him. Only one thing hadn't changed…he still had no true choice. Not if he ever wanted to hold his head high or to die in the glorious knowledge that he had lived his life to the fullest.

And yet…

It wasn't easy, this going. With every step his disloyal feet threatened to turn and carry him back into the sweet snare of Enid's arms.

Con stole into the great hall, not wanting to be accosted by any of the Glyneira folk. His resolve, he sensed, might not be strong enough to withstand much buffeting. He found his harp and scrip just where he'd left them, in a large chest by the door which stored brychans during the day.

Off in a better-lit corner of the great chamber, Helydd sat in close talk with a young man Con didn't recognize. They appeared too preoccupied with one another to spare him a glance. Employing the soft tread that had saved his life more than once, Con crept out of the hall, silently wishing Helydd good luck with her swain. She was a goodhearted creature, a bit too much under Gaynor's forceful thumb. It would not be easy for her to find a husband with Glyneira so out of the way, and herself with little, if any, dowry.

"Con! Con!"

As he emerged into the courtyard, the children's lusty hails made him start, like a thief caught committing a crime.

"It's Pwyll," cried Davy in a breathless voice. "We can't find him!"

"Will you come help us look?" Myfanwy turned soft beseeching eyes upon him, and Con was lost.

With a glance to check how much longer until sunset,

he clapped Davy around the shoulders. "Never fear, lad. Conwy ap Ifan is a tracker of great skill. Besides, how many places can there be in one *maenol* for a pup to hide?"

Quite a few, as it happened. The sun had dropped an alarming distance toward the western horizon by the time Con and the children discovered Pwyll once again in the pigsty doing his best to filch a meal from the old sow. The litter of piglets squealed at a pitch even more shrill than usual, as they tried to crowd out the furry intruder.

Con plucked the pup out of the sty, fanning his nose as he handed the wriggling little creature back to its master. "You'd better go give him a dunk in the river before your mam catches a whiff of him."

"I will. I will." As he headed toward the gate with the pup in his arms, Davy called over his shoulder, "Thank you for finding him!"

"Glad I could help." As Con waved after the small, retreating figure, a queer lump of dismay rose in his throat.

He glanced down to see Myfanwy still standing beside him.

"Hadn't you ought to go after your brother?" he asked. "To make sure he doesn't drown them both?" Hard as he tried to forge a jaunty smile, his lips resisted.

The girl regarded him with a look just as grave. "You're going away, aren't you?"

"Me?" Con struggled with his answer. A harmless falsehood would spare him an awkward parting. He wasn't used to bidding goodbye.

Myfanwy saved him the decision. "You have your harp slung over your shoulder, and your scrip on your belt."

"You have a keen eye, lass." As he'd done so often with her mother in their youth, Con tickled the child's cheek with the end of her golden braid, trying to coax a parting smile from her. "You'd make a fine general."

"Where will you go?" Her steady blue gaze made Con squirm.

"Hen Coed."

"Will you come again?"

"Who knows?" Con shrugged. "I could well."

Myfanwy shook her fair head. "You won't."

It was not an accusation or a complaint, but a plain statement of truth. Yet it struck Con a blow, in the way an ordinary farm tool like an ax or a pike might if wielded as a weapon.

Her shoulders gave a subtle twitch that seemed to dismiss him. "I'd better go keep an eye on my brother, like you said." She set off with a brisk step, calling back with cheerful indifference, "Safe journey to you, Master Con."

"Ah...Myfanwy?"

She glanced back without fully stopping. "Aye?"

"You'll mind what I told you and Davy about the Normans, and keeping close to the *maenol,* won't you?" Con tried to ignore a fierce stinging that beset his eyes.

"I will." She turned from him so swiftly her long blond plait of hair whipped around.

As the child walked away, Con thought he heard her mutter, "Though I don't see why it matters to you."

That made two of them perplexed by the question.

Con tried to shrug it off, the way Myfanwy had his going, but a strange, worrisome hesitation weighed on his shoulders. He pushed himself toward the gate by imagining the timber walls of Glyneira closing in around him.

He was about to cross the threshold into the wide world beyond Enid's *maenol* when a deep, halting voice lured him back again.

"Con...axes. Good and sharp."

Casting a nervous glance toward the horizon, Con turned. "That's fine, Idwal. My thanks to you and to Math. I wish I could stay to help you hew those trees and mend the wall, but...I must be on my way."

Idwal lowered the half-dozen axes he held in one massive hand. "That's...sudden. The day's waning. Bide one more night."

Bide one more night, and he'd never get away!

"I've tarried too long, already, my friend." Though he tried to look and sound casual, Con wondered if Idwal could see through him as easily as Myfanwy had. "I wouldn't be much use chopping trees, anyway. That's a job for big brawny fellows like you and Math. I know I can trust you to see to it."

Though he tried to resist, a pleading note crept into his voice. "You will, won't you, Idwal? It's important."

Idwal nodded his big shaggy head. "I will. Never you... fear."

"Good." Con thrust out his hand. "Then I suppose this is goodbye for us."

Idwal fumbled the axes to free his right hand for shaking Con's. "Aye...well, safe journey. Come again, do."

Trying not to wince at Idwal's hearty grip, Con flashed him a broad grin rather than reply with words the other man might recognize as false.

Again he started for the gate, wondering who might call him back this time. But no further summons came.

Con breathed a sigh of relief when he finally stepped through the gate, free of Enid's wedding threat at last. Yet as he sauntered down a footpath that led to a gap in the trees, he found himself glancing back over his shoulder again and again. Called by a voice only his heart could hear.

* * *

The look on Idwal's face was enough to tell Enid what she wanted to know. Or rather, what she *didn't* want to know.

She made herself ask just the same, to keep any hope from taking root in her heart like the stubborn, bothersome weed it was.

"How long ago did Con leave?"

"Not long." An expectant light kindled in the big man's eyes. "If I rode…I could fetch him back."

The burst of laughter Enid forced came out harsh. "Fetch him back—whatever for? Lord Macsen is on his way, with a good-sized party, no doubt. This will make one less mouth to feed and one less body to house."

"Con brought in…more than he ate." Idwal replied. "And he didn't…take much room…in the hall benights. Wasn't he meant to harp for the guests?"

Enid tried to ignore the gentle reproach behind her brother-in-law's words, one of the longest and most complex utterances she'd heard from him since he'd taken his head wound.

"I know Con was good company for you." She patted Idwal's arm, all the while congratulating herself for speaking Con's name without her voice cracking into tearful splinters. "I'm sorry he couldn't stay longer with us."

Nothing would force her to admit how sorry.

"But," she added in a firm tone before Idwal could suggest some other scheme for fetching Con back to Glyneira, "he had matters to attend elsewhere. If the man chose to go, we can't very well hold him hostage, can we?"

His burst of eloquence spent, Idwal replied with a cryptic grunt.

Enid tugged at his sleeve. "Come along to eat, then, before the food grows cold and Gaynor scolds us both."

That was what she needed—a good, filling supper to

hearten her, and the company of all the Glyneira folk to distract her thoughts from Con ap Ifan.

On both counts, the meal failed miserably.

When the food was served, Enid found she had no appetite to do more than nibble at her *lagana*. Nor did the hall full of people do much to occupy her thoughts. Not since the previous autumn, when Howell had lain dying, had she seen everyone so subdued.

The only ones who seemed not to notice the oppressive mood of the place were Helydd and Lord Macsen's nephew, Rhys. Their lively talk and occasional laughter served only to emphasize the downcast silence of the rest. It was all Enid could do to keep from leaping onto the table and demanding they celebrate Con's going instead of moping about like a party of mourners.

If any of them had cause to celebrate, it was her, Enid reminded herself as she labored to dredge a crumb of satisfaction or even relief from the aching depths of her heart.

After all, she'd set herself to get rid of Con ap Ifan, and she'd done it. Her only fault had been the repeated delays in springing her trap, until she'd fallen so far back under Con's charming thrall that she'd duped herself into believing he might stay.

He'd wasted no time disabusing her of that ridiculous fancy.

Throughout that long dull evening, Enid drank more than her usual share of cider. *Ointment for the heart* was the poetic Welsh term for strong drink, but it provided no balm for hers. Instead it swept through her like a spring flood, demolishing the sturdy bulwark of her pride, and forcing her to admit how much this second leaving of Con's had hurt and humiliated her.

What a simpleton she'd been to lap up his seductive lies! Over the years he'd probably told hundreds of women they filled his *empty place*. Enid's imagination swarmed with tormenting visions of those women.

Buxom and pliant, the way most men liked their conquests. Bejewelled, clad in vibrant-colored gowns made of costly fabrics from the Orient. Beautiful in an exotic fashion sure to eclipse a simple Welsh widow.

Damn Con ap Ifan!

The man had an empty place inside of him—that much was true. An empty place, right where his heart should have been.

Chapter Ten

Were the Welsh heavens as vexed with him as Enid must be? Con wondered when a light but steady rain began to spit from the clouds a while after he'd left Glyneira.

Too bad about them both! He pulled his cloak tighter and trudged on, reminding himself that he'd marched through far worse than a sprinkle of rain countless times in the past thirteen years. On a far emptier belly, too.

Though not in recent months.

As his stomach gave a pitiful growl, Con chided himself for leaving the *maenol* in such haste and agitation that he hadn't thought to pass through the kitchen on his way. There, he might easily have charmed Gaynor out of a cake of *lagana* and a joint of stewed fowl for the road.

Ah well, there was no help for it now.

In a way, Con rather welcomed the rain and his hunger. Such minor discomforts of the body went some way to distract him from the acute discomfort of his heart.

It did no good to remind himself that he'd been forced to quit Glyneira when he'd rather have stayed—that he'd had no true choice in the matter. His troublesome ability to see a question from all possible sides compelled him to view the events of the past week through Enid's eyes.

What he saw made him writhe with shame.

Why *had* he pursued her with such energy when he knew he could not wed her? Had it been because he'd gotten so used to wooing any available woman wherever he found himself? He of all men had reason to know Enid would never settle for a brief tryst, no matter how exciting.

Or had he been unable to stop himself from acting on the attraction that had kindled so long ago and never been quenched? Neither reason cast him in a very flattering light, he decided.

When he could no longer see the path in front of him, Con scrambled up into the branches of a tall oak beside the path. It wasn't a comfortable spot to sleep, but at least the tree's thick foliage kept off most of the rain. If he must sleep out in the open, he preferred the illusion of safety provided by a perch well off the ground, hidden from all but the sharpest eyes.

Straddling a thick branch, with his back braced against the broad rough trunk, Con listened to the soft patter of rain on the leaves. It soothed him like a lullaby, even as it troubled his spirit with a vision of falling tears. On the shadowed, uncanny borderland between waking and dreams, another notion ambushed the Welsh warrior.

Enid had been willing, even eager, to wed him.

The significance of that almost knocked Con out of his leafy perch. He'd been so occupied with why he could not marry her, he hadn't spared a passing thought to this once unimaginable marvel. Her position might not be as high now as it had once been, but within Wales his was scarcely higher than in his youth. He was a rootless, landless fellow in a country where kin and property counted for all.

Now that Enid was no longer reliant on her father, but as independent as she might ever be in this life, she had fixed her choice upon *him*. Even when she had hopes of a much more advantageous match. It was an honor beyond anything Con ap Ifan had dreamed during his downtrodden boyhood.

And how had he received that precious boon?

A bilious spasm gripped his stomach. Hard as Con tried to persuade himself it was only hunger pangs, he remained unconvinced.

He'd scorned the offer that must have cost Enid so dearly in pride and peace of mind. Hurled it back in her face as though *she* were unworthy of *him*.

It would take more than a couple of sword taps on his shoulders from the Empress to ennoble a base creature like him, Con acknowledged with a rueful sigh as he slipped deeper into restless dreams.

No doubt Enid was well rid of him for the second time in her life. The question remained—would he be able to oust her from possession of his heart? For thirteen years he had tried and failed.

What made him imagine he could succeed this time?

For all the rest she got that night, Enid might as well have been sleeping out of doors in the rain. Tossing and turning under her thick woolen brychan, she tried to take vindictive satisfaction from the thought of Con out on such a night.

It was a plight of his own making, after all. If he'd stayed at Glyneira as she'd bidden him—as she'd begged him—he might be tucked up snug with her at this very moment. Enid rolled over again and tried to keep from imagining Con in her bed.

It wasn't any use.

The charming rascal wormed his way in there as he managed to slither into plenty of other places he had no business being. She could almost hear him whispering lyrical flattery as his hands roved up beneath her night smock, anointing her flesh with need and promises of pleasure. She could almost feel him suckling her lower lip or the tip of her bosom, sending a hot tickle coursing down to her loins.

Curse his hide! The mere *thought* of Con ap Ifan ignited a more furious blaze of desire in her than poor Howell's real mating ever had. And what of Lord Macsen? If she wed the border lord, would Con vanquish him on this field of battle, too?

After what seemed like endless hours of such tormenting thoughts, Enid dragged herself out of bed with an aching head, a sour stomach and a heavy heart. She tried to sweeten her humor by reminding herself she'd soon see Bryn. If events unfolded as she expected, she might not have to part from her firstborn again for quite some time.

Yet even the thought of Bryn's coming didn't cheer her as it should have, for the boy would remind her too much of his absent father.

A shiver of apprehension went through Enid.

Now that the Glyneira folk had seen Con ap Ifan, might some of them mark the likeness between him and her eldest son? Might those with long memories recall how the boy had been born right speedily following her marriage to Howell?

She couldn't waste her time worrying about what she could not prevent, Enid chided herself. Instead, she must do what she'd always done when trouble assailed—occupy her hands and at least part of her mind with work.

And there was no shortage of work to do with Lord Macsen's party expected before nightfall. With the help of Helydd and a couple of the other women, Enid swept straw from the hall floor and put down fresh rushes, laced with bay, fennel and other strewing herbs. She looked over the

stables to make sure they were ready to receive the mounts
from Hen Coed. Finally, on her way back to check on the
kitchen, she started at the sound of Con's name being spoken.

"I hope he'll come back soon." From around the corner
of the washhouse, Davy let out a sigh so pitiful it was
almost funny. "He made everything jolly. And he promised to take us up to the ridge."

Though she knew Gaynor might need her help in the
kitchen, Enid lingered out of sight, listening to the children.

"I'm in no hurry to see him again," Myfanwy informed
her brother in a brisk tone. "Sneaking off without a decent
farewell, and after we gave him such a warm welcome.
He promised to take us to the ridge, *today,* then he broke
his word."

"Maybe he had to leave quickly." Davy sounded defensive, as though Con's abrupt departure had bothered
him more than he cared to admit. "Maybe some of those
Saracen fellows were after him."

Myfanwy made no reply for a moment, but Enid could
picture the girl shaking her head and gazing heavenward.
"There's no Saracens in Wales, Davyd ap Howell. Have
some sense!"

"Normans, then," insisted Davy. "Mind what Con told
us about them. Maybe he was leading a whole army of
them away from Glyneira."

"He'd more likely lead them straight through the gate,"
Myfanwy snapped. "Fought for the Normans, that man
did. For pay. Which makes him just as bad as they are.
Worse maybe."

"Doesn't!"

"Does so!"

"Enough of that, the pair of you!" Enid bore down on

her children. Even though he'd gone, Con ap Ifan was still causing trouble in her home.

Her overwrought feelings sharpened her voice. "If you can't find anything better to do than quarrel, I have plenty of jobs I can give you. Davy, go see if Uncle Idwal has any errands he needs you to run. Myfanwy, be a good girl and pen up the geese. I don't want them waddling around hissing at the horses."

"Yes, Mam." Myfanwy pulled a face at her brother.

Davy stuck out his tongue in reply.

"Off with you both!" Enid shot the children a black look that sent them scurrying.

Listening to Davy and Myfanwy had been almost as bad as the contrary voices that swirled inside her own head— one condemning Con, the other taking his part. How she longed for Lord Macsen and his party to arrive! Surely *that* would take her mind off the vexing subject of Conwy ap Ifan…if anything could.

From the fog of a fitful doze, Con heard a deep voice rumble. "My, what big, featherless birds they breed in this part of Powys."

After a chorus of male laughter, a younger voice piped up, "Perhaps the Fair Folk bewitched a sparrow hawk into the shape of a man."

Such an odd exchange could only be part of a dream, but Con pried open one eye just in case it wasn't. What he saw made him start up so suddenly he almost pitched out of the tree.

A party of over half a dozen armed and mounted men loitered on the ground below staring up at him. The fellow who appeared to be the leader of the group bettered even Idwal's impressive dimensions. With his thick black hair and bristling brows over shrewd-looking dark eyes, the huge man put Con in mind of a bear.

Cursing his lapse in proper wariness, Con slid down from his oaken perch. If these men had wanted to, they could have shot so many arrows into him that his corpse would have looked like a giant hedgehog.

He bowed before the big dark man. "Have I the honor of addressing Macsen ap Gryffith?"

So near Glyneira, it had better be.

"That depends, tree-dweller." One corner of the man's wide mouth raised a trifle. "Who's doing the asking?"

"Conwy ap Ifan, from Gwydir in Gwynedd."

"Gwydir, you say?" The big man stroked the dense whisker over his lip as if it aided him in thought. "The lady of the *maenol* not far from here is of that country."

"Aye." Con nodded. "Enid versch Blethyn is distant kin of mine. I just passed several pleasant days at Glyneira. Now I am on my way to Hen Coed to treat on urgent matters with Lord Macsen."

"Then we have spared you a journey, Conwy ap Ifan. I am the man you seek." Lord Macsen trained a challenging gaze upon Con. "Tell me, did you time your departure from Glyneira ill? Or did some accident slow you? In your place, I'd have passed one more warm, dry night under Lady Enid's roof, then made a fresh start this morning."

As Con mentally scrambled for the least incriminating answer, Lord Macsen added, "Better yet, I might have stayed on at Glyneira and let the folk from Hen Coed come to me. My herald must have arrived at the *maenol* before you left yesterday, or did you meet him on the road?"

Con remembered the young stranger he'd spied being entertained by Helydd. "I do believe your herald reached Glyneira safely."

Why had Enid not told him Lord Macsen was due to

arrive so shortly? She must have known. A seed of suspicion found fertile soil in Con's mind.

"As it happens, Lord Macsen, I had...er...hoped to intercept you *before* you reached Glyneira."

Two bushy brows shot up. "Before? Why so?"

Con glanced at the others in the party, six younger men and a boy. Macsen's son? Except for the dark hair and full brows, nothing about the slender lad resembled the border lord.

"If we might talk for a moment, more privately, my lord..." Anticipating a protest, Con raised his hands above his head. "I bear no arms but my eating knife and that you are welcome to take from me."

Lord Macsen exchanged looks with a couple of his men. One dismounted and promptly relieved Con of the knife, handing it over to his master.

The border chief nodded back up the trail, a subtle sign his party was quick to obey. They drew off a discreet distance.

"Talk quickly," Lord Macsen advised Con in the calm tone of a man accustomed to ready obedience. "I'm anxious to reach Glyneira. My visit there has been postponed too often."

The air rushed out of Con's lungs, as though Lord Macsen's massive roan stallion had fetched him a kick in the belly. He knew why the border lord was eager to reach Enid's *maenol*...to beg from her what Con had scorned.

Seeing the flicker of impatience in Lord Macsen's dark eyes, Con forced himself to speak. "It concerns your Norman neighbors in Salop."

"Falconbridge? Revelstone?" The border lord's eyes narrowed. "What of them?"

"I know you have just grudges against them both." Con measured his words. "With the Normans divided amongst themselves over who will wear the English crown, this could be your best chance to strike a blow in return."

"And what concern have *you* in *our* quarrels?"

A canny fellow, Macsen ap Gryffith. Con knew better than to mislead such a man.

"I will tell you that and more besides, sire. All to your advantage, I swear. If you will take me back with you to Hen Coed, we can talk more on the matter."

After an instant to consider, the border lord shook his head. "I have urgent business with your kinswoman at Glyneira, and we are at her very doorstep. Come back with us and speak your piece there. Anything you might say at Hen Coed will not lose its flavor at Glyneira."

Con wasn't certain which dismayed him more—the notion of returning to Enid's house himself, or the thought of Macsen ap Gryffith going there. Clearly Gaynor had not misread the man's intent as far as her sister-in-law was concerned.

"I would just as lief not strain Lady Enid's hospitality with an extra guest she little expects."

Con struggled to keep his pride in check. It galled him to stand on the ground, addressing the border lord on his lofty mount. If Con's mission succeeded and he won further royal favor in the Holy Land, he could be every inch Lord Macsen's equal one day.

"Besides, sire, if you heed the tidings I bring, you might do well to have your men mustered at Hen Coed so you can strike without delay."

Again the border lord paused for thought.

"No." Tossing Con's knife to the ground at his feet, Macsen ap Gryffith wheeled his great rawboned horse, motioning for his men to remount and follow him. "Not even on that account will I come so close to Glyneira without completing my mission."

For all their appearance of mannerly disinterest in Lord Macsen's parlay with the stranger, his men must have been keeping their eyes trained on him. They obeyed his curt, wordless summons without a beat of hesitation.

Over his shoulder, the border chief tossed Con an ultimatum. "If you would talk more with me, return to Glyneira with us. If not, God speed you."

Con bit his tongue to keep from unleashing a torrent of curses. Something about the big, dark-avised border lord put Con in mind of his friend, Rowan DeCourtenay. Both had a vital presence, an air of determination and command. Having made his decision, Macsen ap Gryffith would be neither forced nor swayed from his course. No more than Rowan would have been.

Nor Enid, for that matter.

Perhaps Lord Macsen and the mistress of Glyneira were better matched than Con had first thought. After all, Enid craved permanence and security. Where better to find them than in that sturdy rock of a man? And yet...

Though he had never ventured closer to marriage than in the past turbulent few days, Con sensed that two strong, stubborn wills in a marriage was at least one too many.

Lord Macsen's party trooped by Con in silence, casting glances at him, by turns curious, wary and scornful. Last-but-one in the column rode the boy. When his horse drew beside Con, the lad reined to a halt.

"If you mean to come with us, you may ride with me," he offered.

What choice did he have, Con asked himself, unless he wanted his whole mission for the Empress brought to naught? Surely Enid wouldn't follow through on her threat to wed him by force with Lord Macsen in attendance.

The man riding rear guard scowled at Con, clearly vexed with the delay.

"Thank you, young sir." Con scrambled up behind the boy on a placid old gelding whose rusty hide and black mane were both well shot with white hairs.

Once Con was securely mounted, the boy coaxed his horse into a temperate trot to catch up with the others.

"You seem to be the only one of Lord Macsen's party schooled in proper courtesy." Con praised the lad. Under his breath he muttered, "Including Lord Macsen himself."

"Don't fault them too much." The boy spoke in a clear, pleasant voice that sounded oddly familiar. "They must always be on guard against the Normans. Never more so than out in the country like this. They'll be much better humored once we get behind the walls of Glyneira—you'll see."

"You seem jaunty enough, my young friend." Something about the lad made Con want to smile in spite of all the matters that weighed on him.

"Because I'm going home." The boy seemed to savor that last word as if it was a drop of honey on his tongue. "This will be my first visit since…in a while."

A fleeting chill ran through Con. His clothes were still damp from last night. At least, he tried to convince himself that was the cause.

Without waiting for a reply, the boy continued, "You and I must be some distant relation, if you are kin to my mother."

Having caught up to the other horses, the gelding curbed his pace to a brisk walk.

Con clung tighter to the boy to keep from falling off. "Your m-mother?"

The lad gave a vigorous nod. "Lady Enid is my mother. I'm Bryn ap Howell. She probably told you about me. I have been in fosterage with Lord Macsen ever since my brother was born."

"Of…course," Con heard himself say. "It's an honor to meet you, Bryn ap Howell."

Even as the rote pleasantry left his mouth, Con plundered his memory for any mention of Enid's elder son. Myfanwy or Davy might have made passing reference to someone named Bryn, but Con had paid no heed. Enid, he was certain, had never mentioned having another child besides her two at home.

Bryn looked nothing like his brother and sister, with their fair coloring. He had Enid's dark hair and brows, but nothing of her delicate features. Queer she had not mentioned him. Unless she missed the boy so much, she could not bear to be reminded of his absence. That would be like Enid.

"Has his lordship been a good master to you?" Con asked.

"The best!" There could be no doubt of the young fellow's sincerity. "They use me well at Hen Coed. For all that, home will always be wherever my mother is."

Con might almost have spoken the words himself. He could scarcely recall his own mother, and for years he had been without a home…by choice. Hearing the conviction and warmth in Bryn's young voice, Con suddenly knew that such a home as he had, he would always find with Enid.

"You handle a horse well, Master Bryn. How old are you?"

"Thirteen."

Again Con nearly pitched off the gelding's back. This time he could not blame the creature for slowing or speeding its pace. Half a dozen bothersome, unuttered questions merged in his thoughts, admitting of only one impossible answer.

"*Almost* thirteen," Bryn amended as though repenting his small boast. "In the autumn."

That slight correction came too late for Con.

Already an unwelcome certainty had been born in his mind, writhing, red and squalling. The dubious, disagreeable truth could no more be ignored than an infant could be thrust back into its mother's womb.

This cheerful, well-made boy whom he clutched 'round the middle was not in fact Bryn ap Howell, but...Bryn ap Conwy.

Bryn *son of* Con.

How was that possible? Never, to his knowledge, had he made love to the boy's mother, except in his dreams.

Suddenly Con's vexing ability to assume the outlook of another person reared its troublesome head again. All of Enid's perplexing behavior during that past week finally made a kind of garbled sense. Everything she'd done, everything she'd said, everything she'd *not said* had served only a single purpose—to keep him in ignorance of her son's existence.

She'd even gone so far as pretending she wanted to wed him, in order to make Con flee Glyneira. And he had performed like a well-trained hound.

As they rode through the rain-washed forest, Con saw nothing of the world around him but a blur of green. He scarcely heard the muted thunder of the swiftly flowing river off in the distance. It could almost have been the sound of his own thoughts, churning like white water. He had so many questions he wanted to put to Enid, and demand satisfactory answers.

With each jog of the horse that brought them closer to Glyneira, Con's heart gave a lurch and cried, "My son! *My* son!"

But whether it cried out in elation or alarm, Con could not be certain.

Chapter Eleven

A perfect bubble of joy swelled in Enid's heart when she first caught sight of her son riding into Glyneira.

She should have known such joy could not last any longer than a bubble. When she recognized the man riding with Bryn, her bubble froze, fell and shattered into a thousand jagged shards.

For an instant she clung to the futile hope that Con might be as blind to Bryn's identity as he had once been to her passionate yearning for him. The moment her gaze met his, that brittle illusion also shattered, chilling her with a fear more bleak than any she had yet experienced.

Enid cursed herself for failing to drive Con from Glyneira sooner, when he'd given her so many chances. Amid Lord Macsen's large household at Hen Coed, Con might never have caught more than a passing glimpse of her son.

Of *his* son.

Now she would pay the price for her foolish weakness.

Willing her feet to carry her forward, Enid approached her guests. "Welcome to Glyneira, Macsen ap Gryffith. I hope you and your men will accept water to refresh yourselves."

Though she wished she could withhold the ceremonial

offer of water from Con ap Ifan, Enid knew such action would only rouse Lord Macsen's suspicion and Con's hostility. His icy blue gaze warned her she did not dare add to his ire.

Lord Macsen vaulted from his saddle and greeted her with the kiss of peace. "Well come, indeed, Lady Enid. Though we have arrived on horseback, rather than on foot, my party and I accept your offer of water with thanks. I regret taking so long to return to Glyneira. Every time I prepared to set out, either Falconbridge or Revelstone made threatening moves to keep us on alert at Hen Coed. Add it as another reason for spite against them."

The intensity of his dark gaze sent a ripple of disquiet through Enid. Everything about the man was so large and forceful. He made her feel even smaller and more vulnerable by comparison.

"Your coming is all the more agreeable for being long anticipated." Enid stifled a qualm of conscience.

It wasn't a lie…quite. Though she had told herself time and again how much she wanted to wed Lord Macsen, faced with his dark, potent presence, she found herself thankful he hadn't arrived any sooner to claim her.

He held on to her hand. Enid wished he would release it, but she did not dare ask him to.

The border lord nodded back toward Con ap Ifan, who was helping Bryn dismount. "I hope you won't take it amiss that we've brought a former guest of yours with us for a return visit? To hear him tell it, this Con fellow has some weighty matters to talk over with me."

"Why should I mind?" Enid hoped the false smile on her face and forced cheer in her voice would not betray her true feelings. "All my household enjoyed Con's tales and harping during his first stay. It's only fitting Glyneira should have a bard on hand to entertain you in the evenings while you're here."

"A bard, you say?" Lord Macsen glanced back at Con, his dark brows raised. "For a bard, he talks strangely like a warrior." He shrugged. "I look forward to hearing him play."

To Enid's ears, the words sounded like a threat. For reasons she could not begin to understand, she found herself rallying to Con's defense. "You'll enjoy it very much, I'm sure."

Turning, she beckoned to Myfanwy, who hung back unwontedly bashful, perhaps at the sight of so many strangers arriving all at once.

"Lord Macsen, if you and your men will follow my daughter, she'll show you to the hall. I'll be along in a moment to attend you, but first I must have a word with a certain young fellow in your party."

The border chief nodded and flashed a fond smile that made him look much less forbidding. "Gather him into your arms, if he hasn't grown too manly to permit it. And even if he has, tell Bryn ap Howell his lord commands he submit to his mother's embrace."

"I pray he'll still come willingly." Enid cast covetous eyes toward her son. "But if not, I shall be glad to avail myself of your order, my lord."

As Idwal and the other men of Glyneira led their guests' horses to the stable, Lord Macsen and his party followed Myfanwy into the house.

A little anxious after what Lord Macsen had said, Enid held her arms open to Bryn. His only concession to young manhood was to make certain none of the Hen Coed company was watching before he pelted into his mother's waiting embrace.

"You feel like a *pigwidgeon!*" she cried, gathering him

to her and planting a doting kiss on his still-downy cheek. "All skin and bones. Are they not feeding you well enough at Hen Coed? Have you been ill?"

She couldn't help exaggerating her concern. Not under torture would Enid admit anyone else could possibly look after her son as well as she.

"I'm fine, Mam, and they feed me plenty," protested Bryn. "It's just that I've grown since you last saw me. Why, I'm taller than you now."

"So you are!" Enid wailed, looking *up* into her son's face for the first time.

If only she could make the years run backward, until he was a fat jolly baby again, crowing as he bounced on Idwal's knee. "It's a good thing I got that wool dyed to weave you a new cloak, Master Longshanks. Between Auntie Gaynor and me, we'll fatten you up while you're with us."

If events unfolded as they should, she wouldn't have to part from him again when the time came for Lord Macsen's party to return to Hen Coed.

But Bryn would be a man all too soon, a warning whisper in Enid's mind cautioned her. In a few years' time, he might fly her safe nest for good. Myfanwy and Davy would one day have lives of their own, too. Meanwhile, she'd be committed to Macsen ap Gryffith for the rest of her days.

A fair trade, to keep her children safe until they grew old enough to make their own way in the world, her maternal nature insisted.

Her face must have betrayed the contention within her, for Bryn gazed at her with fond concern. "Is something wrong, Mam? How can I help?"

As quickly as she'd cleaned old rushes from the floor of the hall, Enid swept her troubles from her mind and fixed on a makeshift smile that she hoped would reassure her son. "I'm content as I can be, now that I have all my chicks under my wing again. All you need do to complete my happiness is eat your fill and enjoy your visit with us."

"Bryn!" Davy scampered across the courtyard with the squirming puppy in his arms. "I've got a dog all my own. See?"

"A likely looking whelp he is, too." Bryn petted the little dog, who barked and licked his fingers. "I mind you'll make a fine sheepdog out of him, one day."

Davy replied with a vigorous nod. "If I put him on a leash, maybe Con will let him come along with us to the ridge tomorrow." The child glanced past his mother.

Enid spun about to find Con standing close behind her. A gasp stuck in her throat.

"You *will* take us up to the ridge like you promised, won't you, Master Con?" asked Davy. "Myfanwy said you wouldn't come back, but I knew you'd never break your word."

"It was good of you to have faith in me, Davy-boy." Con's countenance looked more grave than Enid had ever seen it. "Yes, unless something prevents, I'll go along with you to the ridge, tomorrow. Pwyll is welcome to come along if he promises to behave himself. I can't be searching for him the length and breadth of Powys if he wanders off."

"I'll make sure he doesn't get away," Davy vowed, as solemn as if he were swearing a blood oath.

"And I know you'll never break your word. Do you think your brother would care to come along with us?" Though Con feigned a tone of cheerful indifference, Enid marked the intent gaze he bent upon her elder son.

"Aye," said Bryn, at the same instant his mother cried, "No!"

Both boys turned on her with furrowed brows.

"Y-you should ask your foster-father's permission before going off on some lark, Bryn." Enid tried to keep a note of desperation from her voice. "Lord Macsen may have need of your service tomorrow."

She ignored the glare Con shot her.

"You're right, Mam," said the boy. "I'll go ask him, now. Come on, Davy. Let's show Lord Macsen your pup. Race you to the hall."

Letting Davy get a good lead on him, Bryn winked at his mother...and Con. In that instant, the resemblance between her son and his natural father struck Enid like a cruel blow. It was all she could do to keep a whimper from escaping her lips as she watched Bryn chase Davy toward the hall.

From behind, Con's voice wrapped around her, scarcely louder than a passing breeze. His words thundered in her ears, just the same. "You never truly wanted to wed me, did you, Enid? It was only a ruse to drive me away from Glyneira before the boy came."

A palisade of hurt and fear went up around her heart. Archers on the ramparts took aim at Con ap Ifan.

"Yes...it...was." With each lying word, Enid bought back a piece of her self-respect. Not for the world would she let Con guess the truth of it. The man had too many advantages over her without adding the certain knowledge of how much she still wanted him.

Had wanted him. *Had* wanted him.

Con made no move to circle around and face her. Enid did not trust herself to turn and confront him. Anyone watching from a distance might not even realize they were talking to one another. Enid was content to keep it that way.

"I don't know how he can be mine," Con murmured. "But I know he *is*."

The look on his face when he'd entered the courtyard had already told her so, still Enid flinched to hear the words from Con's lips. Though she could not bear to meet his gaze, and it galled her to beg any boon of him, she forced herself to turn.

"You won't tell him, will you?" She stared at the clasp that fastened Con's cloak. "If you ever had any true feelings for me, I beseech you say nothing of this to Bryn."

"We must talk, you and I." Con sounded like a victorious warrior dictating terms of surrender. "I need to know how this happened and why you kept it from me all these years."

If he couldn't guess the answer to that, he was a fool. Though Enid wanted to rage at him, she did not dare for so many reasons. "Tonight, after the meal, we can meet down by the river where there's no chance of anyone overhearing us. I'll make certain Idwal takes the watch himself so our going is not marked by anyone who's apt to gossip."

"Very well. After the meal, by the river." Without another word, Con strode away.

Realizing he had not replied to her plea, Enid ran to catch up with him, grabbing the hem of his cloak with such force it was a wonder the cloth did not rend.

"Say nothing of this to my son," she hissed. "Promise?"

"I will hold my tongue until I've heard you out, tonight." Con wrenched his cloak from her grasp. "After that, I promise nothing."

So it was true.

Con moved through the rest of the day like a reeling drunkard, caught so deep in his own thoughts and memories that his spirit might have been ensnared in the past while his empty husk of a body remained in the present.

Though he did his best not to call attention to himself, he took every opportunity to stick close to Bryn. Observing the boy, Con saw fleeting glimpses of Enid, of her father...and of himself. Was he also catching a peep of the father he'd never known?

"Say, Bryn," Davy pulled his brother over to the dim corner of the hall where Con had taken a seat. "Did you know Con was a soldier in the Holy Land?"

"Is it true?" The lad's eyes, blue like Con's but tinged with his mother's darker shades of purple, fairly glowed with eager curiosity. "How long were you there? Did you ever fight the Saracens?"

"More often the Turks." Sparked by Bryn's avid interest in him, Con launched into a thrilling account of one of his adventures with Rowan DeCourtenay.

These days, Rowan himself was a new father to a lusty infant boy, Con recalled. What would his old friend and comrade make of Con having a son almost grown? Especially one so handsome, clever and good-natured?

Con could hardly wait to whisk the boy off to Brantham for a proper introduction. Perhaps a presentation to the Empress in Gloucester? Or to Prince Jocelin's opulent court in Edessa? Suddenly, Con felt his hunger for advancement hallowed by a higher purpose. To ease the path for his son...and his son's sons.

The notion set him dizzy with wonder. Might there come a day when his descendants, among the first in the land, would hear the bards recite their proud genealogies?

Rhys ap Madog ap Bryn ap Conwy.

From clear across the room, Con felt Enid's glare boring into him as she looked up from washing Lord Macsen's feet. The climax of Con's story fell rather flat, though Bryn and Davy seemed not to notice.

"Whatever brought you back to Wales from such an exciting place?" Admiration glowed in Bryn's young face, shadowed only a little by puzzlement. "I can hardly wait until I'm old enough to take the Cross!"

"Me, too!" Davy's small brow puckered. "Whereabouts do you *take* the Cross to, Bryn?"

His elder brother chuckled. "I guess you take it to the Holy Land. Taking the Cross means pledging yourself to go on a Crusade. It's a fine, noble deed. Tell us more, Master Con."

Though he had his own beliefs about the nobility of his service in the Holy Land, Con held his tongue so as not to tarnish young Bryn's idealism. Perhaps he could convince Enid to let him take the boy to Edessa as his squire.

Until the evening meal was served, Con kept Davy and Bryn occupied with further stories. Though Enid looked daggers at him whenever he glanced in her direction, she did not bid either of the boys away to do chores. Nor did she advance any of the other excuses Con expected to part the lads from him.

It wouldn't matter if she had. He would have balked her. Bryn had grown almost to manhood, never knowing his true father, believing he'd been sired by another. No hard looks from the boy's mother would keep Con from becoming acquainted with his son now.

When the food was brought in, Con reluctantly accepted an invitation from Lord Macsen to dine at the head table. Even from there he kept a jealous eye on Bryn. When he was bidden to sing and recite after the meal, he put on the performance of his life. All to coax his son's smile and awestruck gaze.

To Con's surprise, his singing and harping drew praise from another quarter.

"Well done, Con ap Ifan!" As Lord Macsen clapped his large hands, his rugged visage relaxed from its earlier look of wary suspicion. "If you are even half as fine a warrior as you are a bard, I may do well to heed the counsel you bring me."

"It is honest counsel, my lord. I look forward to sharing it with you." Though his ambition reared, Con found himself conscious of every man, woman and child in the hall. What would his mission to the border lord mean for *them* in the weeks and months to come?

"Tomorrow," said Macsen ap Gryffith, fighting a yawn. "We will speak more of it tomorrow."

While everyone at Glyneira prepared to bed down for the night, Con wandered out into the courtyard with a few other men to relieve himself in the privy. On the way back to the hall, he turned left when the rest turned right, slipping off into the darkness. Idwal opened the gate for Con without a word, as if he saw no one there, but was only glancing outside for his own benefit.

As Con headed for the river, Idwal's tardy whisper pursued him. "Go easy…with her, Con. She's a…good lass."

Con raised his hand to acknowledge Idwal's appeal. But under his breath, he muttered to himself, "She's a lass who has plenty to answer for."

Down by the river he waited and waited, until he began to wonder if Enid had forgotten him. Or if she'd never intended to come in the first place. Even the soothing music of the flowing water could not temper his gathering anger.

He thought about Bryn, growing up as he had—never knowing his father. Con didn't want that for any child, let alone one of his own blood. Did it make it better or worse that the boy had believed Howell was his sire?

Better for Bryn, perhaps, but worse for Con.

How much had he missed during those years he'd been freebooting around Europe and the Holy Land? His son's birth. The boy's first steps. His first hunt. Teaching him to sit a horse and handle a bow. Perhaps even passing on the workaday magic of coaxing oxen.

Enid had robbed Con of all of that. Now she wanted to deprive him of Bryn's company, and keep the boy from learning the truth of his parentage.

"Not whilst I breathe." Con's hands balled into such tight fists, his short-pared nails bit into his palms.

Caught in the undertow of his indignation, he did not hear the faint rustle of Enid's approach until she stood beside him. The scent of her still made him long to pull her into his arms, even after all she'd done to hurt and deceive him. The warrior in Con bridled at this unfair advantage she held over him.

"I came as…quickly as I could." Her words stumbled out on a ragged gasp of breath. "Lord Macsen…detained me for a word."

"A marriage offer?" Though the night was calm and mild, Con fancied his words chiselled in ice.

"Perhaps." Enid settled herself on a tussock of reeds beside Con. "If I'd let him speak. There'll be plenty of time for that in the days ahead, I hope."

"No!" Con wanted to bellow, but he clenched his teeth to imprison the word until it died in his throat.

In the meantime, a tense hush stretched between them.

"Well," said Enid at last. "You bid me come here as the price for your silence, so here I sit. What do you want from me?"

"Answers," Con snapped. "The truth. It's long overdue after thirteen years, wouldn't you say?"

"What would you have had me do—tell the world my firstborn was not begotten by my husband?" Her wrath beat against Con in cold briny waves. "Howell knew and the knowing ate at him. But he was good enough to give my son a name and a place, which is more than you were willing to do."

"Because I never knew I had a son, damn you!" Fearful someone might hear him, even so far from the *maenol*, Con pitched his voice quieter, but not a whit less hostile. "I never knew I had a son until a few hours ago. I still don't know how it came about."

"The usual way." Enid turned her face toward him. The moonlight cast a chill silver-blue light over her fey features. "After all the women you boasted of bedding, I thought you'd know by now how babes are got."

She sounded like a young lady of the estate talking down to an ignorant plowboy. Something she'd never done in their younger years.

Very well, then. He'd answer her like a plowboy. "I knew that long before I bedded any woman. Yet I never saw a ewe give birth to a lamb without first being tupped by a ram. How did you get with my child when we never…"

Con couldn't bring himself to say the words for they were sure to ache with his old yearning.

"We did."

Had Enid spoken? Or had he interpreted a whisper on the wind to say what he longed to hear?

"We…did?" He murmured his disbelief almost as softly. "How? When? I remember nothing of it."

For a man like Con, that last admission did not come easy. Had Enid used some dark magic to rob him of the memory as she had robbed him of the child who grew from their joining?

"Perhaps I should take umbrage." For the first time since he'd rejected her sham proposal, Enid *didn't* sound angry with him. "But I suppose I can hardly fault you for having no recollection of that night. You were very drunk."

"The night before I left Gwynedd to become a mercenary?" When else? He'd never been so drunk before or since.

Beside him Enid nodded as her hushed chuckle sighed on the night air. "I only wonder now that you had enough iron in your loins to do the job."

Con didn't want to laugh with her. It felt like a kind of surrender. But he couldn't help himself. "I've heard other men complain that strong drink makes them want what they're incapable of taking. It's never affected me that way."

Beside him, he felt Enid tense. Suddenly Con's laughter caught in his throat where it almost choked him.

"By all the saints, lass," he gasped when he finally recovered his breath. "Tell me I didn't take you against your will when I was blind drunk?"

The thought of it made him want to retch up his supper.

"No, it wasn't like that," Enid hastened to assure him. Awash in relief, Con almost missed the harsh whisper Enid might not have meant him to hear. "There were times I wished it had been."

"In heaven's name, why?"

"Because then I could blame someone else for all that happened to me thereafter, instead of living with the knowledge that I brought it on myself by my own folly." The words burst out of her with the force of a stopper from a jug of well-fermented cider.

Somehow Con knew he need ask no more questions to coax the whole account from Enid. He must only stay still and open his ears.

"You might say it was *I* who took *you*, Con. Though you didn't put up much resistance."

He could well imagine!

"You must understand," continued Enid. "I was at my wits' end. You were going away and I was so sure I'd never see you again. I felt certain you'd march off and be killed somewhere."

Though he resented her doubting his ability, Con *did* understand young Enid feeling that way. Just as he had always minimized risks, she'd always been prone to exaggerate them.

"I kept hoping you'd speak—give some sign you wanted me as more than a childhood friend or a courtesy sister. Though I knew nothing of what a woman should do to entice a man, I tried. You turned a blind eye to all of it."

He could hear the mounting desperation in her voice. If only he'd realized... "I couldn't let myself believe you cared for me. Can you not see that, Enid? I went away as much to lead myself from temptation as anything else."

"And to deliver *me* from evil?"

"Just so! You were set to wed a man of wealth and princely blood. How could I stand in the way of that?"

A bitter chuckle flew out of her, with a sob clinging to its wings. "Oh, Con. You and your damned ambition. I never cared anything for land or power. I only wanted...you."

Was it possible for one spirit to be buoyed to the moon and flung down to hell in the same instant? Until that moment, Con hadn't thought so.

"I crept into your bed in the barn after you staggered

away from the farewell feast.'' Her words came out fast and clipped, as if she was reciting a dull lesson and wanted to get it over with as soon as possible. ''We fumbled through a mating, then I stole away again.''

''Why did you say nothing of it?''

''I had no notion how drunk you were. I thought you'd remember what we'd done.''

How it must have torn at her when he'd marched away the next morning, too preoccupied with his hammering head and roiling belly to care about anything else. Had he even spared her a word of goodbye?

''The next morning I told my father I could not wed Tryfan ap Huw because I'd lost my maidenhead to you. No one ever struck me that hard before or since.''

''Oh, *cariad!*'' Con wrapped his arms around her. ''I wish I'd been there to come between you and that blow.''

For an instant she yielded to his embrace, then she tensed and pulled away, scrambling to her feet.

''He locked me up until you were gone, then he sold me in marriage to Howell. When I found myself with child so soon after I wed, I wasn't sure if the babe was his, or yours. As time went by, I could see. Howell pretended he didn't, but he never felt the same way toward Bryn as he did to the others.''

Con saw into her heart. ''But you loved Bryn best...'' He rose, quivering with the barely checked need to hold her again. ''...because he's mine?''

''There were times he was all that kept me from sewing rocks into the hem of my gown and throwing myself into this river.'' Her hand snaked out and gripped his hard enough to make Con wince. ''I can't lose that boy. Not now when I've almost got him back again. I beg you, Con, don't tell him you're his father. I'll do anything to buy your silence. *Anything.*''

How could he deny her, after all she'd been through and considering how much she'd meant to him?

Con opened his mouth to swear his secrecy, then closed it again. Even for Enid, how could he surrender the chance to know and acknowledge his son?

Chapter Twelve

Con wanted her son.

Enid had fretted this might happen, but after their talk down by the river, she knew her worst fear had come to pass. A deep, numbing chill settled into her bones. One that neither the hottest fire nor the thickest pile of woollen brychans could warm. It did not help her fitful sleep, that night, to remember it was her own fault.

After all, she had recognized the threat Con posed from the moment she'd spotted him singing and harping in her hall. She had conceived of a plan for getting rid of him, and a good one it had been. If only she'd had sense enough to put it into effect at the first opening Con had presented her. Or the second...or the fifth....

By the time she had frightened him away with talk of marriage, it had been too late. Too late to stop him from blundering into Lord Macsen's party. Too late to keep him from meeting and recognizing their son.

Once Con had seen the boy, Enid could hardly blame him for being drawn to such a lively, handsome lad. She'd have faulted the man more if he hadn't. Now, if only Bryn were not so obviously drawn to the fascinating stranger with his winning ways and beguiling stories of dangerous, faraway places.

The first words out of her son's mouth the next morning made Enid recoil. "Is it true you and Con grew up together, Mam?"

He was hanging about the kitchen with Davy, both of them munching small cakes of oats and dried apples that Gaynor baked for feast days and other special occasions.

It took so much effort to keep her smile from slipping that Enid had no will left over to govern her tongue. She settled for nodding in reply to Bryn's question.

"Why did you never tell us of Con before?" Bryn pressed her. "Him a Crusader and all, that's a friendship to boast of."

"I didn't know he'd gone to the Holy Land." Fumbling noisily with her storeroom keys, Enid turned away from her sons, so she could let her face relax from its false expression of good cheer. "I had no notion Con was still alive until he turned up at our gate two weeks past."

Perhaps her brisk tone warned Bryn that Conwy ap Ifan was not her favorite subject of conversation. Eager to talk about him, nonetheless, the boy turned to his younger brother. "Wasn't that a brave story Con told last night, about spying in Damascus dressed as a woman?"

His mouth still full of oats and apples, Davy gave an enthusiastic grunt of agreement. Once he'd swallowed, the child added, "Tonight you must ask him to sing 'Goat White.' He makes it so comical!"

How could she gainsay the boys their avid interest in Con? Enid asked herself as she checked her household stores and consulted with Gaynor about food preparation for the day. The man charmed most everyone he met—why should her sons be any exception?

Con still charmed her, truth to tell, even when she had reason to fear him, and tried with all her power to hate him.

Last night on the riverbank, for instance. She hadn't meant to admit what a rash, urgent love she'd borne him so many years ago. Warmed to life by his nearness, those memories had set old feelings stirring in her heart all over again.

With his talent for reading people, Con must know Bryn could be his for the asking. How could she possibly compete against Con's cheerful appeal and the lure of his adventurous freebooting way of life? How could she compel her son to remain with her if Con bid the boy to come away with him?

Somehow she must find a way to make Con ap Ifan hold his tongue. But what boon could she offer him, or what threat could she hold over his charming head that might have the slightest effect?

Launched by the force of emotion storming within him, Con's well-honed ax blade bit into the thick tree trunk, sending chips of wood flying.

Fate had sent him this fresh opportunity to shore up the defenses of Glyneira, and now more than ever he felt obliged to undertake the task. What if Bryn should happen to be here during a Norman attack?

The thought of any harm coming to his son bit into Con with a sharp, powerful force, sending chips of his composure flying. Having never given much thought to the prospect of fatherhood, Con had blithely assumed he didn't care much one way or the other. The unforeseen advent of a half-grown son in his life had changed all that. Though Con wasn't sure he liked the change, he was powerless to resist it.

And he hated being powerless.

"Is aught...wrong, Con?" Idwal's question punctured the rhythmic lull as Con swung his ax back for the next loud blow.

"W-wrong?" Con started, making his cut fall awry. "Why do you ask?"

Testing the edge of his ax head, Idwal shrugged. "You look so...grim."

Con let his ax fall idle. "I haven't much practice at woodcutting." His breath came in rapid gusts. "Need to pay attention to what I'm doing so I don't hack off a leg, or send this tree crashing down on top of you."

Idwal stroked his brow as if urging his mind to deeper thought than it was accustomed to. "So it's got naught to do...with you and Enid...last night."

It would have taken a more subtle fellow than Con ap Ifan to speak false while staring into Idwal's steadfast blue eyes.

Con gave a grudging nod. "I'll own, it has been weighing on me."

The look of satisfaction on Idwal's rough-hewn features was almost worth what his confession had cost Con. "Knew it! You don't want her to...wed Lord Macsen, do you?"

Con opened his mouth to assure Idwal that had no bearing whatsoever on his present pensive humor. Try as he might, he couldn't make the words come out.

Though his mind might have been occupied with thoughts of Bryn, the matter of Enid and Macsen ap Gryffith had riddled his heart. From the moment tidings of their expected wedding had tripped off Gaynor's voluble tongue, the whole notion had taken Con aback. As his old feelings for Enid had warmed to life again, hotter than ever, his opposition to the match had grown apace until he'd blurted it out to Enid when she'd asked him.

At the time he hadn't realized that her question and all the rest were only an ambush meant to drive him away and keep him from ever knowing about his son. For all Enid's deception stung him, it didn't change Con's attitude toward her remarriage.

He still didn't care for the idea one bit. Especially since it would make Lord Macsen Bryn's stepfather.

"Knew it," said Idwal for the second time. Clearly, he took Con's mute reply for agreement. "You...can stop her...you know."

"Stop her?" The notion set Con's heart hammering. "How?"

"And some call me...simple in the head." Idwal's mouth stretched in a wide, crooked grin. "Why, bid the lass wed you, instead...Con ap Ifan!"

Yet again Idwal's words struck Con dumb.

Bid Enid wed him? What folly!

He couldn't take a wife just now, for all the reasons he'd given Enid two days past in the orchard. Somehow, since meeting his son, those arguments seemed far less compelling. If he couldn't spoil his plans by wedding now, perhaps once he'd gained all he hoped to...

"Fie! That *is* simple talk, Idwal." Con watched as his harsh words demolished the big man's childlike smile, all the while hating himself for it. "What makes you think Enid would have me when she has the chance of a husband like Lord Macsen?"

What indeed? Yet Enid had confessed to once choosing the lowly plowboy over an even more exalted suitor...on the long-ago night when their son had been conceived.

"I mayn't be...as quick as some..." Idwal hefted his ax with an air of injured dignity, "but I know...what I know. She'd have you...if you were brave enough to ask." He sounded doubtful of Con's courage.

Nonsense! Con wanted to snap, but he couldn't. He already felt like a lump of pig dung for the way he'd treated Idwal.

For all that, Enid's brother-in-law was wrong. True, she had cherished a passion for him during their youth—one he hadn't dared let himself suspect, much less return. But that must have turned to dust ages ago, having died a painful death on the morning he'd marched away from her father's estate without so much as a "God be with you."

As for her recent pretended interest, it had fooled him, just as it had fooled Idwal. Now Con knew better. The depth of feeling he'd sensed had been no more than a measure of how desperately she'd wanted him gone from Glyneira.

Or had it? If Enid married the border lord, Con would never find out.

He struggled to frame an apology that would still shake Idwal from the false hope that had begun a seductive slither through his own thoughts. Before Con could produce one, the underbrush rustled behind him. He spun around to confront the lithe, cheerful figure of his son.

A sensation of wonder bubbled up in Con's chest all over again.

"I beg pardon for interrupting your work," said the boy, "but Lord Macsen sent me to fetch you, Con. He wants to talk over whatever you came to tell him."

"Thank you for bringing me word, lad." When Bryn drew close enough, Con reached out to ruffle the boy's hair.

Somehow it seemed fitting that so sunny and well-made a creature should have sprung from the sweet, forbidden, unacknowledged love that had once shimmered between him and Enid. By heaven, Con wished he could recall the night he'd gotten her with his fine child!

When Idwal hefted his ax once more, Bryn cocked his head a little to one side, exactly as his mother used to when something piqued her curiosity.

"Why are you cutting down these trees?"

Though he knew he should not keep Macsen ap Gryffith cooling his heels, Con could not resist a chance to linger in his son's company.

"They stand too hard by the walls." Con went on to explain the threat they presented to the security of Glyneira.

Bryn interrupted him now and again, asking questions that betrayed the keen insight of a born warrior. By the time they had thoroughly aired the subject of the *maenol*'s defenses, the lad's transparent admiration of him had filled Con with intense pleasure...poisoned by a tincture of shame.

"To think no one here ever noticed that." The boy gazed up into the branches of a towering beech tree as if he could picture a Norman archer perched in the topmost boughs. "Lord Macsen says a skilled warrior must always look to his own defenses before he plans an attack."

Hearing his son quote Macsen ap Gryffith in a tone bordering on reverence, struck Con like a light blow to a sensitive part of his body.

Before he could mouth any words of praise for Lord Macsen that might have burned his tongue, the boy called to his uncle. "Idwal, isn't Con a clever warrior? And a kind man to care how a little place like Glyneira is fortified?"

"Stand clear!" Idwal barked, as though he had not heard his nephew's question. One final swing of his ax sent a lofty white poplar crashing to earth.

In the hush that followed, he answered. "Oh, Con's clever enough...about *some* things."

Bryn laughed, but Con knew the big man's words had not been meant in jest.

"Your uncle's the wise one, Bryn." Though he directed his words to the boy, Con met Idwal's wary gaze. "Warcraft is a child's game compared to the riddles he understands. It's a pigheaded fool who ignores his advice."

Answering that ham-fisted apology with a cryptic grunt, Idwal strode to the tree Con had been chopping and set to work with his own ax. "You oughtn't keep...his lordship a-waiting."

"Lord Macsen!" cried Bryn. "I'd forgotten. Go Con. He's not a patient fellow. Tell him it was my fault for keeping you in talk when I should have speeded you on your way."

"I'll do nothing of the sort." Con propped his ax against a beech tree, then started for the *maenol* gate with swift steps. "You told me I was summoned, yet I tarried. The fault is mine."

Even if it prejudiced Macsen ap Gryffith against him and his mission, Con could not allow any blame to fall on the lad.

Suddenly, words of Enid's echoed in Con's mind. Words she'd hurled at him in anger. *You don't know what it's like to care about someone better than your own life. So that you'd rather take any harm yourself than see it fall upon them.*

Now he glimpsed what she'd meant.

Enid had been talking about her children—Bryn foremost, though Con had not realized it at the time. But had she been talking about something else as well, without meaning to?

How often during their youth had she taken a scolding

or harsher punishment for some mischief of his making? The young plowboy had always been grateful enough to wriggle out of trouble without thinking much about how or why. All these years later, it finally struck him.

Enid had loved him better than herself. She'd been willing to call harm on her own head, rather than see it fall on him. No doubt she had taken harm aplenty bearing his son and rearing Bryn to clever, sturdy boyhood.

No matter what it cost him, Con knew he could not stand by and let her wed Macsen ap Gryffith.

"What's been keeping the pair of you? Lord Macsen's growing impatient."

Meeting Con and Bryn at the *maenol* gate, Enid planted her hands on her hips as she glared from one to the other. The chastened gazes they turned back upon her looked so much alike it took her breath away. How much of the overpowering love she'd borne her son all these years sprang from Bryn's likeness to his natural father?

Too much, Enid found herself suddenly forced to admit. Too much, by half.

Miserable in exile from her Gwynedd home and wed to a stranger, she had searched her babe's plump grinning visage for the slightest likeness to a man she claimed to hate. Once she'd satisfied herself that Con had sired the boy, she'd lived in fear that Howell would also guess the truth.

For all that, the knowledge had nourished something inside her. Hope, perhaps, or strength.

"I'm sorry, Mam. I got Con talking when I'd no business to." Bryn hung his head, casting his mother a glance at once penitent and a trifle cocky, as though he never doubted her eventual forgiveness.

Before she could reply, Con stepped between Enid and her son. "The fault is mine. You'll recall, I never needed much excuse to lose track of time in talk."

Though vexed by the suggestion that Bryn needed to be protected from her motherly displeasure, Enid could not fault Con for jumping to her son's defense—*their* son's defense.

As usual, her mixed feelings for Con flustered her, as did his nearness. Every part of her body he'd kissed or fondled since coming to Glyneira tingled, as if begging for more of the same.

"Tell your tale to Lord Macsen." Though she intended a brisk tone, Enid heard her words tumble out high pitched and breathless. "He's the one you've kept waiting while you minced air."

Not that Macsen ap Gryffith had voiced any great impatience. In truth, he'd appeared eager to seize the opportunity to speak with *her*. About an offer of marriage, perhaps? Some urge, as intense as it was baffling, had sent Enid scurrying away before the border chief could tender his proposal, with the trifling excuse of discovering what had delayed Con ap Ifan.

Con turned to the boy. "Will you carry my apologies to Lord Macsen and assure him that I'll come shortly."

"Aye, sir." Bryn fairly radiated his eagerness to be of service to his new idol.

"Say nothing of detaining me with talk," Con called after the lad as he hurried away.

Enid shot Con a suspicious glance. "Why did you send Bryn, when you could go to Lord Macsen just as quickly."

"Because I wanted a word with you, first." The tone of his voice caressed Enid and set her pulse fluttering in a manner she hated.

"Word?" Her eyes narrowed. "About what? I thought we'd said everything we had to say to each other last night."

Con scanned the *maenol* courtyard, abuzz with activity. Taking Enid's elbow with a firm but gentle grip, he steered her toward the small dairy that stood not far from the gate.

"Perhaps I needed some time to ponder on what you told me."

Once more, fear gripped her with clammy hands. Had Con said something to Bryn? Recalling her son's manner, Enid assured herself nothing had rocked his young world…yet.

Inside the low-ceilinged shed all was dim and still. The dairy maids had dealt with the morning milking, and gone off to other tasks. Enid wrinkled her nose at the sour smell of fermenting curds that hung in the air. Her cheeks warmed as she remembered the fumbling kiss she and Con had exchanged in the washhouse a few days past. That kiss had kindled her dangerous, futile plan to entice him further.

"Well?" She shook her elbow from Con's grasp and faced him. "What is it you want with me?"

Fie, but it felt as if she were trying to balance on the ridgepole of a high roof. On one hand, she could not afford to vex a man who held such power to bring her grief. Yet neither could she bring herself to betray a hint of the stubborn attraction for Con ap Ifan that persisted in spite of everything.

"Has his lordship bid for your hand yet?" Con's bearing and tone both gave him the air of a harp string wound too tight. "Have you accepted him?"

What right had he to know the answer to either of those questions? And why did he care?

The smell of rancid milk turned Enid's stomach. At least she blamed it on the pungent odor.

"Lord Macsen and I haven't had a chance to talk more about it." In her eagerness to keep from adding *if you must know,* Enid bit her tongue.

"Ow!"

Con reached for her. "What is it, *cariad?* Are you all right?"

"It's nothing." Forcing herself to pull back from him, Enid almost tripped over an oaken bucket. "And don't be calling me that. I am not your *cariad!*"

Her eyes had adjusted to the shadowy interior of the dairy shed. She could make out the pensive set of Con's handsome features.

"We may pick and choose which people *we* hold dear." The barest whisper of a sigh escaped from his lips. "But we can't decide who will hold us dear. That, they do at their own whim."

If she didn't soon get out of here, she might take a whim to do something unforgivably daft. Kiss him, perhaps, just to still his beguiling tongue.

"That's all this is to you, then—a whim?" Her vow not to antagonize Con shattered into a hundred sharp splinters. "A fickle breeze blowing hot one day and cool the next? Changing direction without warning, sweeping everything before it?"

"You must own, that sounds exciting." Con gave a tolerant chuckle. "What would you rather have, *Cariad Enid*

Du? A tide whose every ebb and flow you could measure and predict within an inch?''

Dear dark Enid. The very words seduced her, dammit!

''If you value this mission of yours from the Normans, perhaps you should save your quibbles to entertain folks after the evening meal, and go attend Lord Macsen, now, as you were bidden.''

''You speak prudently, as ever.'' Con's teasing grin faded. ''I'll be plain with you, then. Though you weren't sincere in wanting to marry me, I meant it when I said you should not wed Macsen ap Gryffith.''

''Why ever not?'' Only one reason would satisfy her, and that she would not believe if Con ap Ifan were bold enough to advance it.

He seemed to search the redolent air for an answer. ''You don't love him!''

''Love?'' Enid couldn't decide whether to laugh, shriek or retch. ''You talk like an Aquitaine! I've heard tales of that court. Knights vowing devotion to other men's wives—spouting ballads to their beauty, carrying their favors into mock battle. Even those decadent idlers don't wax so foolish as to claim such childish goings-on have any place in a marriage.''

Con wrinkled his nose and pulled a bilious face that nearly drove Enid to laughter, in spite of herself. ''They're worse than that by half.''

Before he had time to draw another breath, his tone and visage turned sober once again. ''Besides, that wasn't what I meant by *love*. I think you know it, too. I pity any man and woman who wed without deep feeling between them. You were cheated of such feeling in your first marriage,

and I'll own the blame I bear for that. I won't stand by
and watch it happen to you again.''

Guilt and pity. Con was meddling in her future out of
nothing stronger than those. She should have known better
than to let herself hope for more. Enid chided herself for
telling Con as much as she had about her life after she'd
seduced him on that late summer evening thirteen years
ago.

Damned if she would let him salve his raw conscience
at the expense of her family!

''What makes you so certain I don't care for Lord Macsen in the way you mean?'' Enid blessed the friendly shadows that shrouded her eyes from Con's ruthless scrutiny.

''Why…you told me.'' He stammered in a manner that
would have made Idwal sound fluent. ''At least…I
thought…''

Had she been fool enough to confess her true feelings
for his lordship to Con ap Ifan? If so, it would not be the
first time Con had cozened her own tongue into playing
her false.

Well, no more.

''You shouldn't set much store by *anything* I told you
when you first came to Glyneira.'' Enid made her voice
as sharp and cold as the long, lethal icicles that hung from
the eaves at Candlemas. ''As you were so quick to discover, it was all part of my plan to get rid of you.''

Surely that would make him leave her alone so she
could do what she must—a task that was proving hard
enough without Con's interference.

''So you do care for his lordship, then?''

Did he mean his question for a challenge…or a plea?

Enid willed her tone not to betray the tempest that raged

inside her. She planted her hands firmly on her hips to keep them from reaching for Con in a moment of weak folly.

"Happen, I do." She flung down the words like a mortal challenge.

His quiet, coaxing reply rocked Enid back on her heels in a way no angry rebuke could have done. "More than you care for me?"

She replied with the only answer she dared give him. "Lord Macsen offers my family as safe and comfortable a home as we could find in this part of the world. He has always treated me with respect and kindness. What have you ever given me to compare with those?"

A son dearer than her own heart, whispered Enid's conscience. More laughter during one golden summer than had passed her lips in all the years since. A sweet, hot rush of desire that she savored, even while she mistrusted it.

Skilled warrior that Con had become under Norman tutelage, he did not try to counter her feint. Instead, he mounted a subtle assault of his own, moving toward her. Though he made no effort to touch her, he stepped so close to Enid that every breath she inhaled overwhelmed her with his scent.

"You haven't answered my question, *cariad.*" His whisper gently ravished her ear.

The fine hairs on the back of Enid's neck rose. Her nipples puckered against the linen of her smock. The inside of her mouth grew wet, forcing her to swallow. The smallest movement on her part would bring their lips into contact.

Just when she feared she could not withstand the dark, potent urge a moment longer, Con murmured, in a voice as insistent as it was beguiling, "Do you care for Macsen ap Gryffith more than you care for me?"

Her soul must be hopelessly damned to perdition by this time. Would one more log on the fire roast her any hotter? Perhaps, for this one would be the size of those trees Con and Idwal had been hewing.

"Yes."

It was not an eloquent declaration, by any means. And her tone lacked conviction. Still, given the forces Con had brought to bear against her, allied with her own traitorous heart, Enid counted that one wavering word a victory.

Relishing the sharp hiss of Con's in-drawn breath, she let her shield fall slack.

"Very well, then," Con whispered, grazing her cheek with his. The delicate rasp of whisker stubble set her flesh on fire. His next words set her reeling.

"Prove it."

Chapter Thirteen

"P-prove?"

Was it his imagination, or did Enid sound even less certain than she had a moment ago when she'd claimed to love Macsen ap Gryffith? Con asked himself why he cared so much, only to discover he couldn't bear to face the answer.

"I owe you no proof, Con ap Ifan." With surprising strength for her size, Enid pushed him away. "Any feeling I have for Lord Macsen is between him and me. No business of yours, that's certain."

Part of him believed so, too, but Con refused to heed the voice of his own reason.

"If you plan to raise *my* son in a household with Lord Macsen as his stepfather," Con stabbed the innocent air with his forefinger, "then you make it my business, woman!"

She flinched, as though he had backhanded her across the mouth.

The thought of visiting such violence on any woman, let alone his dear dark Enid, made Con's gorge rise. For their son's sake, and for the sake of her future happiness, he could not afford to relent.

"You told me how it was between you and Howell—remember? How you wanted to sew rocks into the hem of your gown and throw yourself in the river. Rather than live in such a household, perhaps Bryn would be better off with me."

He hadn't meant to advance such a plan, but once Con spoke the words the notion warmed him. It could be like a return to the good times when he and Rowan DeCourtenay had roistered about the Holy Land. Only this time he would be the mentor, taking Bryn under his wing.

"Never!" If Enid had been holding a weapon, Con knew he might have died where he stood. "You said yourself, you haven't got it in you to be a good father. Besides, I didn't raise that child on my own for all these years only to have you steal him from me, now, and take him off to who knows where."

"When a body takes what belongs to him, it isn't stealing!" Con felt his temper rising. "And who's to know what kind of father I might make if I never get the chance to try."

Perhaps it would serve Enid right if he let her make a mercenary match with the forceful border chief. Try as he might, Con couldn't abandon her to such folly. He'd unwittingly abandoned her once before. That knowledge would be hard enough to live with.

"Bryn isn't yours!" Enid sounded as though she longed to shriek the words for all of Powys to hear…if only she dared. "One drunken fumble in a hayloft thirteen years ago gives you no claim on my son. Besides, you're talking nonsense. How can a body *prove* what they feel in their hearts? You've claimed to care for me. Yet you've brought me more grief than folks who might profess to hate me."

It was true. Con heard it in her voice. He had seen it in her dusky eyes more than once since he'd come to Glyneira. What queer twist of his character let him bring pleasure to women who meant little to him, while visiting distress on the only one he'd ever truly cared for?

He wasn't trying to hurt her now, Con's passion protested to his conscience. He only meant to keep Enid from making a mistake she and her children might regret for years to come. To his surprise, the vow rang true.

"Well, speak up, man!" Enid's sharp demand goaded Con from his musings. "How would you have me *prove* my feelings for Macsen ap Gryffith?"

"I don't know," Con shot back. "But I'll think of something. Until then, I want you to promise me that you won't commit yourself to a marriage with him."

"I'll do no such thing! How long do you think Lord Macsen would let a woman dangle him on a string before he decided the wench was more trouble than she was worth? I cannot risk losing this chance for me and my children on some whim of yours, Con."

Damn! His opposition was only serving to harden her stubborn resolve. From bitter experience Con knew the futility of trying to budge Enid once she got her heels well dug in. Why, he'd have an easier time coaxing a great ox or prodding an ill-tempered mule than swaying this wee slip of a woman against her will.

"I...that is..." It took strong emotion indeed to empty Con's clever mind and tie his facile tongue in knots. Only Enid had ever wielded this terrible power over him.

The worst of it was, at the same time it made him long to run from her as far and fast as possible, it also lured him to draw as close as she would let him.

"I thought as much." Enid crossed her arms in a manner that suggested both wariness and exhausted patience. "You're so fond of spinning quibbles, Conwy ap Ifan, forever putting me in the wrong. When I answer your bluff, see what comes of it?''

She pushed past him toward the wide, low doorway of the dairy shed. ''Lord Macsen isn't apt to have much patience with an envoy from the Normans who keeps him cooling his heels, either,'' she snapped. ''In your place, I'd hie myself to the hall while there's still a chance he might heed you.''

As she strayed within his reach, Con caught her by the arm with the gentlest touch that might still detain her. He had only one coin to barter with Enid. Precious as it was to him, did he dare squander it thus?

The touch of his hand stayed her, though Con sensed it would not last long. Enid canted her face ever so slightly toward him. Hers was a beauty best appreciated in moonlight, dusk or shadow. His reawakened desire for her brought an ache to Con's loins and an answering pang to his heart. What would he exchange for one clear, true memory of that distant summer night when she'd given herself to him?

A notion began to take shape in his flustered mind, if only he could buy enough time to let it ripen. ''Give me one more day, Enid. Surely his lordship will allow you that much leisure to weigh your decision. For as long as you withhold your consent, I promise I'll keep mum about Bryn.''

''Very well.'' Enid responded without a heartbeat's hesitation. ''One day.''

Clearly his silence on the matter was worth a great deal to her. If he promised *never* to reveal himself as Bryn's father, Enid would likely refuse Macsen ap Gryffith for good and all. But that was a higher ransom than Con could bring himself to pay for the privilege of saving Enid from herself.

With a parting caress, he released her arm. "It's of no advantage for me to meddle in Lord Macsen's affairs," he murmured, wishing Enid would not hate him for what he must do. "This is for your own good."

She continued her interrupted way toward the door. At the threshold, she paused, her fine profile crisp and black against the light spilling in from the courtyard.

In a voice tight with anguish she choked out her parting words. "That's what my father said when he forced me to wed Howell. Just once I wish a man would trust me to know *my own good*."

Leave it to Con ap Ifan to disappear from her life for over a dozen years, then come racing back when she was finally on the brink of arranging matters to her own liking. Saints forbid the charming rascal should have grown enough discretion in the meantime to let well enough alone!

As Enid stormed away from the dairy shed, the flesh of her arm smarted, the way it might if she'd drawn close to the fire too quickly after coming indoors on a winter night.

Of course Con couldn't let her content herself with the kind of settled, certain arrangement marriage with Lord Macsen promised to be. Little did Con guess it took no more than his presence in her house, along with the potent memories he stirred, to infect her with vague, bothersome doubts. The last thing she needed was for him to distill those doubts into persuasive words. Perhaps there was one thing she needed less, Enid admitted to herself when she spied Macsen ap Gryffith striding toward her across the courtyard—her own daft yearning to believe that Con wanted her for himself.

That he wanted her, she didn't question. But only as a

meaningless tumble in the grass, not in the honored, lasting way she needed.

Lord Macsen bore down on her. "Has our sparrow hawk flown the nest, then?"

Sparrow hawk? "I beg your pardon, my lord?"

One of Lord Macsen's rare smiles softened his dark, formidable visage. "The harper...or the warrior, whichever he is. Wanderer more than either, I daresay."

"You mean Con." Enid glanced back over her shoulder toward the dairy, but saw no sign of him. Was he still skulking there, or had he rambled away? "I spoke with him only a moment ago and bid him attend you in the hall. Perhaps you and he missed one another coming and going."

"That could be." The border chief's smile faded, replaced by the kind of intense gaze that never failed to make Enid squirm. "For a fellow so eager to bend my ear, he's been backward enough about doing it."

She must not speak a word in Con's defense. What Lord Macsen said was perfectly true. But after so many years of shielding Con from her father's displeasure, it had become second nature to her.

"Do not judge him too harshly, my lord. Con has been laboring to make Glyneira more secure in case of attack." Before she could regain control of her tongue, Enid heard herself telling Macsen ap Gryffith all about Con's venture to cut back the trees that pressed too close to the *maenol* wall.

His lordship's dark brows rose as he listened. "I daresay Glyneira is safe enough while Hen Coed stands between it and the Normans. But enough about this. I came here to escape such worries for a few days."

Taking Enid's slender hand, he tucked it into the crook

of his elbow. "Walk with me and let us grasp this chance to speak of the reason for my visit."

Enid forced a wan smile. "As you will, my lord."

Behind the meek mask, she raged at herself. *Love this man, damn you! Love him as you swore to Con you did. Macsen is everything you require in a husband, everything your children require in a father. He will keep your family together and keep you all safe.*

As they ambled toward the *maenol* gate, the border lord swept a glance around the busy courtyard. "You've managed well at Glyneira since you lost Howell."

"Aye, my lord." Life was so much easier when the men were here to work, instead of constantly mustering to fight. "It was a quiet winter."

Lord Macsen nodded. "The snow falls, then the spring rains come. Time passes."

Emerging from the *maenol,* they strolled away from the sound of Idwal chopping trees.

The border lord inhaled a deep breath. "Pardon my awkwardness of speech. I am a fighter, not a bard. For some years now, I have admired you more than any man should admire the wife of a comrade in arms."

Her eyes fixed on the ground as though she feared a fall, Enid concentrated on hearing Lord Macsen's words over the thunderous pounding of her heart. Could that be why she found it so difficult to rouse any warm feelings for this man—because she'd been aware of his unsettling attraction to her while Howell was still alive?

Lord Macsen fell mute for a moment, perhaps waiting for a reply. When none came, he pressed on. "I would never have spoken while your husband lived, but now…"

Part of her wanted to ease this ordeal for him, but how could she and still keep her promise to Con?

They walked a little farther in anxious silence, then Lord

Macsen came to an abrupt halt, beside a blackthorn bush swathed in soft white blossoms. He turned to face Enid, enveloping her slender fingers in his vast grasp.

Swallowing a lump of panic that threatened to choke her, she made herself look up at him.

"I held the wife of my youth very dear. Though I knew it was my duty to sire sons to secure my line, I delayed wedding again. Now, I am ready and you are free. I want you for my wife, Enid. Will you have me for a husband?"

A look of relief eased his tense features, as though he had finally tackled a much-dreaded chore and was glad to have it done.

Macsen ap Gryffith wanted her in a way Con never would, Enid realized as she moistened her lips to reply. What matter if she did not return his feelings? At least she was acquainted with the man and thought well of him. She had wed Howell ap Rhodri with far less than that. Over the years they had built a solid, workable partnership that might have floundered if she'd given her husband the power to hurt her.

"You do me great honor, my lord." Enid tried to look more receptive to his offer than she felt.

In spite of the dangerous doubts Con had spawned in her, she could not afford to turn from the course she had chosen. She must forestall Lord Macsen without discouraging him.

"I pray you will not take it ill if I beg a little time to think on your offer, and on what is best for the future of my family."

Enid doubted the border chief could have looked better pleased if she'd given him her swift, ardent consent. He must know how she was bound to answer for her children's sake. Clearly Macsen ap Gryffith did not possess

Con's disturbing ability to divine the true feelings she might hide from the rest of the world.

Enid added that in his favor as a future husband.

"I wish I could grant you all the time you need," Lord Macsen said, "but I dare not tarry away from Hen Coed more than a few days."

"One is all I need," Enid assured him.

"Perhaps this will sway your decision in my favor." As he leaned toward her, Enid willed herself not to flinch from his kiss.

Behind her Con's cheery voice rang out. "Lord Macsen, I have found you at last! I fear we've been chasing each other in circles today."

At the last instant, the border lord checked his advance. Though his lips barely glanced Enid's, the sensation still made her gorge rise. Spinning around to face Con, she insisted to herself that she resented his ill-timed intrusion.

Yet some traitorous part of her felt as though he'd rescued her in the nick of time.

Fool! Con ap Ifan cursed himself. He could read the glowering set of Lord Macsen's features as easily as he might glance at a darkening sky and tell a storm was brewing. The present climate of the border lord's humor did not bode well for their talks.

"For a bard, you could stand to improve your timing, Con ap Ifan." Lord Macsen's deep voice rumbled with the soft menace of distant thunder.

"So I could, your lordship." Con forced a chuckle, pretending to take the remark at its surface meaning. "And in battle, too, no doubt. The timing of an attack is vital."

This was his latest blunder in a campaign he could not afford to lose, Con chided himself. When he'd spied Enid and Lord Macsen in confidential talk, reason had warned him to turn on his heel and march back into the *maenol* to await the border lord. Enid had agreed to delay in accepting any offer of marriage from Macsen, and Con trusted her to keep her word.

But when it became clear that the towering border chief meant to claim a kiss from *his* Enid, a great wave of protective, possessive madness had swamped the spinning coracle of Con's self-control. Try as he might, he had not been able to hold his tongue.

He steeled himself for a black look from Enid, but none came. She appeared flustered, though, blushing red as an October apple and avoiding his gaze. Whether she was troubled more by his sudden interruption or by Lord Macsen's aborted kiss, Con could not tell.

That very uncertainty fertilized the seed of a plan their earlier talk had sown in his mind. If it worked, his strategy promised to make Enid face her true feelings for Macsen ap Gryffith, and keep her from accepting his marriage offer. But how could Con persuade her to accept his challenge? Unless…

Picturing all he stood to gain if only he could coax Lord Macsen to take action that would benefit the Empress, Con wrenched his thoughts away from this personal matter and forced his feet backward. "Forgive my interruption. I'll go back to the hall and await your lordship's pleasure."

"No!" The urgency of Enid's cry seemed to surprise her as much as it did the two men. "I mean, no…need to run off, Con. Lord Macsen and I were about to head back of our own accord. I must go see how Gaynor is getting on in the kitchen."

She sniffed the air. "I think I smell meat burning!"

Before either of the men could say anything to detain her, she brushed past Con and fled toward the *maenol*.

When Macsen ap Gryffith glared at him, Con replied

with a shrug and a rueful grin. "She always was overly mindful of her duties as a hostess—even when we were young."

"You've known her a long while." The border lord's threatening scowl eased. "Was she always so…?"

Con's imagination rushed ahead. So beautiful? So radiant? So loyal and kindhearted?

Lord Macsen seemed to grasp for a word that eluded him, finally settling for "…so singular?"

If that was the best this man could do to describe Enid, he must not properly appreciate all she offered. "My lord?"

"Singular." The border lord defended his choice. "Not like all the others. I've never met a woman quite like her—have you?"

The notion ambushed Con. "I—I suppose not, now that you remark upon it."

He'd always supposed that Enid held a unique place in his heart because of the past they'd shared, and because she had been his first love. Macsen ap Gryffith had no such connection with her, yet he recognized her as a unique, special woman. Somehow that threatened Con worse than a drawn weapon.

Caught in a current of powerful unwelcome feelings, Con almost missed Lord Macsen's next question.

"Whatever made her throw herself away on this poor *maenol?*" The border chief seemed to muse aloud. "And a man like Howell ap Rhodri?"

Me. With difficulty, Con managed to bite back the word, but he could not purge the conviction from his heart. Enid had ended up here, far from the safe home she'd so cherished, wed to a stranger, almost driven to despair because she'd loved him unwisely. That he hadn't meant to get her with child hardly mattered.

What if he'd drunk a little less on that long ago summer night, enough that he'd had a few of his wits about him when she stole into his loft bed? Would he have denied her what she wanted, and what he'd long burned for? Not by half!

And when morning had come, would he have had the courage to face her enraged father, or the character to turn his back on his life's ambition to satisfy honor? Much as Con wished he could say yes, he knew better.

"Not that there was anything *wrong* with Howell, you understand," Lord Macsen said. "The man was brave in battle and loyal always. For all that he didn't seem worthy of such a wife."

His voice fell to a whisper, but Con's sharp ears picked up something that sounded like, "Perhaps I'm not, either."

There! A righteous certainty swelled in Con's chest. If the border lord himself entertained doubts about his suitability as a husband for Enid, Con would be doing them both a favor by preventing the match.

"Enough of this." A heavy scowl pulled down Lord Macsen's firm mouth and thick dark brows. With a motion of his head that invited Con to follow, he turned and marched farther away from the *maenol*. "Tell me more of the urgent matter you sought me out to advance."

Here was his chance. Con's ambition, his ruling master for so many years, bid him put aside trivial matters and make a compelling case for the men of Powys to war against King Stephen's allies, the Marcher lords of Falconbridge and Revelstone.

He rushed to catch up with Lord Macsen. "How much do you know, my lord, of the quarrel that divides the Normans?"

"Only that it is good for Powys." The border chief checked his stride so Con could fall in step with him.

"Since the old king died, we have been able to claw back some of the territory these *Marcher lords* wrested from us. If it was in my power, I would toss another stick on the fire to keep their feud merrily boiling for years to come."

Con nodded. "Wise words, my lord. But I am well enough acquainted with the Normans to assure you this struggle for the throne will spend itself, and sooner than any of us may guess. Stephen of Blois is no longer a young man, and the time he spent as a captive of his cousin the Empress did his health no good.

"Even among Stephen's supporters there is talk of Maud's boy, Henry, succeeding the king. Sooner or later the Angevines will have the English throne, and once they clean up the mess in their own kingdom, they will go for the throat of Wales again."

"They will have to get past me first." Macsen ap Gryffith muttered the words in a tone of grim resolve.

In spite of himself, Con felt a stirring of admiration for the embattled Welsh warrior. The Normans would have their work cut out to defeat him.

"When that day comes, my lord, even an Angevine might think twice before attacking one who'd done his family service when their fortunes were low."

The border lord's black brows rose. "Indeed? And what service could a humble Welsh chief perform to win the favor of this Empress and her Angevine spawn?"

Poised for a receptive hearing, Con wet his lips and marshaled his arguments. Instinct told him it would not be difficult to enlist Macsen ap Gryffith and the men of Hen Coed to harry Stephen's loyal Marcher lords in Salop.

With all his heart, Con believed such a campaign would hold the best hope for the future of Powys. Lord Macsen stood to regain lost territory, since Falconbridge and Revelstone could not appeal to King Stephen for assistance.

In turn, the pressure of Welsh raids would keep the Marcher lords from bleeding their own garrisons of troops to fight for the king.

Best of all, it would put Con ap Ifan in an agreeable odor with Empress Maud and yield him all the juicy plums that lady had promised. But what might such a heightening of border hostilities mean for Enid and her children? The question gnawed at Con's conscience.

What might the consequences be for his son?

Chapter Fourteen

What mischief was Con ap Ifan up to now? Enid wondered as she spied him returning to the *maenol* with Lord Macsen after their talk. Both men looked grave and pensive—an accustomed disposition for the border chief, but very much out of character for Con. About time he experienced a little worry weighing on his carefree, irresponsible mind!

Hard as Enid tried to take vindictive satisfaction from it, her hand trembled with the stifled impulse to smooth away the furrows from his brow, and her arms ached to enfold him. She had always brooded enough for both of them, relying on Con to lighten her spirits, which he seldom failed to do. Somehow it seemed an offense against the natural order of life that Con should be troubled or cast down. Enid couldn't help feeling it must portend some calamity.

As if his presence in her house wasn't calamity enough! Between fretting over what he might be advising Lord Macsen, fending off his demands that she refuse the border chief's marriage offer and fearing that he would lay claim to her son, little wonder she scarcely had a thought to spare for anyone or anything *but* Con ap Ifan.

At least, those were the reasons Enid gave herself for being unable to shake him from her thoughts.

If she caught herself smiling more often than a sensible woman ought with so many worries to vex her, it must be because she had her dear son under her roof once again. And if she took greater care with her appearance than she had in years, it must be for Lord Macsen's benefit.

But why her dreams writhed with sweet, searing visions of she and Con cavorting naked in a lazy-flowing stream or exploring each other's bare bodies on a bed of new-mown hay, Enid did not dare try to explain. It made no sense for her to yearn for a man who had brought her so much heartache in the past and from whom she had so much to fear in the future. Then again, when had reason ever swayed her feelings for Con?

Lord Macsen called his men together in the courtyard where Con directed them to a variety of tasks aimed at strengthening Glyneira's defenses.

Did this mean Con's parley with Macsen ap Gryffith would put her modest, isolated estate in danger? If so, it would be more important than ever for her to secure the border chief's protection.

She didn't dare flout her bargain with Con by accepting his lordship's marriage offer before the day had passed. But she could signal her forthcoming consent by the fine feast set before Lord Macsen and his party this evening. And by the well-groomed appearance of her family. At least those preparations were both under her control, unlike so much of what had been happening around Glyneira of late.

Not least her own wayward emotions.

When Enid entered the kitchen, Gaynor immediately bustled over.

"Well?" Below a moist-looking brow, Gaynor's hazel eyes glittered with curiosity. "Has he asked you yet?"

"Has who asked what?" Enid inhaled the savory steam rising from a cauldron suspended over the fire. "I thought I smelled something burning."

"Not from *my* kitchen!" The suggestion distracted Gaynor for a moment, then, like a hunting dog on the scent of game, she returned to her question. "Besides, you know very well who asked what, so don't torment me. Did Lord Macsen ask you to wed him?"

The harder she tried to divert her sister-in-law, the worse she would pique Gaynor's curiosity. Enid knew from past experience. "He asked."

Before she could utter another word, Gaynor seized Enid around the waist with stout arms and twirled her in a dizzying circle. "This calls for a fine celebration! Why don't we broach those flasks of mead Howell took on trade from the wool merchant last summer?"

"I haven't given his lordship my answer yet." Enid wrenched herself out of Gaynor's hearty grip before the spinning made her ill.

Seeing the look of horror on her sister-in-law's broad face, she hastened to add, "I mean to accept him, of course. The mead sounds a fine idea. I'll go fetch the flasks from my stores."

"Have you gone daft?" A quick step put Gaynor in Enid's path of escape. "If you mean to have Lord Macsen, why did you not tell him so straightaway?"

If Gaynor knew the truth of it, she'd probably flay Con alive! "This is an important decision. I have my children to consider as well as Glyneira. Why, I'd be daft to give my consent without a little thought on the matter."

It was just the sort of reasonable-sounding argument

Con ap Ifan might have advanced. Enid couldn't decide whether to feel proud of herself…or disgusted.

Gaynor made no secret of siding with the latter. "A little thought? You must have lost your wits, woman! It's not as though his lordship surprised you with this out of a blue sky. Every soul within these walls has known what was coming for months. *That* was the time to make up your mind."

"And so I did, however…"

Fie but Gaynor was harder to budge than a badger sow from her den. The woman reminded Enid of…herself. How would Con dance his way out of this?

"…Lord Macsen had no way of knowing his marriage offer came to me as anything but a surprising honor." Fumbling with her keys, Enid brushed past her sister-in-law, heading for the stores. "I didn't wish to appear over-eager. No man wants what he can gain too easily, least of all a man like Macsen ap Gryffith."

"I suppose…" Gaynor sounded more than a little dubious.

As she headed away, a sense of relief bubbled up in Enid, as though she'd dodged a swift-flying arrow. Over her shoulder she called, "Tonight, Lord Macsen can drown his impatience for my answer in a flagon of well-aged mead."

As for her own lurking worries, it would take an ocean of mead to make an end of them.

After securing that special libation for the meal, Enid made sure her children were well scrubbed and combed. Then she set about grooming herself for the evening. Surely if she donned her best garments and dressed her hair in a becoming style, it would signal Lord Macsen how she meant to answer his offer of marriage.

Stripping out of her clothes, she swept a glance down

her naked body, wondering if her new husband would find it worth all she stood to gain from their union.

Apart from a few faint red lines that childbearing had imprinted on the skin around the base of her belly, her flesh was unmarked. Motherhood had wrought some improvements in her form, too—wider hips and riper breasts. Enid tried to imagine Lord Macsen's firm mouth closed over one of her rosy paps, his massive hands fondling her backside.

Her breath quickened and a faint heat simmered in her loins. But when she pictured the border lord's vast, dark frame poised above her own slight body, a weight of panic threatened to smother her.

The sound of a masculine voice from the entrance to her chamber made her gasp. She plucked a discarded smock from off her bed to cover herself.

"If you'd had such a fine pair of breasts back when we used to swim naked as youngsters, you wouldn't have needed to wait until I was blind drunk to ravish me, *cariad.*"

A blistering rebuke rose in Enid's throat, only to strangle there when her gaze met Con's. Seeing those once-beloved blue eyes shining with shameless admiration for her bare body throttled her beyond hope of speech, or even breath. At the same time it provoked a raging fever within her, many fold hotter than the tepid flush she'd stirred with her fancies of being bedded by Lord Macsen.

At last, by dint of will, she managed to choke the words out. "H-how dare you slink in here and spy on me without announcing yourself?"

Her sputtering mixture of outrage and embarrassment did little to quench Con's teasing charm. What had happened to the ridges of brooding worry that had furrowed his brow such a short time ago. Enid had wanted to dispel them—but not like this!

"Whoever left the room last didn't latch the door as well as they might have." A grin of brazen devilment threatened to break wide across his face as Con pointedly tugged the solid oaken portal shut tight, with himself on the wrong side of it. "Besides, it isn't as though I crept in here while you were asleep and invited myself into your bed."

The full meaning of his words thrashed her with the disturbing awareness of what she'd done to him on that sultry summer night, years ago.

"You can't stay here, Con."

"Oh, I won't be long." His gaze fairly crackled with desire. "Much as I'd relish the chance to linger."

Demon! He would stay just long enough to turn her life upside down again, then flee at top speed the moment she needed him. Macsen ap Gryffith might not rouse such a fiery tempest inside her, but at least he would be there— tomorrow, next week and next year. His land, his people, his duties and *her* would be enough to fill his life. The need to climb higher or venture farther into the wide world would not tempt him away from her.

"If you won't leave, at least have the manners to turn your back so I can cover myself decently."

Heaving an exaggerated sigh, Con did as she bid him. "It seems an insult to the Almighty, covering up such beauty that he created."

"Save your flattery." Enid pulled her fine linen smock over flesh warmer from Con's admiring gaze than it might be from another man's ardent touch. "You must have come here to do more than catch me undressing."

Even though his face was averted from her, Enid sensed a change in Con's jesting manner. When he began to speak after a telling hesitation, his tone of voice confirmed the shift.

"Worthy as that reason might be, I'll own I did have another. May I turn 'round again? You've had time enough to don a full suit of armor."

If it promised to protect her heart from his blandishments, she would put on a coat of mail. "Turn, then, and speak your piece. What do you want from me now, Con?"

"One night."

The uncertain significance of those two brief words sent an anxious shiver through Enid from heel to crown. "Don't talk in riddles! What do you mean by *one night?*"

"One night to prove you love Macsen ap Gryffith enough to make a good home for my son."

"I told you, it's impossible to prove—"

Con cut her off. "If you can spend one night alone in my company without giving yourself to me, I'll take that as all the proof I need."

The thought of it set her heart tumbling down a steep slope. "You must be clean mad! Where could we be alone in a *maenol* crowded with guests? My children share this chamber with me and I can't very well turn them out. Is this some trick of yours to turn Lord Macsen against me by making it look as though I'd play him false?"

"You know me better than that, Enid." The hurt that shadowed Con's clear candid eyes reproached her. "Just because I can't refashion myself to be the kind of man you want, doesn't mean I'm a faithless blackguard. I only seek what's best for you and for our boy.''

"You have a fine way of showing it."

"Do you think I'd run such a risk if I could see any other way?'' When that beseeching note wove a plaintive harmony in Con's fine mellow voice, stones might sprout violets for him. ''I swear I will find us a private place where none will disturb us, nor be a whit the wiser.''

"I *could* perform this ordeal.'' Were her bold words meant to convince Con, Enid wondered...or herself? ''But why should I, just to give *you* peace of mind?''

Con felt his Adam's apple bob wildly in his throat. What had he expected? Enid was too canny a woman to accept his challenge without a powerful inducement. Would what he was about to offer prove potent enough? And if it did, was he so bold as to wager his flimsy charm against Enid's formidable stubbornness?

Inhaling a deep breath, Con reminded himself that he hadn't risen this far in life by doubting his abilities. ''Of course I mean to make it worth your while. If you can prove your feelings for Lord Macsen, I will give your marriage my blessing...and promise never to tell Bryn I'm his father.''

At any other time, Enid's dumbstruck look would have sent Con into peals of mirth. But never in his carefree life had he felt less inclined to laughter.

"You mean...'' Enid leaned against her bed for support, as if she might otherwise wilt to the floor ''...if I can pass the night in your company without—''

"It will be your choice,'' Con assured her. ''You know I would never do aught to force you, but be warned, I will do everything in my power to entice you.''

Enid gave a wooden nod. "But if I can resist, you will *never* tell Bryn you are his father." She sounded reluctant to believe it.

"I will swear on my mother's soul, or anything else you name. But if you give in to me, you must admit you do not love Lord Macsen enough to wed him."

Enid's face blanched to the sickly gray-white of chalk. "Then—?"

"You'll be bound to refuse his marriage offer," said Con. "And I'll be free to deal with young Bryn as I see fit."

She stood there for a long time neither moving nor speaking, staring at Con with cold revulsion in her eyes that made him fear for the success of his challenge.

At last, when he'd begun to doubt she would answer, Enid spoke. "It must be tonight."

Tonight? Surely he'd misheard her. He would need more time than that to prepare.

"Tomorrow," he countered.

Enid pulled herself erect. "No, Con. I told his lordship he would have my answer by tomorrow. I will not forestall him any longer than that. Besides, we'll be serving mead with the evening meal in honor of our guests. I trust everyone will be sleeping too soundly to mark where you and I go."

For once, Con could not argue with her reasoning, no matter at how great a disadvantage it placed him.

As if speaking to herself alone, Enid murmured, "I want this settled. For good or ill, once I know my way I have the courage to tread it. But I hate to have it hanging over me like a headsman's ax."

For good or ill. Enid's words tore into Con like a hail

of arrows. By *ill* she meant seeking delight in his arms—
something they had once both burned to experience.

Yet nipping at the heels of that bitter regret and setting
it to flight came a heady urge to prove himself. Laying
gentle siege to Enid's fortress of resentment and stubborn
resolve, he would need to ply every sensual weapon in his
pleasure-giving arsenal.

Not only that. He would also need to put himself firmly
in Enid's place, Con realized, to see the world and himself
through her eyes. Only then might he find the key to un-
lock a secret door and gain access to her most private
sanctum.

"Very well, then. Tonight it shall be."

With those words, he slipped out of Enid's chamber as
stealthily as he had slipped in, making certain her door
shut tight behind him. He did not want anyone else to
blunder in and catch her disrobed.

"Tonight, by heaven," he chided himself in a whisper.
"What have you let yourself in for this time, Con ap
Ifan?"

Enid's words of protest returned to haunt him. *Where
could we be alone in a* maenol *crowded with guests?*
Where indeed?

It must be someplace special, well nigh magical, for him
to succeed in besieging Enid's formidable will. Where
would he find such a spot in all of Wales, let alone on this
modest estate? His countrymen were not given to the kind
of luxury Con had experienced and enjoyed in the Frankish
courts or Byzantium.

If only he had an enchanted flying carpet, Con mused
as he wandered out of doors, like the ones he'd heard about
in tales from the East. Then he could transport Enid away

to some opulent setting worthy of her. The chamber of a certain Constantine noblewoman glittered in his imagination, complete with its lavish tiled bath.

The din, the smell and the bustle of workaday activity in the *maenol* courtyard sent the magic carpet of Con's fancy plummeting back down to earth.

Damn his arrogance! He was going to lose the chance to acknowledge his son all because…might as well own to the full extent of his folly. All because he couldn't bear the thought of Enid as another man's wife. Not even a fellow as worthy as Macsen ap Gryffith.

"Is something wrong, Master Con?" asked a melodious young voice.

As his bemused gaze lit on Enid's daughter, Con wondered that Myfanwy had a jot of sympathy to spare him. Ever since his abrupt departure from Glyneira and his equally abrupt return, she'd paid him as much mind as if he was invisible, and smelled foul besides. Not that he blamed her. From his own childhood he recalled the sharp disappointment of adult promises broken.

For her own reasons, it appeared Myfanwy had decided to give him another chance…regardless of whether he deserved one. If only her mother still possessed such a supple young heart, Con might stand a chance tonight.

For a moment he basked in the child's blue-green gaze, that put him in mind of the Mediterranean on a tranquil day. Then he winked and flashed her a rueful grin. "*I* am the matter, lass. Hard as I try, I can't seem to put a foot right."

"Don't worry." Myfanwy reached for his hand and gave it a heartening squeeze. "Everybody makes mistakes sometimes."

Not on his scale, they didn't.

"My mam told me so," added the child, "when I first took up the harp. She said it's all part of learning."

"A wise woman, your mam."

Myfanwy gave a ready nod. "Mam said she got into all sorts of muddles when she first began to work with the wool. She said as long as you learned how you went wrong and didn't make the same mistake over again, you'd run out of missteps by and by."

"That's sound advice. I'll have to heed it."

Had he kept repeating old mistakes where Enid was concerned? Con asked himself. And if he failed tonight, would he ever have the chance to correct them?

"I know what'll take your mind off your troubles." Myfanwy tugged him toward the forge. "Help me find Bryn and Davy. We're playing a hiding game."

Con opened his mouth to decline her invitation. He'd done enough searching around Glyneira for Davy's wandering puppy. Besides, just now he needed solitude to reflect on the impossible task he had set for himself tonight. Quiet to plan his approach.

But he'd disappointed Myfanwy once. That was not a mistake Con wanted to repeat. "Let's have a look, then. Have you checked the pigsty yet?"

They dashed off to the pen where they found the old mother sow suckling her piglets, undisturbed by the puppy Pwyll or his young master.

Myfanwy towed Con back toward the smithy. "Let's ask Math if he's seen them."

The blacksmith had indeed seen both boys a while before, heading toward the washhouse.

"They're likely hiding in the big tub where mam soaks the wool," cried Myfanwy as she bolted across the courtyard.

Con wandered after her at a slower pace, still mulling over the problem of Enid and how he might win her tonight with so little in his favor. The more thought he gave the matter, the less it seemed to admit of a solution. As much as he longed to win their wager, Con acknowledged, he longed even more for one sweet tryst with Enid. A night to remember, since he could recall so little about the first time she'd given herself to him.

He reached the entrance to the washhouse just in time to hear Myfanwy mutter a mild oath for which her Auntie Gaynor would surely have scolded her.

"They aren't here, either." The child set her winsome young mouth in a determined line. Though Myfanwy might take after her late father in looks, she clearly favored her mother in character. "They'd better not have broken the rules by venturing beyond the walls, or so help me I'll flay them both."

"Have you given this place a thorough search?" Con struggled not to grin as he peered into the dim outbuilding.

The faint tang of dye plants and the mellow aroma of tallow reminded him of the morning after he'd arrived at Glyneira, and the brief feverish kiss that had overtaken him and Enid.

"Look for yourself." Myfanwy budged out of the narrow doorway to let Con enter. "I was that sure they'd be in the cauldron. Mam sometimes lets us bathe there in the winter."

Squatting over a fire pit dug into the earthen floor, the shallow tub was large enough to hold two boys, Con judged as he peered into it. True to Myfanwy's word, it was empty even of the water in which Enid had cleansed and dyed Glyneira's wool clip.

A far cry, this, from the luxurious bathhouses Con had known in the Holy Land.

"I think I see them!" Myfanwy squealed. "Come on!"

"I'll be along," murmured Con, as his gaze swept the rude little building and his thoughts began to swirl.

Before he composed himself enough to follow the child, Myfanwy returned with her brothers.

"I found you," Myfanwy insisted.

Bryn shook his head. "Davy and me got tired of hiding is all, so we came out."

"You *never* would have found us, Myfanwy," agreed Davy. "Say, Master Con, why don't you hide and we'll see if Pwyll can track you after we let him get a good sniff?"

Con scooped up the puppy, who was already giving his feet a careful smell. "I have a better idea for a game."

Three young faces turned their expectant gazes toward him.

"What kind of game?" asked Bryn.

An unlooked-for spark of hope kindled in the black ashes of Con's fancy. Each new idea that blew through his thoughts, coaxed it to burn hotter and brighter.

"We'll pit two teams against one another to see who can fetch water the fastest." He hoped his enthusiasm would communicate itself to the children. "Bryn and Myfanwy against Davy and me. What do you say?"

Davy's small nose wrinkled. "It sounds a queer sort of game to me."

"It might be good fun all the same." Bryn shot Con a

probing glance, as though he guessed this was more than a game, but could not fathom what.

"Go!" Myfanwy snatched a wooden bucket from the floor and sprinted off to the well.

The boys ran after her, and Pwyll scampered behind them barking like mad.

"Hurry, Con!" Davy called back over his shoulder.

"Coming." Con swept one more glance around the washhouse as he hefted a bucket.

Perhaps he stood a chance with Enid tonight after all... however slender.

Chapter Fifteen

If Con ap Ifan thought he stood a chance with her tonight, the man was fooling himself! That grim conviction ran through Enid's mind as she poured mead for Lord Macsen and his men prior to the evening meal.

True, Con still made her burn for him the way she had as a girl. But she was many years past girlhood, with many scars on her heart to prove it. Both the oldest and the most recent of those wounds had been inflicted by the same arrogant fellow who believed himself capable of seducing her before the sun rose tomorrow morning.

Let him try!

Lord Macsen took a deep draft of the amber liquid in his cup, then nodded in approval. After another drink, he glanced around the crowded hall.

"Will our bard honor us with his presence tonight?" One full, black brow rose and the dark eyes beneath seemed to pierce Enid's placid surface, to the turbulent depths beneath. "Good mead and good music go together...like a well-matched bride and groom. Who knows but the drink may even put my feet in a humor for dancing?"

"No doubt he'll turn up when the fancy takes him, my

lord.'' Enid struggled to maintain a tone of cheerful indifference to Con's comings and goings. "I've never known him to miss a meal if he could help it. We won't wait the feast on him, that's certain.''

Where *had* Con got to and what was he up to? A welcome sense of annoyance nagged at Enid. She added it to the stout bastion of suspicion, fear and old festering grievances already ranged around her heart. She knew Con and herself well enough to realize she'd need every possible defense tonight against the battering ram of his charm.

Fortunately she'd have time as her ally, for it always favored the patient…or the stubborn.

As she threaded her way through the crowded hall, dispensing the mead with a liberal hand, Enid gradually noticed an absence that bothered her far more than Con's.

Where were her children?

It wasn't like them to be late to table, especially Davy, who had the ravenous appetite of a fledgling.

"Have you seen my young ones?'' Enid whispered to Gaynor as her sister-in-law bustled within earshot.

Gaynor craned her short neck to peer around the hall. "I've been so busy, I never noticed. Now that you mention it, I haven't clapped eyes on any of them since Davy came poking about the kitchen before noon. Shall I go call them?''

"No, I'll round them up.'' Enid passed Gaynor the flagon of mead. "Once everyone's been poured their drink, you can start serving the food. I'll only be a moment.''

So she hoped at least.

Catching Lord Macsen's gaze upon her, Enid flashed him a false, fleeting smile of reassurance. Privately she wondered if Con had anything to do with her children being tardy for supper.

She did not have to wonder for long.

Just beyond the threshold of the hall she found all four of them, sporting identical shamefaced grins and flushed cheeks.

"Where have you been? I was growing worried." She shot Con a glare to inform him that *his* absence had not caused her an instant of concern.

"I'm sorry, Mam." Myfanwy slipped past her mother into the hall. "We didn't notice how low the sun was getting."

"Supper smells good." Davy charged by on his sister's heels. "I'm hungry!"

"There's nothing new in that." Enid caught her youngest son in a quick embrace.

Relief at finding her children none the worse for being a trifle late lightened her spirits…until her hand came in contact with Davy's damp garments.

"Davyd ap Howell, did you fall into the river?" She touched a suspicious dark patch on Bryn's tunic and found it wet as well. "What have you been up to?"

"Only a game, Mam." Bryn gave her a quick peck on the cheek then pulled his little brother into the hall. "Come sit by me, Davy."

"But you need to change clothes," Enid called after them.

"It's only water, *cariad.*" Con's garments looked as though they had undergone a similar baptism. "They'll dry out quick enough. The three of them had a jolly time and they're no worse than a little wet, so no need to borrow trouble, is there?"

"I suppose…" It would be like him to excuse some dangerous lark on the grounds that no harm had come of it—dismissing the harm that *might* have come if undeserved luck had not been on his side.

Con shrugged. "Besides, it kept them out from underfoot while you were busy preparing for tonight."

"I suppose you think that merits my thanks."

"Perhaps." He cast her an impudent grin as he stepped into the hall. "I know better than to expect it, though."

She might have clouted him on the ear if there had not been so many folk watching, including Lord Macsen. Instead, Enid reined in her temper and reminded herself she'd soon be well rid of Con ap Ifan's troublesome company.

Pity, the thought did not bring her the satisfaction she'd hoped it would.

Con suppressed a rueful sigh.

Would Enid ever come to see that he meant her no harm? If by some unmerited grace he managed to prevail tonight, would she grant that he'd acted out of care for her and their son? For Myfanwy and Davy, too, Con reminded himself. Over the past fortnight, Enid's younger children had rapidly come to mean as much to him as the one he'd begotten.

"So our harper has arrived at last." Lord Macsen patted the bench beside him. "Come oil your tongue and loosen your fingers with a drop of mead, Con ap Ifan."

"It'll be a pleasure to oblige you." Con helped himself from the flagon set before Lord Macsen. While pretending to fill his cup, he barely let a trickle wet the bottom of it.

"We'll expect a fine performance from you tonight." Lord Macsen drank deeply.

Con made a convincing pretense of guzzling his mead. "I'll do my best to oblige you in that, as well."

He refilled Lord Macsen's cup to the brim, then dribbled a trifling measure into his own.

"Let us drink to the promise of happy news," said Lord

Macsen, looking more relaxed and affable than Con had yet seen him.

The mead must be a potent batch, for the big border chief did not have the look of a man who'd be easily inebriated.

"To happy news." Con feigned a hearty swig, which in truth scarcely wet his lips.

He wished he dared drink more, for the brew tasted like distilled sunshine, but Con soon had reason to be glad of his clear head.

When Enid ventured near the table, Lord Macsen grabbed her around the waist and pulled her down to the bench beside him. "You've been a fine hostess, *cariad,* but now that the food is coming you should sit and keep me company."

The sound of his own endearment for Enid on another man's tongue made Con itch to reach for his dagger. If he'd drunk half as much of the mead as he'd pretended to, he might have landed himself headfirst in a boiling cauldron of trouble. Even sober it took every crumb of self-control to keep his temper in check.

Instead he took out his spite on the meal, biting into his bread and meat with almost savage force. As soon as he dared, Con excused himself from the table on the pretense of needing to tune his harp. After a few purposely tortured notes, he settled down to playing softly while the rest of the company ate, drank and talked among themselves.

At last Lord Macsen swept a commanding glance around the room. In spite of the drink in their bellies, his men immediately heeded it and fell silent. The Glyneira folk were quick to follow their example.

When the hall had fallen so quiet Con fancied he could hear a beetle crawling through the rushes, the border lord ordered, "Play for us, bard."

"As you bid, my lord." Con ran a thrill on his harp strings and shot a glance at Enid.

Perched on Lord Macsen's broad knee with his large hands around her waist, she was making a valiant effort not to appear ill at ease. From what Con could tell, she was also losing a subtle battle of wills with Lord Macsen, who kept trying to ply her with mead.

Though Con knew it would make Enid more receptive to his wooing later, that was not how he wanted to win her.

He began his performance with several rousing battle songs that encouraged the rest of the company to drink. Then he played a few especially favored by the children, knowing Enid would soon send hers off to bed. The lusty singing and boisterous laughter of the adults told Con they would sleep soundly in their brychans tonight.

When the last rousing chorus of "Goat White" ended, Enid pried herself from Lord Macsen's grasp and beckoned her children. "Time for bed, Myfanwy, Davy."

"Just one more, Mam?" The children looked to Con for support.

"The hour grows late." Con shrugged to suggest he was powerless in the matter.

"Stay put and take your ease, Enid." Gaynor jumped from her place at the end of the high table. "I'll see the young ones to bed."

Lord Macsen beamed at Gaynor as he pulled Enid back onto his lap. "A skilled bard like you must know a few love songs," he called to Con.

"So I do, my lord." Could he think of one that would not choke him as he watched the big border lord fondle *his* Enid?

Perhaps he did…

"If she were mine and loved me well," Con sang, *"life would be naught but pleasure."*

Macsen ap Gryffith nodded his approval.

"I would not care for sacks of gold, nor other earthly treasure."

Liar! The accusation blazed in Enid's eyes.

Con knew himself guilty, yet an uncanny certainty resonated in his voice as he sang, *"Her winning ways, her laughing eyes, throw such a charm about her. She must be mine, yes mine alone. I cannot live without her."*

He gazed into Enid's eyes, certain that he touched her in a way Macsen ap Gryffith could not with his powerful hands. *"If she were mine, my aim would be to make her love me dearly. That all her heart and all her thoughts belonged to me sincerely."*

The words of the ballad forced Con to look deep into his heart. What he discovered there confounded him.

Remembering why he had chosen his song in the first place, he sang the final words as a warning to Lord Macsen. *"But should I find to my dismay, that I had cause to doubt her, then were she mine and loved me not, I'd rather be without her."*

If Macsen ap Gryffith heard and heeded, he gave no sign. The last bittersweet notes of the melody trailed off into silence, followed by a soft refrain of snoring.

Just then Gaynor returned from settling the children. Looking around at the nodding, dozing company, she asked in a giggly whisper, "What did you play, Con ap Ifan? Some enchanted lullaby that puts all who hear it to sleep?"

Con pulled a rueful face. "It's a poor bard who sets his listeners all snoring."

Dislodging Lord Macsen's slack hand from around her waist, Enid rose—a mite unsteadily, or so Con judged. She ignored him altogether, addressing herself to her sister-in-law. "Let's collect all the cups, then unpack the brychans to bed everyone down for the night."

"Aye." Gaynor yawned deeply. "The sooner the better." She poked Helydd and a few of the other women who were not fast asleep to help with the task.

As Enid headed for the corner chest where the brychans were stored, Con stole up behind her and whispered in her ear, "When you're finished here, meet me out in the washhouse."

She started, then spun around to face him. "The washhouse? Have you gone daft?"

"The washhouse," he said again, making an effort to mask his uncertainty. "I'll be waiting."

Had he gone daft? Con asked himself as he slipped out of the hall to put the final touches on his preparations. Was it too much to hope he might win Enid tonight?

Win her in a way he'd never intended—in a way he probably didn't deserve?

She didn't dare delay any longer.

Enid glanced around the great hall, bathed in the soft blush of the fire's glowing coals. A peaceful chorus of rumbling snores and whistling breath in a slow, steady rhythm enticed her to sleep, though she knew she must resist.

With all her guests and family bedded down for the night at last, she had no more excuses to stay in the hall. She must make her way to the washhouse where Con awaited her. If she did not come, or even if she dallied too long, her subtle-minded opponent might not be above declaring himself the winner of their wager by default.

As she tiptoed past Lord Macsen's slumbering form, she fought the urge to fetch him a well-placed kick. She settled for a black look that relieved her feelings without waking him.

The way he'd bid her drink from his own cup of mead, made her wonder if the border chief might be in league with Con. Though she'd let only a tiny amount of the potent golden liquor pass her lips, it had still been enough to leave her limbs warm and heavy, her mind dazed and dizzy. Too easy a target for Con ap Ifan's practiced wiles of seduction. At least, he might imagine so.

Enid knew better.

Even with hogshead of mead inside her, she would never give herself to a man who'd abandoned her twice for the lure of gain and glory. No matter how desperately she'd once loved him. She would not throw away her whole well-mapped future and the unity of her family for one fleeting night in Con's arms.

Especially not on the dirt floor of some dark, cramped, smelly little shed where she washed and dyed wool!

As she stole out of the house and made her way toward that outbuilding, Enid recited under her breath the long litany of her grievances against Con. Heading the list came his arrogant presumption in setting her this challenge.

The night air cooled her flushed cheeks as she crossed the courtyard. Enid welcomed the chill, for it promised to cool any ardor Con might kindle in her before morning.

Something drew her gaze to the heavens where a swath of stars cast their ghostly glimmer, far beyond mortal reach.

Perhaps the mead she'd sipped with such reluctance was making her fanciful. For she imagined the Fair Folk offering her and Con some magical means to travel into the night sky and harvest a fortune in star jewels.

Con would leap at the chance. Not only for the promised riches and the acclaim that would attach to such a feat, but

for the opportunity to venture where no man had ever gone
and do something no other man had ever done. And if the
Fair Folk demanded a price, as they often did for such a
boon, Con would pay it…even in blood.

And Enid? She'd pay an equally high bounty to be
spared such a rare "gift" and all the risks that must come
with it. She'd ask nothing more than to keep her feet
planted on safe, familiar ground with her loved ones held
close.

Little wonder she and Con had never been able to forge
a lasting bond, in spite of their feelings for one another.
A soundless sigh seeped out of Enid to mist in the crisp
night air. Ahead in the darkness, the door of the washhouse
thrust ajar a little way. A soft, warm light spilled out
through the narrow opening.

"Is that you, *cariad?*" Con's whisper floated out to
wrap around Enid like an enchantment, drawing her toward the shed.

"'Tis I, and a good thing for you." She tried to keep
her tone as crisp and cool as the night air. "Imagine the
trouble you'd be in if Lord Macsen or Gaynor had staggered out here instead."

As she spoke those last words a chuckle ambushed her.
Damn that mead! And damn Lord Macsen for making her
drink it!

Con held the door open wider. "Come in before you're
chilled to the marrow."

Wait until he got a taste of her response to his wooing.
As she stepped over the threshold of the washhouse, Enid
put the garrison of her resolve on alert to repulse Con's
amorous assault. She'd show him a chill to the marrow!

Her every thought bent on resisting Con, Enid scarcely
noticed her surroundings at first.

When she finally wakened to them, it was more like slipping into a dream.

"Merciful Mother, Con," she breathed, "you've bewitched the place." Or bewitched her, perhaps. How else could the mean little shed where she washed and dyed wool have been transformed into such a cozy, fragrant bower?

A bed of glowing coals warmed the place, coaxing wisps of steam from the water-filled cauldron above it. Petals of apple and cherry blossoms floated on the surface of the water, perfuming the air with their wholesome sweetness. A carpet of brushed fleeces covered the bare earth floor and a single tallow candle cast its flickering golden light over garlands of lush spring greenery.

"Do you like it?" A mellow note of hard-won satisfaction warmed Con's words. "It's not as opulent as some bathing chambers I've seen in the East, but it was the best I could do in a pinch."

He shut the door behind her, then strode to the cauldron. There he dipped a finger into the water, nodding his approval of its temperature.

When she saw Con's bare chest, Enid's body grew far too hot for her liking. The first breathless delight in her surroundings ebbed as she realized its purpose.

"So this was the game you and the children were playing before supper?"

"Aye. They helped me. So did Helydd." Con gestured toward the fleeces. "And Idwal." He nodded toward the greenery.

Had her whole household allied with Con against her— even the familiar countryside she loved?

"Come on." Con held out his hands to her as he flashed his most inviting smile. "Let's shift you out of those clothes. I'll be your bath attendant for tonight and pamper you the way a princess ought to be.''

Shift her out of her clothes, indeed! Enid wrapped her arms around herself, digging her nails into the sleeves of her kirtle. ''You must be clean mad if you think I'm going to strip naked so you can have your way with me.''

''It won't be like that, I swear.'' Though his stance and the look in his eye proclaimed a desire to approach her, Con kept his distance. ''I'll concede victory to you in our wager if I touch you anywhere and any way but as you direct me.''

Enid cast him a wary glance, but her firm grip on the fabric of her sleeves eased.

''Upon my life,'' Con vowed, sweeping her a deep bow. ''You may think of me as your humble eunuch bath attendant.''

''Eunuch?'' Enid cast a pointed stare at the lap of his breeches where his manly desire flaunted itself. ''I fear my imagination has its limits.''

Con's cheeks blazed and he began to laugh.

Hard as she tried to resist, Enid found herself laughing, too. Some tightly clenched bud inside her began to unfurl its petals.

The blossom-strewn water in the tub called to her.

''I suppose it would be a shame to have all this work of yours go to waste.'' She wriggled out of her kirtle, resisting Con's offer to help her. ''Since we must spend this night together, one of us might as well get some pleasure out of it.''

Why not both of us? The twinkle in Con's eyes seemed to ask.

''Purge that thought from your mind straightaway.'' Enid peeled off her undergown. ''I mean to be the only one taking any enjoyment tonight, and not the kind you intend, either.''

As she loosened the necktie of her thin linen smock, Enid reminded herself she had no need to feel bashful of baring her body before Con. After all, he had made that rash promise not to touch her except where and how she bid him. If he grew too bold, he would forfeit their wager.

Arming herself with that thought, she removed her final undergarment with deliberate care.

"Ah, *cariad.*" Con swept an admiring gaze over her, making Enid's naked flesh quiver as if he *had* touched it. "Whatever else does or doesn't happen between us tonight, I will take pleasure from feasting my eyes upon you."

The flatterer! Enid steeled herself against Con's powerful weapons. No doubt he'd cozened his way into more than one noblewoman's bed with such charming words. Or perhaps their opulent bathing chambers, of which he appeared to have such intimate knowledge.

She tested the water with her forefinger, then eased herself into its hot, wet embrace. "Mmm. This is one foreign indulgence I might learn to like."

"There are others you'd relish, too, unless I miss my guess." Con picked up a washcloth. "Shall I tell you about them while I scrub your shoulders, my lady? By your leave, of course."

What could it hurt if Con swiped a cloth over her shoulders or prated on about the Holy Land? It would pass the time till morning.

"Very well." She stole a glance at Con's well-shaped torso and the firm-muscled forearms of an archer. "To both."

Con dipped his cloth in the bath, then squeezed it gently to let rivulets of water trickle down over Enid's neck and shoulders. A sheen of sweat broke on her brow as she imagined him playing the water over her breasts.

''Your upper arm, may I wash there, too?''

''You may.''

The water's warmth seemed to leach something out of her. Something tight, angry and unyielding. Something she'd never much liked about herself, but had been unable to let go.

True to his word, Con did not touch any part of her body she had not given him leave to touch. But it hardly mattered.

When he swiped the soft damp cloth over the crook of her elbow or the sole of her foot, it felt as intimate and arousing as if he'd fondled her breasts...or elsewhere. How Enid wished she dared let him.

For years she'd settled for whatever life dealt her, then struggled to make the best of it. For the sake of her children. For the sake of Glyneira.

Just once could she not indulge her own desires?

''Will you grant me one boon, *cariad?*'' Con's smooth, delicious murmur caressed her ear.

''That depends on what it is.''

She hadn't forgotten all the reasons she must resist Con, tonight. Drowsy, buoyant and roused as she was just then, those reasons had lost their urgency—floating away from her toward a distant horizon.

Of all the things she imagined Con might ask, she did not anticipate what came.

''Tell me about the last night you and I passed together.''

Perhaps Con sensed her confusion, for he added. ''The night we made that fine boy of ours. I want to remember, *cariad.* I want to sort it out from all the times I only dreamed of you and me together. Will you give me back that much, at least?''

She had stolen his seed to get her son, and the drink had stolen his memory of it. She couldn't bear to yield Bryn up to Con, but she could restore the other to him, as much as it was within her power.

''Very well. I'll tell you.''

The telling would come at a price to her, Enid sensed as she unlocked that trunk of memories and began to rummage through it for the first time in years.

This night and this wager were not turning out at all as she'd expected. She'd believed her challenge would lie in resisting Con's overtures. Instead, she'd discovered a far more difficult test—resisting her own desires.

Recalling in detail the long-ago night when she'd given herself to Con might whet the edge of her yearning for him…until it grew sharp enough to slice her in two.

Chapter Sixteen

His distant mating with Enid was not all Con had forgotten. As she restored that memory to him, piece by piece,
word by whispered word, he began to forget the reason for
his present tryst with her. The years between then and now
began to blur...fade...dim.

On his travels to and from the Holy Land, Con had often
stared off into the mysterious western horizon beyond
which none but the Fair Folk sailed. He'd watched the
gray-blue expanse of sea merge into the blue-gray sky until
it became one vast baffling vista. Tonight past and present
blended together in much the same way, with *Cariad Enid
Du* his only constant star by which to navigate.

Their destination? Paradise.

When she'd first looked around the wash shed and declared it enchanted, Con had felt his heart swell within
him until it fairly pained his ribs to contain it. Who'd have
thought a little greenery, a few fleeces and an armful of
apple blossoms could transform such a humble workaday
structure into a bower of striking, sensuous beauty? One
to rival the most lavish lady's bath chamber he'd ever seen
in the East?

And did he find it all the more pleasing because it

sprang from the peculiar charm of his native land? Con could not deny it.

No matter how exotic or elegant, every other place in which he'd made love to a woman had been missing something—something vital but elusive. He had been missing something, too, all these years without ever realizing it. The memory of his first time with a woman.

"I recall the scent of hay and clover," Enid murmured. Suddenly Con could smell it, too, in all its lazy, mellow sweetness.

Enid's eyes slid shut, the better to go back in time and take him along with her. "I remember the sounds of the horses in the barn below—swishing away the flies with their tails, shaking their manes and nickering."

She gave a quiet chuckle. "It was a wonder I could hear anything over the buzz of your snoring. The loft was dark as pitch, so I crawled toward that sound until I found you."

Con could almost hear the faint creak of boards and the rustle of straw. A girl's breath, coming fast because she'd just climbed the ladder. Because she was frightened…and eager.

Abruptly Enid sat up in the tub. Drops of water sprayed off her back, a few falling to hiss on the coals beneath the cauldron. "I must get out of this water before my skin wrinkles like a dried plum."

"T-to be sure." Con shook his head to clear the daze from his abrupt jolt back into the present. He felt as though he'd fallen out of his old hayloft onto the hard barn floor below. "It'll be…easiest if I lift you out. May I?"

"No harm in it, I suppose." A subtle hitch in her breath betrayed Enid's sense of the danger.

As he rose and bent toward her, she reached for him, locking her arms around his neck. His left arm slid under her back and the right one beneath the crook of her knees.

She didn't weigh much, but Con found the angle of the lift awkward. The slight pressure of her breast against his bare chest and her hip against his belly set his head spinning. He lurched back onto the fleece-draped floor with Enid in his arms. The next thing he knew, she sat nestled in his lap, covered with a brychan, her slick, bare skin in tempting contact with his own.

To keep her occupied so she would linger there, he prompted Enid in a whisper, "I was snoring?"

It worked!

She nodded, making her smooth dark hair rustle against his breastbone. Her voice took on a liquid, dreamy quality. "You were."

One of her arms stayed anchored around his neck, but the other drifted downward, caressing his bare chest as it fell. Con's blood beat a hot, rushing tattoo in his ears.

"Your body felt all loose and boneless," said Enid in a drowsy drawl. Then a trill of laughter rippled through her, making the soft rounding of her backside bounce against the straining lap of Con's breeches. "Most of it, anyway."

Something told him he should chuckle or trade her a quip, but his throat had squeezed so tight Con could scarcely force breath through it.

Even that grew more difficult when Enid raised her face to his. "I tried to kiss you awake."

He stared at her lips, full and red-ripe with a promise of untasted sweetness. Why, they might beguile a dead man back to life. Just looking at them made Con's whole mouth burn with the need to kiss Enid.

But if he kissed her, she would speak no more. And he wanted to hear.

"Did it work?" he managed to croak. "The kiss?"

He raised his gaze, hoping to distract himself from her

tantalizing lips, only to tumble headlong into the dark am-
ethyst depths of her eyes. The slight span between her face
and his felt alive, somehow—watchful and waiting, as if
a colony of invisible winged insects hung there with tiny
wings aflutter.

"I...thought it did. You moved. Your arms went 'round
me and you kissed me back."

He *did* remember! Remembered the clean, sweet taste
of her maiden lips and the cascade of her unbound hair
through his fingers—a thousand magical harp strings that
played a rich, wild music of delight within him. Was it
any wonder he'd dismissed it as a wishful dream when
he'd woken the next morning, cold and alone?

Con had reason to wonder if he was dreaming again
when Enid whispered, "Kiss me, now."

He swallowed hard to clear his throat. "Do you mean
it, *cariad?*"

With a subtle nod of her head, she closed the brief gap
between her lips and his.

"Now." As she spoke, Con could feel her lips forming
the words and the warm whisper of her breath against his
chin. "While you know what you're about and so do I."

Con needed no further urging.

With tender restraint, he caught her ripe lower lip between his, then played his tongue across it.

He could half imagine, half recall the raw, fumbling tempest of that long-ago kiss and all that had followed. Though
he desired Enid even more now than he had then, Con
wanted to offer her something better this time. Perhaps to
prove he was no longer the crude plowboy who had once
lusted after her. Even then there had been more to it than
that. But he'd been too young and too drunk to demonstrate
his true feelings in the way he made love to her.

Tonight would be different. Tonight, by her leave, he would make it right for them both.

The sensations Enid experienced that night were different than the ones she recalled in such vivid detail. The scent of sheep and apple blossoms instead of horses and clover. The flickering glow of a tallow candle instead of the darkness of a windowless loft. The soft caress of fleece instead of the rustle of straw.

Con was her only constant, but even he seemed different—his body larger, more weathered, scarred in places. His touch and his kiss were no longer those of a lusty, green lad, greedy for his first maiden. Instead, they were deliberate…lingering. As lazy and luxurious as the warm bath he'd treated her to.

Though her mind could scarcely function while her senses were under Con's delicious siege, somehow Enid knew it was not the years alone that had wrought this change in his approach. The day they'd gone fishing with the coracles, not long after he'd arrived at Glyneira, Con had chased her, caught her and kissed her in the wild way of the boy she remembered.

She had steeled herself against something similar tonight. But the seasoned warrior had changed tactics.

Part of her tried to resist. But when she struggled to recall why, her memory swarmed with potent images of that other night in the hayloft. The only time she had ever given herself to a man without reserve.

The very temperance of Con's kiss made her more demanding. Enid pressed her lips harder against his as she caressed the firm flesh of his chest to rouse him.

It worked.

His breath rasped in her ears, fast and harsh. A keening sound rose from deep in his throat—a wordless plea in answer to the one that strained beneath every inch of her own skin. When Con broke from their kiss with obvious reluctance to ask her a question, she knew what it would be…and how she would answer.

"Did I hurt you that night, *cariad?*"

Caught off guard by words so unlike the ones she'd expected, Enid scrambled to frame a reply.

Before she could couch an answer, Con spoke again in a tone that ached with regret. "A daft question, that. Of course I hurt you—your first time and me too drunk to realize I didn't know what I was doing."

He ran his hand over her hair in the way someone might comfort an injured or frightened child. "I'm sorry, *cariad.* Sorry for all of it. You deserved better from me…and from life."

He'd hurt her far less with his rough lust than he had by marching away the next morning. The reproach burned on Enid's tongue, but she refused to give it voice. What had happened that night had been her choice and the consequences hers to bear.

Blaming Con for all the troubles in her life had been a desperate ploy to oust him from her heart, Enid realized. It had been a matter of survival, otherwise the longing for him would have gnawed her to pieces. That did not give her the right to condemn him for the bitter consequences of *her* actions.

"I'm sorry, too, Con." She cradled his face in her hands and kissed him again.

It was not a kiss of desire, though that still burned hot within her. It was a deep, tender kiss that acknowledged all he had once meant to her. Celebrated the bright colors and joyful music with which he'd filled her girlhood. Honored the precious gift he'd given her in their son.

Con wrenched his lips from hers. His breath came in

ragged gusts. "Just once...let me love you...as you deserve."

How could she deny him? How could she deny herself?

Con had stirred up the glowing embers of her memories
into a raging fire beneath the simmering cauldron of her
old passion and set it boiling again. Scarcely aware of what
she was doing, Enid groped for his hand and raised it to
her breast.

Accepting her consent, he played the tips of his fingers
over the sensitive flesh. A firm, kneading caress on the
rounded fullness. The barest graze over the straining peak.
When he finally withdrew his touch, Enid writhed and
whimpered with need.

"Hush now, *cariad*." Con lifted her from his lap,
spreading her supine on the carpet of fleeces. "I won't
abandon you unsatisfied."

How could he possibly satisfy the dark, urgent hunger
he provoked in her? Enid asked herself as Con hovered
over her, his mouth so close to her nipple that the vapor
of his breath seared it.

"May I?"

Not certain what he meant, but past caring, Enid heard
herself gasp, "Do!"

Slick and hot, his tongue swiped over the rigid nub,
stoking a blaze of sharp urgent pleasure in her bosom and
her loins.

"Mmm, you like that, don't you, my angel?" Con's
voice sounded warm with satisfaction and husky with his
own desire.

Then he closed his lips over her nipple and suckled.
Enid found she could not reply with anything more than a
gurgle of delight.

In time she did find her voice again, inviting Con to

touch her and kiss her in places she'd had no intention of allowing him. As the shadowy hours of the night stretched taut with longing, Con stripped away the layers of restraint in which she'd swaddled herself over the years. Until she was once again the passionate rebellious girl who'd dared to give her heart where she had no business giving it.

When she could not stand the exquisite torment of his touch a moment longer, she arched toward him, crooning, "*Cariad, cariad,* come to me. Make us one."

"You are ripe for it, aren't you?" Con's fond blue gaze seemed to penetrate her heart and soul, as he prepared to enter her. His voice held a tight, fervent edge, as if he was holding back a powerful force with his waning strength. "I've never wanted to delay the end of it like I do now."

Enid knew what he meant…or thought she did. Long ago she'd braved the pain of losing her maidenhead gladly for the wonder of that joining between them. Now, she would even forsake the fevered bliss of Con's love play to experience it again.

But when he eased himself into the slick, sultry fissure between her thighs, a mewling cry broke from her lips.

Con froze. "Have I hurt you, *cariad?*"

A sigh shuddered out of her. "If this is hurt, then go ahead and kill me with it, I beg you."

"Who knows but we may both die before we're through." Con gave a warm, breathless chuckle on his way to claim her lips.

It proved no idle threat…or boast. With Con poised over her, filling her, coaxing her to scale the peaks of ecstasy, Enid marvelled that her body could survive such intense sensation. Then a palsy of pure pleasure shuddered through her again and again as her spirit soared to the friendly stars, all a-sparkle with the familiar laughter in Con's eyes.

* * *

A while later, Con woke abruptly to a sense of chill and emptiness where warmth and softness should be. He groped for Enid, but his hands met only a barren expanse of fleece.

Could he have dreamed last night, the way he'd dreamed their first encounter?

Con shook his head to clear it. Their first encounter had not been a dream, after all, but a true mating that had produced a child. Besides, he was no longer a yearning boy prone to carnal fancies of the night. And yet…

He could not deny that his stolen tryst with Enid had taken him beyond anything he'd previously experienced with a woman.

Prying his eyes open, Con peered around the dim wash-house. The candle flame guttered in a puddle of tallow, making it just possible for him to discern the figure of Enid pulling on her kirtle.

Con yawned and stretched his languid limbs. "Where are you off to at this time of night, *cariad?*"

She started at the sound of his voice, but did not turn to face him. "Back to my own bed, where else? So my children won't be alarmed when they wake and there won't be any more gossip about us than can be helped."

"You worry too much." Con chuckled. "Always did."

"I've had plenty of cause to worry." She lobbed the words back over her shoulder at him. "Still do."

He didn't want their magical night together to end on a sour note. "The children won't wake for hours yet, nor anyone else after the mead they put away at supper. Linger with me awhile, won't you? There are things we need to talk of, you and I, and who knows when we'll get a moment alone once Glyneira's stirring? I'd much rather do it with you soft and naked in my arms."

That made Enid spin about to look at him, her dark unbound hair billowing 'round her like a lustrous cloak of black silk. Even in the faint, fitful light of a dying candle, one glance at her face made Con wish she'd turn away again.

"You've won your game, Con. What more is there to say?"

So *that* was the trouble! In truth, he'd forgotten their wager in his single-minded quest to bring Enid pleasure. Who had touched whom, with or without express invitation, he could no longer recall.

He held out his hand to her, offering his most inviting smile along with it. "I thought we both won, *cariad*. Are you sorry for what we did together?"

Ignoring his outstretched hand, Enid leaned back against the door. "You gave me something rare and wonderful, Con. I wish I could blame you or pretend I didn't know what I was doing, but that would be a lie. I'm not sorry on my own account, and I'm not sorry at this moment."

She expelled a sigh that sounded too large to have come out of her small frame. "I will be sorry, though, for what all comes of it. For what it may cost my children and Glyneira."

Damn! He'd only wanted to heal an old tainted wound from the past. Instead he'd struck Enid a fresh blow.

She pulled herself upright, squaring her slender shoulders as if to bear the heavy weight of what she'd done. That tiny gesture smacked Con harder than any reproach she might have hurled at him.

Enid pulled the door open a crack, letting the chill draft of reality in upon their enchanted cocoon. "I'll speak to Lord Macsen as soon as I can get him alone for a moment."

Then, as if giving voice to her private thoughts, she

murmured, "I hope he won't think I've been leading him on all this time, and take it ill. He deserves better than a wife who only wants him to bring her family together and protect them."

Something he didn't quite understand propelled Con up from the fleece-strewn floor before Enid marched out of his life, as he had once marched out of hers. Naked and roused anew, he caught her between the door and his body, pressing her back until she pushed the door shut again.

"Don't fret, *cariad*. I'll bring your family together. I'll take care of them." It wouldn't be easy, but he would find a way. "You and I, we'll have a lifetime of nights together, as fine as this one and better."

The candle sputtered out just then, but not before Con glimpsed a look of relief and wonder in Enid's eyes that made his heart soar.

"Do you mean it, Con?" She spoke in a whisper, as if she feared her asking might change his mind.

"More than anything in my life, *cariad*." He wrapped his arms around her, partly to signify his protection and partly to anchor himself to the ground in case the rapidly inflating bubble of joy in his chest should waft him straight up to the roof.

In the darkness he fumbled to locate her lips with his own, only to find them raised to meet him. He and Enid kissed long and deeply, without the least reserve. A kiss at once fondly familiar and deliciously fresh. A destined kiss that seemed to fill the empty place in Con's heart to overflowing.

"We'll be a family." The thought of it set him so drunk with happiness, he gave way to giddy laughter as he hoisted Enid off the floor and twirled her around. "You and me. Bryn and the young ones."

Like a magical carpet, his enthusiasm seemed to lift him

off the ground and fly away with him. "I want to wed you as soon as we can arrange it with Father Thomas. Once my mission for the Empress is done, I'll come back to collect you and the children. Then we'll sail to the Holy Land where I'll set you up with a fine house in Edessa."

Caught in the sweet, silken web of his own fancy, Con barely noticed how Enid tensed in his arms. "I promise, *cariad,* you'll have the most luxurious bath chamber of any lady in that city."

"What nonsense are you talking, Conwy ap Ifan?"

The sting of Enid's tone and the force with which she wrenched herself from his arms sent Con's flying carpet hurtling to the hard earth.

"Is that your notion of protection? Carting my children off to some far corner of the world, away from everyone they've ever known to plunge them into the middle of a holy war?"

He had offered her the precious treasure of his fortune and his future, and here she was flinging it back in his face as if it was a reeking pat of sheep's muck!

"They're in the middle of a war, now, in case you haven't noticed. And the Normans have the upper hand. In Edessa we'd be the ones in a position of strength."

"Living among Franks and heathens."

"And what's wrong with that? They may be different than us, but there are good people among them. Besides, who's to say our ways are right and theirs are wrong? It's a big, exciting world out there, Enid. Our children will be all the better for venturing out into it."

"They're *my* children." Enid jerked the door back open. "And I know what's best for them."

For a moment she froze there in the open doorway, a dark slender shadow against the faint light of approaching dawn. When she spoke again, the outrage had fled her voice, leaving behind a wistful note that tugged at Con. "Why must we go away? Why can't you stay here with us? You've seemed so happy at Glyneira."

"I am...I was." Con groped on the floor for his discarded garments. Even in the dark, he felt at a disadvantage arguing with her fully clothed while he stood bare. "But we've plowed this furrow before and nothing's changed. How can I stay at Glyneira with no authority and nothing in my own right? You'd still be the mistress and me little better than a hired plowboy again."

"No authority?" Enid's words rode a wave of scornful laughter. "You came here as a travelling harper and had the whole *maenol* doing your bidding in a week. Why is it so important for you to be a big man in the eyes of the Normans? Will gold and glory warm your bed at night? Will they tend you when you're ill, or weep for you when you die?"

Dumbstruck, Con struggled into his breeches, trying to think of something, *anything* he could say that might convince Enid to wed him on his terms.

For once it was her turn to have the final word.

"You vex me to death by times, Con ap Ifan. For all that, I think the world of you and I'd sooner have you for my husband than any lord or prince. If you thought half as highly of yourself as I think of you, you'd have nothing to prove to anyone."

Without giving him a chance to reply, she closed the door of the washhouse, plunging it once again into stifling darkness.

"I have nothing to prove." Con tried to believe it, but the words rang false in his ears and the empty place inside him gaped wider than it ever had before.

Chapter Seventeen

"A word with you, my lord, if I might?" Enid fought down a spasm of panic that threatened to make her retch up what little she'd eaten for supper the previous night.

"What?" Lord Macsen rubbed his temples as he glanced up at her from his seat in the hall.

A pair of contrary sensations ran through Enid at the sight of his fierce visage. Foremost came alarm, wondering how this proud, powerful man might respond when she rejected his marriage suit. Yet deep in her heart a feeling of relief unfurled its fragile wings.

However she would manage without his protection, at least now she would not have to wed a man capable of stirring such disquiet in her.

"I—I would speak with you, my lord. Somewhere more private, if we may."

Lord Macsen stared at her face for a moment, then seemed to recollect who she was. "Your pardon, Lady Enid. There is a fog in my head this morning. I'm not accustomed to such potent spirits in the quantity I put away last evening."

He staggered a little while getting to his feet, then

flashed Enid a rueful look. "I hope I did not make too great an ass of myself."

"A man who carries so heavy a burden has a right to take his ease and make merry when he gets the chance." She dithered for a moment, trying to decide where best to break the news of her decision.

Perhaps Lord Macsen guessed what she was thinking, or perhaps he didn't feel up to much walking. "This is as good a place as any for us to talk. I will make it private for us."

He beckoned one of his men at arms, then muttered a few words to the fellow. Like late snow on a mild day, the small crowd in the hall melted away until he and Enid were all alone.

Her galloping heart beat faster still. "Can I fetch you aught, my lord? Cider? Ale? Strong drink often provokes a great thirst afterward."

As Enid backed away, Lord Macsen reached out, grasping her wrist to stay her. His hand was so large and her arm so small, his clenched fingers reached from her hand nearly to her elbow.

"My curiosity is sharper than my thirst just now." With firm but temperate force, he drew her down to the bench beside him. "I hope you'll quench it in a manner to my liking."

If only she could! Enid toyed with the notion of accepting Lord Macsen's offer, despite that benighted wager with Con. How could he hold her to it, if she chose to do otherwise? By indulging her own selfish desires, she had forfeited his silence in the matter of her son. Now he would claim the boy whether she wed Lord Macsen or not.

Gathering her breath, Enid forced herself to meet the border chief's intimidating gaze. "I am honored that you offered for me, my lord. But after careful thought, I fear I must decline.''

"Damn!" Lord Macsen pounded his leg with his fist. "I *did* make an ass of myself last night. I was too familiar in my speech and actions. I offended you."

"Not so, my lord."

He did not heed her tepid assurance. "I swear it is not my custom to take strong drink, for I need to keep my wits about me. Last night I only took the mead because I did not wish to disdain your hospitality."

The urge to hide behind this excuse tempted Enid sorely. Lord Macsen must recall that Howell had often drunk more than was good for him. His lordship would blame himself, not her, if she refused him on that account.

But she had resolved to shoulder the consequences of her actions.

"Do not fret yourself, my lord." Enid spoke to him in a more forceful tone than she ever had. "How can I fault you for accepting the drink I offered? Besides, there was nothing in your conduct last night to give offense. Please believe me, it had no bearing on my decision."

Lord Macsen's brow folded into deep furrows, as if he had trouble believing her or was searching for another explanation. "Did I ask too soon? It took me years before I was ready to wed again, but my rank allowed me the luxury of waiting. I can wait longer yet, if you will abate your answer. I ask only that you tell me when you are inclined to take a new husband so I may put myself forward again."

Why could she not love this man? Enid wanted to pound her head against the thick timbers that framed the hall. For all his unsettling size and fierce aspect, he had never failed to treat her with earnest consideration. As a husband, he would be constant, reliable, protective—all the qualities Con ap Ifan would never have.

Now he offered her the means to delay the confrontation she dreaded. She would be honoring her agreement with Con, yet not creating a costly breach between Glyneira and Hen Coed.

"Very well, my lord." It shamed her to give him false hope, but what choice had Con left her? "If I find myself inclined to take a husband, I will consider your offer first."

Her smarting conscience goaded her to add, "I will not hold you bound by this. If you grow weary of waiting and choose to take another bride in the meantime, the loss will be mine for hesitating when I should have jumped."

"Do not be too harsh with yourself." He enveloped her hand in his. "You only do as your heart bids you. I would be the last to gainsay that."

Enid's gaze flinched from his. "You show me more patience than I deserve, my lord."

"Patience is the twin sister of persistence." He released her hand with a show of reluctance. "They may not be a comely pair, but they stand a man in good stead over the years. For now I am content to bargain your *no* up to a *perhaps*. In time I hope it will become a *yes*."

"I wish I could oblige you now, my lord."

If only her traitorous body had not led her stubborn heart into rebellion against her will.

As Con tidied the washhouse of any evidence that he and Enid had passed a night of pleasure there, the courtyard rapidly filled with Lord Macsen's men. Curious, he sauntered over to a pair of them. From what he could see, they appeared to be suffering the ill effects of last night's mead.

"What's all this?" Con nodded around the courtyard.

"A sorry sight you lot are. You should get back in under Lady Enid's roof before you frighten the beasts."

"Would that I could." The taller of the two Powys lads shielded his eyes from the sun's glaring light. He looked decidedly green and spoke in a halting way, as if barely holding his gorge. "Our lord and your lady are talking in the hall. He ordered us out."

Your lady. The words set a bittersweet echo ringing in Con's heart. It was how he thought of Enid, and had during all the years he'd adventured in the Holy Land.

Now he wanted to make it the truth for all to know, but she would not have him except on their old terms with him as servant and her as mistress. Even for a prize like Enid, he could not cast aside the foundation he'd built for himself in the past dozen years, nor the fine life he might build upon that groundwork in the years to come.

If she felt for him even half of what she claimed, how could she scorn the splendid future he offered her for the sake of a modest acreage the Normans would likely seize one day? How could she expect him to bury himself here with her until the *maenol* walls closed in tighter and tighter around him, and the deadly sameness of one day after the next suffocated him?

The other of Lord Macsen's men spat on the ground at Con's feet, wrenching him out of his bitter musings.

"Why do two people need so large a hall to talk in?" the fellow demanded of his companion. "Can they not find a private corner out here and leave the hall to them who need more rest?"

"I daresay they won't be long." The taller man looked better for a few minutes in the open air. "Rhys told me Lord Macsen proposed to the lady yesterday. She's likely giving him her answer now."

"Let us hope she'll have him." The shorter one elbowed Con in the ribs. "Then we can make merry at the wedding feast."

Before Con could retch out a reply, the other man spoke. "She'll have him right enough and plenty glad of it I daresay. This is no time for a widow woman to be running a *maenol* on her own. Besides, it's plain how our lord dotes on her. I reckon he'd do most anything for her and her brood."

Those words struck Con with the force of a mailed fist in the stomach, knocking the air out of him. Macsen ap Gryffith had nothing like the bond with Enid that he did. The border lord could not have known her more than a few years, and those only as another man's wife. He was not the father of her son. Yet even his men at arms knew Lord Macsen would do most anything for her.

Was that not the true measure of love?

The taller of the two men caught his friend's eye, then nodded toward the *maenol* gate. "Why don't we take a walk down to the river and douse our heads in cold water?"

"A fine idea. Will you come along, Master Bard? You looked to have put away a vast quantity of that mead last night. For all it may taste like honey, the morning after is worse than the sting of a hundred bees."

The tall fellow clapped a comradely arm around Con's shoulders. "Gerriant speaks right, harper. You do look about ready to flay the goat."

Con certainly felt ready to retch his guts up, though it had nothing to do with the few sips of mead he'd drunk last night. "You two go ahead. I'll catch you up in a bit."

The one called Gerriant shrugged. "Please yourself."

They set off toward the gate with hesitant steps, as if anxious not to jar their tender heads or bellies. Con watched them go, his own head spinning with regrets and his belly queasy with shame. He had thrown the word *love* around far too freely since coming to Glyneira. Now he asked himself if he'd ever truly known its meaning.

A loud, urgent cry from the watch platform rescued him from his rueful thoughts. "Bar the gate!"

The order seemed to effect a miraculous cure on Gerriant and his friend, who ran the last few steps and threw their backs into pushing shut the great slab of lashed timbers.

Con sped toward the forge, hoping to lay hands on a bow, a sword, or even a pike.

The children! Might they have been caught outside the walls? A choking fear such as he'd never known on his own account chilled Con's blood.

When he rushed back into the courtyard again with a bow in one hand and a full quiver slung over his shoulder, the gate had been opened just wide enough to admit a lone rider who clung to the neck of his lathered mount as if exhausted…or wounded.

Lord Macsen's men swarmed around the rider, whom they clearly recognized. Some eased him from the saddle while others held and calmed his horse. The men of Glyneira flocked to the courtyard, each with some manner of weapon in hand, while the women swooped down to pluck their children to safety.

In all the commotion Con spotted Myfanwy dragging her little brother toward the house. His heart began to beat properly again.

Macsen ap Gryffith strode from the house with Enid hurrying close on his heels. Her gaze swept the courtyard. Spying her younger children, she rushed toward Myfanwy and Davy, clamping them in her protective embrace even as her eyes continued to search for her eldest son.

The border lord's deep resonant voice rang out over the

tumult around the gate. "How now? Are we under attack?"

"Not Glyneira, my lord," came a reply, "but Hen Coed has been taken by the Normans of Falconbridge. Aled roused himself to deliver the warning before he fainted from his wounds."

"Bring him into the hall," called Enid, pushing Myfanwy and Davy toward the house. "I will tend him."

At a curt nod from their lord, Gerriant and his friend carried the wounded messenger where they'd been bidden. Con plunged into the milling crowd and pulled Bryn clear.

"Aled is only two years my elder," the boy murmured as he let Con lead him away. "He's another of Lord Macsen's fosterlings."

Staring with unblinking eyes, Bryn walked with a wooden, stumbling gait, as if his young mind was in too much turmoil to properly control his body.

Con tried to stifle visions of what might have happened to his son if Macsen had not thought to oblige Enid by bringing the boy with him.

"Your mother needs your help, lad." Con shook the boy by his slight shoulders. "You must collect Myfanwy and Davy, then take them somewhere they'll be safe and out from underfoot. Can you do that?"

With a twitch, Bryn seemed to waken to the world once again. "Myfanwy and Davy." He gave a vigorous nod. "Aye, Con, I'll see to them."

"Good lad." Con clapped him on the back. "I'll come check on how you're faring as soon as I can."

The boy took a few steps toward the house, then paused and looked back at Con. "Mam will make Aled better, won't she?"

Con replied with a nod—one he prayed would look

more certain than he felt. It must have, for Bryn ran off without another backward glance.

Now Con turned his attention to Lord Macsen. In the midst of a tight circle of his own men and those of Glyneira, the border chief was issuing swift, decisive orders.

"...ride north and bring word to our kinsman, Madog ap Merydudd. If he can spare us men and arms, have them muster at Banwy Ford. Dylan, Cass and Onfael, rally men from all the cantrevs within a day's ride."

Con could picture the Empress rubbing her hands with glee when she heard the news. No doubt she would account his mission a grand success, and make plans to reward him accordingly. The prospect of a pitched battle between the Powys folk and their Norman neighbors made Con break out in a cold sweat.

"My lord." He caught Macsen's eye. "An attack to regain Hen Coed two or three days hence is just what your enemy will expect. You may prevail, but at what cost?"

The border lord drew himself up to his full, intimidating height and glared at Con. Clearly he was not a man to tolerate having his commands interrupted, much less questioned.

"You talk as if I have a choice, Con ap Ifan. The Normans have filched what is mine while my back was turned. Now, I must take it from them, whatever the cost. You yourself urged me to be watchful and ready to repel Norman treachery. Would that I had heeded you and turned back to Hen Coed when I had the chance."

The man felt guilty because he'd let down his guard for a few days to press his suit with Enid. Con understood. He also understood that guilt might drive Lord Macsen to strike back without his usual forethought.

"Don't fret for what might have been, my lord. Who can know if your presence and an extra handful of men would have made any difference. As it stands, you are safe and at liberty to regain what is yours. I gave you honest counsel before and I will again, if you'll heed me. My time in the Holy Land has taught me there is often more than one way to shear a sheep.''

"Very well, then, speak your piece." Lord Macsen made a marked effort to contain his impatience. "I will hear you, though I make no promise to heed."

Con gathered his breath and his thoughts. There were times, he realized, when a persuasive tongue and a cool head could prove superior weapons to bow or blade.

"As I said, my lord, FitzLaurent will be braced for an attempt to recapture Hen Coed. What he will not expect is for you to mount an assault against Falconbridge in his absence. I urge you to ride there as swiftly as possible, mustering men from the cantrevs we pass on our way. I wager we will find the Norman keep easier pickings than Hen Coed."

Lord Macsen gave a slow nod, his expression still wary. "Then what? I hold FitzLaurent's fortress and he holds mine."

"Then I will broker an exchange for you, my lord." With every word, Con's voice took on greater confidence. Never, in all his years fighting abroad, had he felt this fire burning deep in his gut. "I know the Normans—their tongue and their ways. I will strike a barter to your advantage…I swear it."

As he waited for the border lord's answer, Con found himself wondering what Enid had said to Lord Macsen before their talk had been interrupted. Would the Powys chief trust a man who had cost him a much-desired bride?

Heaving a deep sigh, Enid ran her hand in a motherly caress over the downy sweat-streaked cheek of the boy sprawled unconscious on the table before her. Why, he looked little older than her Bryn. Had she only been mincing air when she'd told Con that familiar danger was better than foreign?

Any threat to her children would be as bad as another.

As if summoned by her worries, Bryn appeared in the hall. "Will Aled be all right, Mam?"

"I hope so." She beckoned her son near. When he approached within arm's length, she gathered him to her. "He's lost some blood where an arrow grazed his arm, but he doesn't look to have taken any worse harm, saints be praised. I've stanched the bleeding and applied herbs to help the wound bind."

Bryn's soft young features took on the harsh cast of a man's righteous wrath. "I'll make the Normans pay for hurting Aled, and for attacking Hen Coed."

"You'll do nothing of the sort!" Fear gave Enid's voice a sharper tone than she'd intended. "Who's put such foolishness into your head?"

One name burst off her tongue in a fury. "Con?"

"No!" Bryn pulled away from her. "He didn't say a word about it. He said you needed me to help by keeping Myfanwy and Davy out from underfoot, and I have. They're in your chamber with Davy's little dog."

"Oh." Con might not have planted rash notions in her son's head, but he had sown them long ago in the boy's blood. "That was wise of him to suggest, and good of you to do."

"I do have the odd prudent notion." Con's voice wafted into the room.

Its warm teasing timbre stirred a sense of lightness in Enid's bosom, despite her regrets about last night and the fresh fears borne to Glyneira by the unconscious boy on the table. She welcomed that queer feeling almost as much as she mistrusted it.

"You know, Bryn," Con added, "your Mam and Idwal are going to need a good strong garrison to keep Glyneira safe in case the Normans grow bolder. I'd stay myself if I was a better fighter who'd be of any use to them."

Few people knew as well as Enid how hard it could be to resist Con's sincere-sounding flattery. Now she thanked God for his dubious talent and prayed her son would yield to it.

"Pig swill!" The boy glowered at Con. "You're a great warrior—a Crusader. You wouldn't let anything keep you from going with Lord Macsen, and neither will I."

"Bryn ap Howell!" Enid cried. "I did not raise you to spew such talk. Apologize to Con at once."

Her son was not so far gone in youthful rebellion that he could ignore a rebuke from his mother. Bryn hung his head, directing his scowl at the floor as he scuffed the reeds with one foot. "Your pardon, Master Con."

"That's better," his mother said. "As for your going with Lord Macsen, I will not permit it and neither will he, I daresay."

"Of course he'll take me." Bryn ventured a defiant glance. "I am a part of his household. I have friends at Hen Coed, and I want to help free them from the Normans."

"Lord Macsen will have enough to worry about without minding a boy of twelve years."

"I'm near thirteen, and I don't need minding!"

"You need a rod taken to your rump, saucy whelp."

Con came between them. "Now, now, save your spleen for the Normans, both of you. Enid, the lad is to be commended for his boldness—"

"Whipped for his insolence and folly, you mean."

"Fie, woman. I doubt you've ever laid a hand on this young fellow in anger." Con reached toward Bryn, tilting the boy's chin to meet his gaze. "Your mother only wants to keep you from harm."

"Keep me in swaddling clothes!"

"Go cool your temper, now." Con gave the boy a gentle nudge toward the door. "Nothing's been decided. Lord Macsen is still laying his plans. If he wants you with his party, I'm sure your mother will not gainsay him."

Before Enid could sputter a denial, Con shot her a warning look. To her own surprise, she held her tongue.

"In the meantime," Con said, "why not prove to your lord how useful you can be by making certain the horses are well watered and otherwise ready for a long swift ride?"

Bryn mulled over the suggestion, his gaze fixed on the floor except for a single fleeting glance from Con to his mother. Finally he muttered a word or two that Enid could not make out, though his tone suggested assent. Then he bolted from the hall.

After a moment's stunned hush, the fear-fuelled anger in Enid found a natural target. "What daft talk was that? If you think I will let you or Lord Macsen put my babe in the middle of a battle with the Normans, you are—"

Her next words were lost in the folds of Con's tunic as he gathered her into his arms and held her tight. Her rage demanded she pull away, but the maternal worry that fuelled it sensed an answering concern in Con.

"Don't fret, *cariad*," he crooned, running his hand over her hair in a gesture of loving comfort she so desperately needed. One she had never received from any other source. "I won't be taking him anywhere, and neither will Lord Macsen. But the lad's more apt to heed an order from his lord than a scolding from his mother."

It felt like the world had turned upside down, for her to be taking wise counsel from Con. When had he grown discretion and prudence?

"I don't know what's come over Bryn. He was always the sweetest-tempered, most obliging child in all the world." Resisting the intense urge to weep out all the strong feelings that battled inside her, Enid wrenched herself out of the safe circle of Con's arms. With Con ap Ifan, that safety could only be an illusion.

"Blood will tell." He chuckled.

Enid ignored the familiar attempt to lighten her mood. "Now all of a sudden he's so…"

"Willful?" suggested Con in a whisper. "Stubborn?"

"Blood *will* tell." Enid expelled a deep sigh. "My blood."

Had her father felt just as helpless, just as furious in his helplessness, facing down a heedless child bent on bringing herself to harm?

Her eyes searched Con's, looking for guidance with no true expectation of finding it. "What am I to do with a boy who's as reckless as you and as stubborn as me?"

"Treasure him." A proud gleam in Con's eyes told Enid he did. "Shield him when you can, but do not try to hold him too tight…"

As he spoke, Con took her hand and squeezed it gently. His grasp felt warm and heartening…at first. Little by little, he increased the force of his grip until Enid jerked her hand out of his.

"…or you will drive him away."

Was that part of what made her draw back from Lord Macsen, Enid wondered, the sense that he would try to hold her too tight?

"I never thought the day would come when I'd look to you for advice on how to raise my children, Con."

He shrugged and flashed a smile that could charm fish out of the water. "I'm not the boy I was, *cariad*. By all that's holy, I swear I'd do everything in my power to protect you and the children from harm if you come away with me to the Holy Land."

She wanted so badly to believe him, but how could he promise such a thing? And how could she leave behind everything familiar and dear to her?

Con held his arms open. "Once I've helped Lord Macsen settle this business with the Normans, may I come back and ask for your hand again?"

"You may come." Something drew her toward him, something she could not control. That frightened her worse than any Norman war party. "But I cannot promise how I will answer."

"I'll take my chance as I find it," murmured Con as his lips found hers and exchanged a wordless vow.

Chapter Eighteen

A light rain began to fall not long after Lord Macsen's party quit Glyneira. On they rode through the mist-swathed countryside at as swift a pace as their mounts could sustain for the day. There was not rain enough in all of heaven, however, to quench the small but stubborn spark of hope that lit Con's whole being.

Enid had acknowledged his wise advice in dealing with their son. Events had unfolded to show her that dear, familiar Wales could be every bit as unpredictable and dangerous as any foreign place. To cap it all, wonder of wonders, his *cariad* had promised to revisit a decision she'd made.

The decision to refuse his marriage offer.

With a glow of certainty he'd seldom felt in his life, Con knew he could change her stubborn mind if she gave him a fair hearing. For the coin of stubbornness had two sides, and the other face of it was constancy. Whether she knew it or not, Enid had remained constant in her love for him all these years, in spite of what it had cost her.

Con had never thought himself capable of inspiring that depth of feeling in anyone. All his life he'd striven to win favor by being amiable and amusing. Only with Enid had it been enough just to be himself. Perhaps that was why no other woman had ever displaced her in his heart.

"You look in fine fettle, Con ap Ifan." Rhys, the young nephew of Lord Macsen's who had been paying court to Helydd, let his horse fall into step with the chestnut mare Idwal had lent Con for the journey. "Spoiling for a fight with the Normans, are you?"

Con pondered the notion for a moment. Could there be more to this strange eagerness inside him than the high hope of winning Enid once all was settled between Falconbridge and Hen Coed?

In his years as a hired warrior, a wind of anticipation and challenge had often filled his sails on the eve of battle. Today, some righteous passion thrummed in his veins, deeper and stronger than the familiar lust for adventure and glory. For the first time in his life, he would draw his bow in defense of his native land.

"The Normans have done well enough by me over the years," he said at last. "But I do look forward to outwitting that fellow FitzLaurent. By all accounts, he thinks pretty well of himself."

"Do you truly believe we can overrun that big stone keep of his?"

They were travelling in a great arc moving north, then east, giving Hen Coed a wide berth and gathering as many men as could be spared from the small cantrevs they passed.

"I hope *he* believes we cannot." Con patted the neck of his borrowed mare. After so many months afoot, it felt good to have a mount under him. "Or better yet, has discounted the possibility that we may try. Even if it does not yield easily, the battle cannot be as hard as the one we would have to fight for Hen Coed. And no danger of your families getting caught in the fray."

"Lord Macsen is right about you, Con ap Ifan." The young man urged his mount to overtake the next rider in line. Over his shoulder he called, "Your skill as a warrior is even more subtle than your touch on the harp."

Con laughed. "I hope you fight as well as you flatter, friend!"

Lord Macsen's party rode on through the hilly green borderlands. Along narrow paths through old but vital forests. Past slender brooks that spilled over stony outcroppings. Except for the odd word passed when another horseman rode by him, Con was alone with his thoughts and his hopes.

The challenges before him—to help Macsen ap Gryffith regain his stronghold at the lowest possible cost in Welsh lives, and to win Enid as his bride—suddenly mattered far more to him than any honor Empress Maud could bestow.

"Glyneira feels so empty this evening." The words slipped out of Enid's mouth before she could check them.

On her right at the high table, Helydd made no answer but a faint sigh as she nibbled on a morsel of *lagana,* lost in thought. Idwal chewed his food in a sullen silence that mirrored young Bryn's. Clearly their spirits rode north with Lord Macsen's troop, though their bodies had been prevented.

Only Gaynor remained her usual cheerful, voluble self. "I should be mighty surprised if it didn't, between all our company going away and a good many of our own men riding with them. Not even the bard left to amuse us of an evening."

Enid tried not to wince at her sister-in-law's words. If she could be honest with her heart, she must admit it was not the absence of Lord Macsen's party that made the place feel empty. So many familiar faces of Glyneira men missing from the evening meal did not leave a void inside her that even the reunion of her family failed to fill.

It was Con ap Ifan she lacked and yearned for.

Looking back on those first bleak months when she'd come to Glyneira in exile, Enid let herself acknowledge for the first time the true nature of her despair. Sharing her bed with a stranger had only been part of it. For years she had blamed it on homesickness for the cherished people and routines of her family's estate in Gwynedd. Now she understood whom she'd most sorely missed.

Gaynor's remark about the missing bard sent Myfanwy scrambling up from her place. "I can fetch my harp and entertain. Con taught me a new song. He said I have a fine voice."

"So you have, my pet," Gaynor clucked. "By all means, play for us to lighten our spirits."

Enid exchanged a smile with her sister-in-law as Myfanwy ran off to fetch her harp without even a token show of reluctance. The child returned as quickly as she'd gone. Taking Con's accustomed spot by the fire with a proud toss of her golden-brown braids, Myfanwy began to sing of a Fair Folk castle beneath the waters of an enchanted lake.

Gaynor slid closer to Enid and whispered, "In all the excitement, did you and Lord Macsen reach an understanding before he rode away? Will we celebrate his return with a wedding?"

Perhaps, but not the wedding Gaynor had her well-intended, meddling heart set on. This might be the best time to break the news to her, Enid decided, in the midst of a roomful of people.

"I know you only want what's best for me and the children, Gaynor, but I can't wed Lord Macsen. I don't love him."

Gaynor's eyes grew as big as two rounds of *lagana,* and she looked as though she was suffering a silent fit of the palsy.

She said not another word about Lord Macsen or anything else until the household had settled down for the night. Then, she clamped a forceful hand around Enid's wrist and hauled her toward the deserted kitchen.

"Have you lost all sense?" she hissed. "Lord Macsen finally offers for you, just as I said he would, and you turn him down? Surely you don't doubt he'll get Hen Coed back."

"No, I don't doubt it." Now that she had finally reconciled her head with her heart, no matter how imprudent her decision might appear, Enid was quietly resolved. "If I loved him the way a wife ought to love her husband, I wouldn't care whether he regained Hen Coed. I'd give him the running of Glyneira gladly."

Gaynor wrung her hands. "What's to become of my poor lambs, now? Powys up in arms again and no father to defend them?"

Enid gnawed on her lower lip. Gaynor had struck at her most vulnerable misgiving. On her own account, she was willing to endure the possible hardships of the path she had chosen. But for her children...?

What if she could not convince Con to give up his lofty dreams of foreign glory and make his humble but loving home here with her? What if the raid on Falconbridge went awry and Con did not return?

Perhaps Gaynor sensed her advantage, for she hastened to press it. "What is all this maiden talk of *love* from a woman with three children? You managed well enough with Howell, though you didn't have any great fancy for him at first. The way you acted when you first came here,

I was amazed you let him get you with child so soon, and...by *Dewi Sant!*

"What is it, Gaynor?" Enid reached to support her sister-in-law, who looked ready to hit the floor with her ample weight at any moment. "Are you ill?"

"Only sick to my belly!" Gaynor pushed her away. "Bryn isn't Howell's son, is he? That's why you came here so unwilling—to save your family from disgrace when you bore a misbegotten babe."

Enid bowed her head under the accusations of which she had lived in daily fear for the past dozen years.

Once Gaynor's trusting, unimaginative mind had made that shocking leap to the truth, it vaulted beyond. "It was that Con ap Ifan who got you with child, wasn't it? That *dear, old friend* from your girlhood. How could I have been so blind to it? I must be simple-minded!"

"Keep your voice down, Gaynor! Everyone in Glyneira doesn't need to know. Yes, Bryn is Con's son. And I mean to tell Bryn so as soon as I find the right words." After years harboring that corrosive secret, the notion of revealing it frightened and relieved Enid in equal measure.

Gaynor leaned back against the wall, shaking her head as if she could not bring herself to believe the outrageous charge to which she'd made Enid confess.

"God have mercy on you," she whispered as she made a hasty sign of the cross. "My poor lambs. What'll become of my poor lambs?"

"Go to bed, Gaynor, and try not to fret over it more than you can help. We'll sort all this out when Con comes back."

After treating Enid to a reproachful stare, Gaynor shuffled off to her brychan, shaking her head and muttering to herself.

Exhausted by their encounter as she never had been by

a hard day's work, Enid retired to her own darkened chamber for a restless night's sleep that only deepened in the early hours of the morning. The children were up and gone by the time Gaynor's wailing woke her.

She ran out of her chamber barefoot, wearing nothing over her smock. "What's wrong? Is Glyneira under attack?"

Idwal glanced up from his harried efforts to console his wife. "It's Bryn. The boy's…gone."

"The folk at Glyneira will be rising for the day, now," Con reminded Lord Macsen as the two of them inspected Falconbridge Keep, three days after they'd ridden from Enid's *maenol* in such haste. "I wonder what they'd say if they knew we were in possession of FitzLaurent's castle with scarcely a scratch among us?"

"Probably the same thing I say." The border lord gave Con a hearty clout on the back that almost brought him to his knees. "That you're the wiliest warrior Wales has raised in many a year."

Con thought back over their audacious ruse. How he had ridden up to the gate of the keep just before dawn in Norman armor he had *borrowed* from a Revelstone messenger who'd blundered into their party. "The luckiest, perhaps."

In Norman French he'd bellowed a call for reinforcements to ride to their lord's aid at Hen Coed. Con could not fault the speed with which FitzLaurent's remaining garrison answered the bogus summons. He had gambled everything on the Norman penchant for obeying an order without question.

They had not disappointed him.

"Don't be modest." Lord Macsen flashed one of his rare, brief smiles. "Leave that to the priests. I'll own, I sweat a bucketful while we waited to see if they would take the bait.''

But take it they had. And when the last horseman had ridden out of Falconbridge, half of the Powys force had stormed in, disarming the skeleton of a garrison before they knew what was happening. Outside the stout keep walls, the mounted ''reinforcements'' found themselves surrounded by a ring of stout Welsh archers with short bows drawn, and had seen the prudence in a swift, bloodless surrender.

''I owe you more than I can repay, Con ap Ifan.'' The border chief shook his head, as if he still couldn't quite believe it. ''When all this is over, you have only to name your reward and I will do anything in my power to grant it.''

''No need for rewards or even thanks, my lord.'' Con's conscience smarted. If not for his interference, this good man might have been wed to Enid by now. What he had done so far scarcely began to atone. ''This serves me at least as well as it serves you.''

Since Lord Macsen had not been the first to attack at his provocation, Con could still live with himself. ''FitzLaurent need never know how we came by that armor from Revelstone. Instead, let us hope he'll suspect his Norman neighbor of treachery and be so busy guarding his back that he will have no attention to spare for further attacks on Powys. Any falling out among Stephen's allies will please the Empress.''

They climbed a steep stair and gazed out over the battlements toward Wales.

''Are you still set on returning to the Holy Land when your mission for the Empress is finished?'' Lord Macsen glanced sidelong at Con.

Around campfires on the two nights of their journey, the

border chief had drawn Con out about his past mercenary service and his future plans. Con had talked at length, in part to prove he knew a thing or two about warfare, and in even greater measure because he found himself drawn to this quiet, formidable man now that the smoke of jealousy had cleared from his eyes.

"Why do you ask?"

Lord Macsen nodded toward the faint line of Offa's Dyke away in the distance. "Wales needs men of your cunning, my friend, if we're to have any hope of holding the Normans at bay in the years to come."

Gazing west, toward the rolling English countryside, Con shook his head. "I've lived among the Normans too long. I'd be caught between the ocean and the rocks every time."

It also went without saying there would be no gold and little glory in defending this small, endangered land. A line in some ballad, perhaps, that would be forgotten in a hundred years when tiny Wales had finally been conquered and her people no longer even spoke their own tongue.

Somehow, Con found himself ashamed to voice such reasons in Lord Macsen's hearing. So he did what glib folk always do in an awkward situation—he changed the subject. "Now that you've seen Falconbridge from within, are you sure you want to exchange it for Hen Coed?"

The border lord levelled a wry gaze at him. "I am."

"And do you trust me to drive a hard bargain with FitzLaurent on your behalf?"

"I do."

For some reason, those curt words made Con's eyes sting. He hid his feelings behind a mask of hearty banter. "In that case, I reckon I had better set out for Powys while I have plenty of daylight to find my way. Just to be safe, I hope you can spare me a guide or two."

Lord Macsen started down the steep steps to the bailey. "Take your pick."

A few hours after he had ridden into Falconbridge, Con rode out again on one of Martial FitzLaurent's own steeds, along with Gerriant ap Owain and Lord Macsen's nephew, Rhys ap Rhys.

After a day's hard riding, they presented themselves at Hen Coed where they were hauled, none too gently, before the Marcher lord, Martial FitzLaurent of Falconbridge.

"What manner of pitiful war party is this?" FitzLaurent wrinkled his aquiline nose at Con, Rhys and Gerriant as if they stank to high heaven. "I expected little enough, but three men is an insult."

Though the Norman equalled Macsen ap Gryffith in his impressive height, his body was far leaner and his face composed of straight planes and sharp angles—a Norman wolf to the Welsh bear. He had hair the shade of ripe acorns and eyes the cool, dangerous gray of freshly whetted iron. At a glance, Con knew the man was not an opponent to trifle with.

Sinking into a bow so deep it verged dangerously on mockery, Con answered in his best Norman French. "Macsen ap Gryffith means no insult to your lordship. He has not sent us to fight, but to parlay with you."

The Marcher lord quickly hid whatever astonishment he might have felt at hearing a Welshman address him so fluently in his own language. "Is that so, indeed? Pray, what is there to negotiate, except perhaps his surrender?"

Oh, this fellow was as arrogant as Con had heard. He bit back a smile at the thought of what a necessary lesson in humility Martial FitzLaurent would soon receive, concentrating instead on the job he must do for Lord Macsen and for Powys. A job that felt as though he'd been training for it all his life.

"Lord Macsen does not intend to surrender, sire. He sent me to work out an exchange with you for Hen Coed."

"The gall of the fellow!" FitzLaurent seated himself on a large chair with intricate carving on each of its stout legs.

He made a dismissive gesture around the hall that was larger and better appointed than the one at Glyneira. "I'll own it is a mean place and worth little, but what can he possibly have to bargain with?"

"He has Falconbridge, sire." Con fought to curb a gloating tone that his voice wanted so badly to take. "I trust you would like to get it back."

"Ridiculous!" The Marcher lord surged up from his seat again, as though it burned his backside. "Does your master think I am a simpleton to give back what I have taken for the sake of so wild a claim? I should have your tongue cut out for this impudence!"

Gerriant and Rhys had clearly understood little of what had passed between Con and the Marcher lord, but they recognized the tone of a threat when they heard it. Both stepped closer to Con and adopted a menacing stance that announced anyone wishing to harm him would have to deal with them first.

"Be easy, now," Con cautioned them in Welsh. "Once he understands that we truly hold his castle, this haughty fellow will learn some manners, I daresay."

He dropped back into the Norman tongue again. "Naturally, sire, my master knows you would not credit a claim of this kind without proof."

From the scrip on his belt, Con drew out a number of small objects and handed each one to the speechless Marcher lord: an ivory miniature of the Virgin, a letter bearing the King's seal, and a lady's hair ornament wrought in silver.

"If you pay a visit to the stables," Con said, "you may

recognize the gelding I rode here on. The beast does you credit. I found him surefooted and good-tempered.''

FitzLaurent stared longest at the hair ornament, all traces of mockery erased from his aristocratic features. "You... took this from my lady sister?''

"She gave it, sire, and most obliging, too, once I explained the need. You mustn't fret for her. Lord Macsen is an honorable man and the lady has her confessor to bear witness that no one transgressed against her virtue.''

The full meaning of what he held in his hands seemed finally to dawn on the lord of Falconbridge.

"Welsh treachery!'' He hurled the innocent objects to the floor. "You will pay for this!''

"Treachery is it?'' For an instant, Con let his tact slip. "We have a saying in *my country,* Lord Falconbridge, that the hearth shouldn't call the soot black. Remember who attacked first.''

The Norman looked ready for another outburst, but managed to master his temper. "So this Macsen wishes to make an exchange of his stronghold for mine? And who are you to bargain on his behalf?''

"Conwy ap Ifan at your service, sire.'' Con bowed again, but less deep. "Lord Macsen bid me deal for him in this matter since I speak your tongue. You must recognize that we can hardly make a straight trade, Hen Coed for Falconbridge. As you said yourself, this is but a mean place and worth little compared with your fine stone keep.''

For the first time since they'd arrived, Lord Falconbridge looked at Con with something akin to respect. "You may speak one civilized language, Welshman, but you have an impudent tongue in your head, like all your race.''

"Thank you, sire.''

"That was no compliment."

Con grinned. "Not to you, perhaps."

Again the Marcher lord swallowed the worst of his ire. "What is it you want?"

"No more than a fair bargain, sire." Con tried not to gloat. "I feel bound to point out that Hen Coed seems to have suffered some damage before it fell to your capture, whereas Falconbridge has not a hinge bent nor a chip in the mortar. You are welcome to inspect it yourself."

"So Macsen may snatch me as a hostage? I think not. Now state your terms."

"I strike a more generous bargain when my belly is full and my throat well dampened, sire," suggested Con.

FitzLaurent stabbed his forefinger toward the three men. "Do not push too far, Welshman."

He turned away from them and remained silent for a moment. Then, as if to demonstrate the idea was his own, he called to one of his men at arms who stood guard on the door, "Bring us food and drink if there is either fit to consume in this glorified pigsty."

A short time later the food and drink arrived in the hands of an older woman, who exchanged a fond look with Rhys. While the Welshmen dined, Con and FitzLaurent traded offers and counteroffers. At last, when Con judged he had wrung all the concessions from his opponent that he was likely to get, they struck a bargain.

After a night's sleep they began a second round of talks. This time to work out the details of *how* an exchange would be effected between two enemies who distrusted one another so profoundly. Once again Con bargained hard and came away pleased with what he had secured for Macsen ap Gryffith and the Welsh in this border area of Powys.

He liked this diplomacy business, Con admitted to his surprise. He found it every bit as exhilarating as armed warfare but far less bloody. In some ways, it seemed like the kind of combat he'd been born for. His middling stature and spare frame were no handicap in this contest of wits and nerve, while his knack for languages, his amiable manner and his ability to see both sides of a question had proven clear advantages.

"One last thing," FitzLaurent said as Con's party prepared to leave for Falconbridge where they would begin the exchange of holdings.

"Sire?" Con plundered his memory in an effort to recall if there'd been anything he'd neglected to include in the negotiations.

A slow smile of triumph curled the corners of the Marcher lord's thin lips. "A small matter of the boy."

As he heard those words, every hair on the back of Con's neck bristled.

Chapter Nineteen

Her boy, alone and fleeing headlong into the middle of a border battle—the notion made Enid's belly churn as her white pony jogged along beside the stocky brown beast that belonged to Father Thomas. If she'd let Bryn go with Lord Macsen's party, under Con's protection, her son would probably be safe now. And if she'd told him the truth about his father, the shock of overhearing her and Gaynor would not have sent him hurtling into danger.

Maternal instinct told Enid that must have been what had happened. She'd clutched her son too tightly, as Con had warned her against, with just the consequences he'd predicted. Now regret gnawed at her heart.

When she could no longer bear the weight of such thoughts, Enid tried to distract herself by addressing her escort. "How soon will we be there, Father?"

Since she'd come to Powys thirteen years ago, she had never ventured so far from Glyneira. Along with the regrets and fears for her son, an unexpected sense of liberty stirred within her. For once, instead of cowering behind the timber walls of the *maenol* and sending men out to deal with the world on her behalf, she was sallying forth to meet the challenge head-on.

For the first time, Enid acknowledged a grudging sympathy for Con's need to be engaged with the wide world beyond any family hearth. Though she would never fully share it, a least it no longer seemed like willful madness.

"Less than five miles until we reach St. Mynver's." Father Thomas looked pleased with the chance for a jaunt away from his isolated parish.

They had taken refuge the previous night in a small priory and now they were bound for a Benedictine abbey not far from Hen Coed. If Bryn had any sense, he might have gone there to seek food or information. Much as she hoped so, Enid doubted her impetuous son had exercised such prudence.

"I pray they have some news for us of my boy, or at least of how matters stand between Hen Coed and Falconbridge, so I can begin searching for him."

Father Thomas drew back his cowl to let the spring sun warm his round, tonsured head. "If anyone hereabouts knows aught, you may be certain Abbot Peter will have made it his business."

"A little worldly for the cloister, is he?" Enid cast a sidelong glance at the priest. "If he has news of Bryn, I'll forgive Father Abbot for being the worst busybody in all Powys."

They rode the rest of the way to the abbey in silence as Enid kept a sharp eye out for any sign her son had passed that way.

The porter of St. Mynver's opened the wicket to admit them. "The abbey is buzzing with guests today. Father Abbot will be as happy as a pig in a warm wallow."

As Father Thomas laughed at the jest, Enid's anxious gaze searched the cloister. "Your other guests, Brother Porter, was one of them a dark-headed boy, a little taller than me?"

The monk shook his head. "No boys, Mistress. But the chief of Hen Coed and the lord of Falconbridge, both. I'm not privy to what that's all about. Some trading of captured domain, I hear tell."

Just then a familiar figure emerged into the cloister garth.

"Con!" Enid dashed toward him. "Thank God you are safe, at least."

She threw her arms around his neck, pressing her lips to his with a shameless fervor that had little business inside cloister walls.

Could she let him go again, even if he refused to abandon his ambition to return to the Holy Land?

Remembering her urgent errand, Enid forced herself to break from their kiss, though she kept her arms clasped about Con's neck.

"Bryn ran away," she gasped. "I think he overheard me admit to Gaynor that you are his father. I should not have delayed in telling him the truth. I should have listened to you."

"Hush, now, *cariad*. Don't fret." Con wrapped her in his embrace.

This was her true home, Enid realized. Anywhere could be her home as long as it housed her circle of loved ones.

"Bryn's safe," Con crooned as he stroked her hair. "He'll be back with you as soon as Falconbridge and Hen Coed are exchanged."

"Saints be praised!" Sweet tears of relief flooded her eyes as she kissed him again.

But something was badly amiss. Enid sensed it beyond doubt, though she could not determine what it might be. Con had never held her or kissed her in quite this way before, as though something compelled him to push her away when he most longed to hold her close.

She pulled back, just far enough to gaze into those lively, clever blue eyes. "What's the matter, *cariad?* You and Bryn are safe. You've got Hen Coed back, or soon will. You ought to be turning tumbles for joy in the cloisters."

All traces of boyishness had left Con's lean, mobile features. Though he had never looked more attractive to her, Enid missed that air of youthful confidence and good cheer. His eyes held a steely resolve, tempered by a faint shimmer of wistfulness.

"There's a little bench by the door of the chapel, *cariad.*" He drew her toward it. "We can talk there."

"Were any of the men from Glyneira killed?" Enid clung to Con's hand. "Brother Porter said Lord Macsen is here at the abbey. Is he wounded?"

"Lord Macsen is well." Con's mouth curved upward at the corners, but the result fell far short of a smile. "Not a drop of Glyneira blood was spilled."

Before she could once again demand to know what was wrong, Con launched into an account of how the Powys men had captured the Norman castle.

"FitzLaurent and Macsen ap Gryffith are hostage here until the exchange of men between Falconbridge and Hen Coed has been made. Then both will be free to return home."

"My son...*our* son? Where is he? When can I see him?" Could his fears for Bryn be making Con behave so strangely?

"The Normans have him at the moment." Con hastened to add, "You'll see him soon, though. Bryn must not have heard that we planned to attack Falconbridge, for he rode straight to Hen Coed and into the hands of the Normans."

There, with the reckless bravado he'd inherited from his newly discovered father, Bryn had boldly informed his captors that he was the son of Conwy ap Ifan and the fosterling of Lord Macsen. Con did not share this distressing information with the boy's mother.

Enid crossed herself. "Thank heaven you were able to ransom him." Head bowed, she glanced up at Con through her lashes. "Bryn will need a father's firm guidance if he ever hopes to curb this heedless streak of his. Will you return with us to Glyneira when this is over?"

"No, *cariad*. I must go away."

"B-but you said—"

"I know what I said well enough." Con surged up from the bench, putting a small but unbridgeable distance between them. "But I've had a change of heart since then. The past few days have shown me what's most important in my life."

Had she truly believed a man with his abilities and opportunities could be content in some little Welsh backwater?

Pride told Enid to hold her tongue, but for once in her life she paid it no heed. "They've shown me what's important, too, *cariad*. If you must return to the Holy Land…then, perhaps I could—"

"Listen to yourself, Enid!" Con turned away from her and for a long moment he did not speak.

When he found his voice again, its harsh tone rasped in her ears…and on her heart. "You'd be miserable where I'm going. There's no sense trying to pretend any different."

"How can you be sure, if we don't try?" Even as she spoke the words, Enid heard the doubt in her voice.

"I am sure, *cariad*." His voice fell to such a soft hush, she wondered if Con had really spoken, or if she had just imagined it. "And we can't take the chance of trying, for there's more than you and me to consider."

Thirteen years ago Con had walked out of her life and it had never been the same. Back then, neither of them had spoken words of love. Neither of them had guessed she would bear his child. This time, Con knew what he was leaving behind, but leave he would just the same.

"One other lesson this past few days has taught me." Con turned toward Enid again, with an awkward, forced gait, and knelt before her. "It was selfish of me to stand in the way of your wedding Lord Macsen. He's a fine man. I see that now. He'll be the kind of husband you need and a good father to your children. I release you from your promise to refuse him."

"But, Con—"

Before she could protest or plead, he kissed her. The soft, tender play of his lips against hers told of love and longing and lament.

Enid's whole world tilted. Her arms closed around Con's neck, clutching him tighter and tighter until she realized what she was doing. Then, contrary to every urge that raged in her heart, she let him go.

Contrary to a stubborn flicker of hope within her, he rose and marched away, without a word or even a glance back over his shoulder.

The urge to turn back and tell Enid the truth tore at Con like a pack of hunting hounds at a wounded stag, but he refused to surrender to that impulse.

If Enid knew where he was bound and why, she might do something foolish that would mean hardship for her and the children. Better far if she believed ambition and wanderlust had lured him away from her. Then she might turn to a man who possessed the kind of steadfast heart and quiet honor she needed.

Part of him wished Enid had never come here in search

of their son, for it made what he shrank from doing still harder to undertake. And yet, the chance to hold her one last time had felt like a visitation of grace.

Conscious that the Powys men and Normans might arrive at any moment to complete the exchange of hostages, Con crossed the cloister garth with purposeful stride. When he reached the abbot's parlor, he informed the lay brother standing outside the door of his identity and something of his errand. The lay brother knocked, then entered. He returned almost at once with an invitation for Con to join Father Abbot and Lord Macsen.

As the door swung open again to admit Con, a gleeful cry rang out followed by a volley of hearty laughter.

"So this is your crafty war leader, Macsen?" The abbot pressed the tips of his wizened fingers together as he looked Con up and down. "I might have mistaken such a fresh face for one of our novices."

Con made a deep reverence to the tiny man whose rusty red tonsure was frosted with white. "I doubt I would be much of an asset to St. Mynver's, Father Abbot."

The walls of the abbot's snug parlor felt as though they were closing in on him. Con tried not to gasp for air. A bottomless pit of fear opened up in his belly as he contemplated what might be in store for him at Falconbridge. At the hands of a man he had not only defeated, but humiliated into the bargain.

"That may be." The abbot's deep-set eyes twinkled with unholy mirth. "For all that, a man who can successfully defend his country without spilling a drop of blood is heaven-sent, whatever way you look at it. Here in the cloister we're meant to be above such worldliness, but I have enough Welsh blood in me to rejoice in your roundabout victory over our Norman brethren."

"*Our* victory, Father Abbot," Con corrected him. "I

only sowed the seeds. Macsen ap Gryffith and the men of Powys brought the enterprise to bear fruit. Now, if I might beg a boon of you, Father, my time here draws short and I have a few words I wish to speak privately with Lord Macsen.''

''Of course, my son, of course.'' Abbot Peter rose from his chair and headed toward the door. ''It is time I summoned the brothers for Chapter. Make yourselves at home here for as long as need be. If I do not see you again before you depart, may God go with you, my son.''

''Thank you, Father.'' For no reason he could explain, Con felt his apprehension ease.

Once Abbot Peter had shuffled away to Chapter, Lord Macsen poured Con a cup of wine from the flagon that stood on the low table between his chair and the one in which the abbot had sat.

''What is this private talk you would have with me, Con?'' He held out the cup with one hand, while gesturing toward the chair with the other. ''Your face is as white as chalk, man. Has something gone amiss with the exchange?''

''Nothing like that.'' Con dropped into the chair the abbot had vacated and quaffed a long heartening drink of Malmsey. ''Enid has come in search of Bryn.''

''Fool boy to have fretted his mother so.'' The unmistakable glow of fondness for both mother and son belied Lord Macsen's hard words. ''I'd warm the young whelp's breeches if I didn't think he'd already learned his lesson at the hands of the Normans.''

''The boy needs your firm guidance, my lord, but he also needs the softness of his mother's care.''

''Don't expect me to gainsay that.'' Lord Macsen took a deep drink of wine, then held his cup as if weighing the wisdom of revealing a confidence. ''I had hoped Enid would consent to wed me, if only to be under the same roof as her son again.''

Con gazed into the pool of rich red wine in his cup, too ashamed of how he'd behaved to meet Lord Macsen's discerning gaze. ''She meant to accept you. I convinced her not to.''

''Why?'' The news clearly came as a surprise to the border chief.

''There…was something between us when we were young.'' Con measured his words. He did not want to taint what he was about to do with outright lies. But neither could he afford to blurt out the whole shabby truth.

''When I saw her again after all those years, it hit me afresh, and I wanted her for myself.'' Soon enough Macsen would learn that Con had fathered Enid's eldest son. Con could not bring himself to confess it now.

''Indeed?'' Lord Macsen glanced up. For an instant his dark gaze met Con's before they both averted their eyes. ''I can hardly blame you for being drawn to her again.''

A deep sigh heaved out of him. ''I promised you a reward for helping me regain Hen Coed. She is not mine to grant, but if Enid will have you, expect no trouble from me over it. I may not have the heart to dance at your wedding, but I will wish you find happiness together.''

Con had judged this man right. But the knowledge came as hard comfort to him. ''You mistake me, my lord. I have come to see that Enid and I have no future together. We have always wanted very different things from life. I fear we could never reconcile those differences.''

Con tossed back another drink to fortify himself. ''I care for her all the same, and I want a better life for her than she's had since first we parted. The reward I would ask of you is to make Enid your wife, and to help her raise her children as if they were your own.''

For several long moments, the border lord did not reply. Con clenched his lips to keep from recanting his petition.

When Lord Macsen spoke at last, his tone sounded strangely wary. "I will do it gladly, if Enid consents."

"She will."

"And if you are certain this is what you want?"

"I...am." Con rose and headed for the door. "Now I must make ready to complete the exchange of hostages."

What he did not tell Lord Macsen was that he would be one of those hostages. In a secret exchange for the freedom of his son, Con had forfeited something more precious than his life.

His own liberty.

She had set Con at liberty when she had most longed to hold him tight. Yet he had still flown from her.

Though her heart reeled, a flicker of hard-won wisdom assured Enid she had done right. Part of her wanted to wrap herself in the protective armor of bitterness she'd worn for so many years, blaming Con for any unhappiness in her life. That would not be fair, though.

To her children, to Con, or most of all to herself.

If Con had cared for her less, he would have dragged her family across the world to be with him, no matter what it cost them. And if his craving for freedom and adventure ran as deep as her hunger for the safe and familiar, she loved Con too much to hold him captive.

A flurry of activity at the abbey gate pulled Enid from her daze of shock and hurt. Three horsemen rode in— Normans. She could tell by their helms, mail shirts and clean-shaven faces. Pillion behind one of the riders sat a boy.

"Bryn!" She raced across the cloister garth, her regrets swamped by joy and relief at seeing her son safe.

"Mam!" Bryn slid to the ground before the horse had fairly come to a stop. He dashed into his mother's open arms.

"Praise heaven you're alive." In spite of Con's advice she clutched her son as tight as she dared. "Those Norman dogs didn't mistreat you, did they?"

"They didn't hurt me, Mam." His face crumpled until he looked no older than Davy. "I'm sorry I ran away, Mam, and caused so much trouble for everyone. Is it true what Auntie Gaynor said about Con being my father?"

Enid nodded.

"But how can that be?"

"I'll explain about it later." Enid smoothed back his hair and tried to reassure him with a shaky smile that all would be well. "For now, though, we have to get you home."

A blunt-fingered hand landed on Bryn's shoulder and would have jerked him out of her arms if Enid had not been holding onto him so firmly. The Norman behind whom Bryn had been riding barked some words in a sharp, ugly language that had none of the sweet musical cadence of Welsh.

Enid wrenched Bryn away and thrust him behind her. "Keep your hands off my son, you vicious Norman viper!"

Though her legs trembled beneath her skirts and her heart thundered like a war party at full gallop, Enid made herself return the Norman's belligerent stare. "Must you terrorize Welsh women and children because the men of Powys can fight and think circles around you?"

The Norman made to push her out of the way and seize the boy. An order bellowed in French made him freeze.

The next thing Enid knew, Con had thrown himself between her and the Norman. He rattled off a string of words she did not understand, but which sounded too menacing to question.

The other riders strode to the aid of their comrade until an order shouted from the cloisters stopped them. Enid spun around to lock Bryn in her protective embrace. All eyes turned toward a tall, grim-looking man who stalked into the garth.

The three Normans began protesting to him, speaking rapidly in their own tongue and pointing at Con. The man raised his hand for silence, then rapped out a question to which Con replied at length.

What where they talking about?

When Con finished, the Norman commander gave a curt order to his men, who withdrew to the gate. Con exchanged a few more words with the tall man, perhaps expressing gratitude, before the Norman commander spun on his heel and retreated to the cloisters again.

Meanwhile, the three riders trained wary gazes upon Con, Enid and Bryn.

"What was all that about?" Enid asked.

"I told them I'd vouch for the boy, that he would not run off before the exchange was completed." Con shifted his weight from foot to foot, clearly awkward in the close company of the woman and son he would soon abandon for the second time.

"Why don't you and Bryn go sit outside the chapel until all this business is over. I imagine Lord Macsen will want you to spend the night at Hen Coed before he sends you home with an escort of Glyneira men."

"Will you come back to Hen Coed with us?"

Con shook his head. "Once the exchange is made, my work here will be done. The Empress will be anxious for a report from me."

"I understand," said Enid. At least her mind did. Her heart remained baffled.

"Well, I don't understand why you cannot stay," cried Bryn, pushing free of his mother's embrace. He spoke in a voice reedy with fright, yet still defiant. "Do you know I'm your son?"

Con winced. "Aye. From the first hour I met you."

"Then why did you not tell me?"

At the risk of estranging her son, Enid spoke. "Because I asked him to keep silent."

"Why, Mam?"

A fair question, but how could Enid hope to explain it to her son, when she was no longer certain she understood her reasons. Over Bryn's head, his mother and father exchanged a look.

"We'll talk over all this when we get home."

"I don't want to go home." Bryn thrust out his chin. Clearly his brush with disaster had not chastened him as much as Enid had hoped. "I want to go to the Holy Land, with my father."

Enid's heart seemed to freeze in her bosom. From the moment she had spied Con in her hall playing the harp with Myfanwy, she had dreaded the prospect of this moment. She'd done everything in her power to prevent it coming to pass, including a number of things of which she was now heartily ashamed.

Her lips parted. The words that came out shocked her at least as much as they surprised Con and her son. "That is for your father to decide."

She'd had Bryn for his young years when a boy most needed a mother. Now perhaps it was time Bryn learned the lessons only a father could teach. Doubtless the time was long past due for Con to enjoy the company of his son.

Even if the boy's going broke her heart.

For an instant Con's comely features twisted, betraying pain. Then his lip curled in a sneer, making Enid wonder if she had only imagined the other.

"Do I look like a wet nurse?" Con backed away. "I will have my hands full enough where I am going without a child to tend besides."

"I'm not a babe." Bryn's out-thrust lower lip belied his brave words. "I would be no bother, I swear. I can look after myself."

"The way you looked after yourself by running straight into enemy arms?" Con demanded. "I can do well without such bother."

Bryn hung his head, but not before Enid spied tears in the eyes so like his father's. Though her mother's heart rejoiced that she would not lose her son—at least not to-day—she felt puzzled and hurt on Bryn's behalf that Con had refused him in so harsh a manner.

"Stay in Wales where you belong, boy." Was it her fancy, or did Con's voice falter? "Mind Lord Macsen and your mother."

While they'd been talking, a trio of Welsh riders had entered through the abbey gate. Enid recognized two of Lord Macsen's men and Math, the blacksmith from Glyneira.

Con marched past them without a word, mounted a waiting horse and rode off. Not once did he look back at Enid or his son.

The Norman commander joined his men, after which the party soon quit St. Mynver's.

Enid turned to her son. "I'm sorry, Bryn—"

A high, tight sob belched out of the boy as he turned from her and bolted in the direction of the chapel. His mother watched him go, wishing she, too, could run off and vent her feelings with a burst of tears.

Lord Macsen's deep voice rumbled behind her. "Leave him be for now. I'll go find him and talk to him before we leave."

"Thank you." She turned to find a pair of strong arms held open to her.

Though they were not the arms she longed for just then, Enid stepped into their too-tight embrace just the same.

Chapter Twenty

A few miles from St. Mynver's abbey, the three Normans and their Welsh captive halted to let their horses drink.

Con approached Martial FitzLaurent. "Sire, I owe you a debt of gratitude for not betraying our...arrangement to my friends."

The Marcher lord scowled, as though he had been insulted, rather than thanked. "Do I want that Macsen fellow mounting raid after tiresome raid against Falconbridge in a vain effort to free you? He will be bother enough, now that he has seen the defenses of my keep, without knowing I hold you prisoner."

Con hoped Bryn and Enid had not seen through his own performance as easily as he saw through FitzLaurent's.

"It is no sin to show mercy, sire."

The Norman trained his steel-gray gaze on Con. "Perhaps not, but it is often folly. If you think this means I will dance to your piping while you are my prisoner, Welshman, you mistake."

"What do you plan to do with me?" Con willed any hint of a tremor from his voice. He had seen the tiny, airless cells in the lower levels of Falconbridge and his courage failed at the thought of being locked inside one of them.

FitzLaurent considered his answer for a long moment before he replied. "I mean to discover what manner of price you will fetch, Welshman, and from whom."

Would anyone part with a brass farthing to ransom him? Con wondered. While desperately bargaining for the life of his son, he had painted himself a great prize—former Crusader, friends with the likes of Lord DeCourtenay, emissary from the Empress. Privately, Con acknowledged himself all but worthless to anyone on the English side of Offa's Dyke.

By the time FitzLaurent figured that out and released him in disgust, the Empress would scarcely recall his name, let alone the extravagant reward she'd once promised him. He'd thrown away his freedom, his future, and his one chance at lasting love. And all for what?

Enid's parting words after their tryst in the washhouse came back to haunt Con as he rode east with the Normans. *If you thought half as highly of yourself as I think of you, you'd have nothing to prove to anyone.*

Unlike the people he'd spent the latter part of his life trying to please, Con knew Enid would give or do whatever it took to ransom him. And if twenty years passed before he won his release, she would still remember and care for him. At least, she would have, if he hadn't pushed her and young Bryn away so harshly.

On a bit of high ground ahead, Falconbridge Keep loomed, its stout stone walls waiting to imprison him.

If he had it to do over again, Con asked himself, would he?

Yes, he decided. Not without thought, without fear or without regret. But he would do it.

Glancing back over his shoulder as a golden spring sun

set beyond the Welsh hills, Con ap Ifan realized that he had just proven something very important to the one person who truly mattered.

Himself.

Conwy ap Ifan. Enid heard men speaking and singing his name out in the great hall of Hen Coed. She had better get used to it, for Con would likely remain a subject of heroic ballads in these parts for some while to come.

Still, every repetition of his name bit into her heart like a switch.

Kneeling beside her bed in a small guest room off the hall, Enid prayed to the Blessed Virgin and to all the female Welsh saints for guidance. So far, she'd received no response.

What would those holy maidens make of a man like Con ap Ifan? Enid wondered. Could they bring themselves to intercede for all the mistakes she'd made and all the sins she'd committed in the name of love?

A soft, almost timid, knock sounded on the door behind her.

"Come in."

The door eased open far enough for Lord Macsen to poke his head through the crack. "Forgive my interruption. I see you're at prayer. I'll come back later."

"Wait, my lord!" Making a hasty sign of the cross, Enid scrambled up from the floor before he could pull the door shut again. "My prayers are finished."

Could any petition ascend to Heaven, when weighed down by such a load of grief and regret?

Lord Macsen cast a wary glance around the little room. "You're certain?"

Enid nodded as she beckoned him inside. Though she

could not bear to join the celebrating throng in the great hall, she had found no peace in solitude, either.

"I would be glad of some company."

"I hope you find this lodging tolerable." The big border lord looked ill at ease in such close quarters.

"It is snug and safe. I could ask no better." Since the room had no chairs, Enid settled herself on the edge of the bed and gestured toward a low trunk that might serve Lord Macsen as a bench.

Gingerly he lowered himself onto it. "I had a talk with young Bryn, about the folly of what he did, running away from Glyneira. I saw no useful purpose in punishing him further."

"Thank you, my lord." Between the indignity of being captured by the Normans and the sting of being rejected by his father, her son had been punished enough.

Lord Macsen inhaled a deep breath, then spoke in a rapid burst. "The boy tells me Con ap Ifan is his…natural father. Is that true?"

"It is, my lord." Enid stared at her lap as a stinging blush crept into her cheeks. "I was no maid when Howell brought me to Glyneira. I had lain with Con in hopes it would keep him from going away, and force my father to let me wed him."

"Indeed?" Lord Macsen sounded as though he doubted her capable of such willfulness. "Con told me there had been something between you once upon a time, but I did not imagine…" The secret she had guarded so jealously for so many years would soon be common knowledge. Whispered behind raised hands, with eyebrows lifted and sly looks exchanged. Though the shame of it stung Enid's pride, a curious sense of relief buoyed her.

After an awkward pause, Lord Macsen cleared his throat

and continued. "Con also told me you refused my marriage offer at his behest."

Enid hesitated. Had the answer she'd given Lord Macsen been solely in payment of her wager with Con?

The border lord did not wait for a reply. "I offered Con any reward of his choosing for all he'd done to help me recover Hen Coed. He asked me to wed you...if you would."

Damn that man and his meddling! Had Con looked back on all the missteps she'd made over the years and assumed she could not govern her own life?

Faced with her silence, Lord Macsen quickly added, "I am not doing this only because Con bid me. You know I have long wanted you, Enid. What you've just told me of your past does not change that. If you agree to marry me, I will send at once for the younger children to join us here."

He hunched forward and reached out to envelop her hands in his. "Will you?"

There it was, the offer she'd set her heart on before Con had barged back into her life and turned it over its head and ears. The chance to reunite her family and to keep them safe under the wing of a fierce protector.

Fighting an almost overwhelming urge to nod her acceptance, instead Enid shook her head. She needed to cultivate the strength to protect her children, and nurture in them the strength to protect themselves.

"I cannot, my lord." She owed him a better answer than that, but since she could not give it, she must offer an explanation in its place. "I had no choice but to wed Howell ap Rhodri. While I kept faith with him and always strove to be a dutiful spouse, I did not love him in the way a wife ought to love her husband. He knew it and I believe it plagued his heart until the day he died."

For the first time, Enid ventured a glance at Lord Macsen. Something deep in the wells of his dark eyes told her he knew she spoke the truth.

"Howell deserved better than that, my lord, and so do you. You deserve a wife who will give you her whole heart, even when reason tells her it is folly."

With a gentle squeeze of parting, Lord Macsen released her hands. In a hoarse voice, he asked, "The way you gave your heart to Con ap Ifan?"

"Aye," she whispered. "Twice."

"For all his cleverness, the man was a fool to turn his back on you."

"Perhaps." Enid sighed. "Then again, perhaps he only wanted to spare me what I want to spare you. What I wish I could have spared poor Howell."

And one day, perhaps, if Con grew tired of novelty and adventure, he might come seeking the quiet, constant joys of hearth, home and heritage. If that day should arrive, and Con should find himself drawn to Glyneira once again, he would find her waiting.

The secret to keeping sane in captivity, Con discovered as the border spring gave way to summer, and summer to harvest, was not to wait.

If he had waited for his freedom, counted each passing day, paid heed to the messengers despatched from Falconbridge and lamented the ones who returned empty-handed, then he might have scaled the battlements of the keep and hurled himself to his death in despair.

Instead, Con had grudgingly resigned himself to captivity, and in doing so he'd learned a few things about himself. To begin with, he'd discovered a deeper attachment to his homeland than he had ever suspected. He'd also come to realize that he thrived, not so much on adventure and danger, but on any challenge to his abilities, however modest.

Perhaps most importantly, he'd grown to understand it was not the affection others bore him that filled the old gnawing void in his heart, but the love he nurtured for them.

On this fine autumn day, not long after Michaelmas, Con passed a piece of harness he'd mended to the fellow in charge of the Falconbridge stables.

The stable master eyed the work, then jerked it tight between his powerful hands to make certain the repair would hold. "You've made a good job of it, Welshman. Is there aught you can't turn your hand to?"

Con pulled a droll face. "Marriage?"

Missing the barb of truth in Con's jest, the stable master slapped his muscular thigh and brayed a laugh. "Don't let Lady Albina hear you say so. From the soft eyes she casts at you, a body would think you were an honored guest of the house rather than her brother's prisoner."

Con had read the signs well enough. A few months ago, he might have found some way to take advantage of the lady's partiality. These days he behaved himself—giving a respectful answer when addressed, telling her stories of the world beyond her brother's keep when asked. He sensed a restiveness in her such as had once bedeviled him.

Which of them was more a prisoner of Falconbridge? he often asked himself.

Not wanting to make the young lady a subject of gossip, Con ignored the stable master's quip. "Have you any more jobs for me today?"

By being helpful and agreeable, he'd won himself decent treatment as well as a certain measure of liberty within the castle walls. His recent offer to coax the Falconbridge oxen in fall plowing had been refused less from fear that he might escape, than because the Normans could not imagine a means of working oxen other than driving them with a goad.

"We're well enough, for the moment," replied the stableman. "Perhaps the blacksmith can use you for a spell on the bellows. Will you play your harp for us tonight, again, Welshman? I mind I'm beginning to pick up a word or two of your tangled tongue."

A warm sense of satisfaction heartened Con. The Normans would never retreat from the Welsh borderlands. If his country was to survive, the marriage bed might prove a more favorable battleground. Every Welsh lass who learned a few words of French and every Norman soldier who mastered the odd Welsh endearment furthered that subtle campaign.

Just then, the watchman at the keep gate called down a challenge to someone outside.

Con and the stable master exchanged a look. Could this be another raid from Revelstone? Ever since Con had gained access to Falconbridge wearing Revelstone armor, the two Marcher lords had been at one another's throats.

The confident but mannerly reply to the watchman's challenge assured them this wasn't a raid after all. Though Con could not make out the visitor's words, something about the timbre of the voice struck a chord inside him.

He warned himself not to raise his hopes on the strength of a voice he fancied familiar, but he could not help himself. Shading his eyes against the autumn sun, he glanced at the broad-shouldered horseman who rode into the courtyard.

"Rowan!" Con bolted across the bailey and launched himself at his friend, who vaulted out of his saddle.

DeCourtenay caught him in a bone-punishing embrace.

"Con ap Ifan, what's this? I expected to find you shackled and starving, not well fed and wandering FitzLaurent's bailey at will."

"When have you known me not to land on my feet?" Con dug an elbow into his old friend's ribs only to bruise it against Rowan's mail shirt. "Tell me you haven't come all the way from Berkshire on my account?"

Though the unexpected advent of his friend lightened Con's spirit and touched his heart, he could not bear to picture Rowan impoverished or compromised in order to ransom his sorry hide.

Rowan thumped Con on the back as he began speaking in broken, badly accented Welsh. "As it happens, I'm here at the behest of a certain royal lady who is interested in your return to her service. This fighting between Stephen's supporters pleases her even better than if they were busy battling the Welsh. But let's not mention that to your *host*."

Empress Maud had ordered Rowan away from his strategic castle in Berkshire just to secure Con's release? The notion flooded him with surprise and satisfaction…and regret. If he'd valued himself enough to believe this might happen, would he have been so quick to commit Enid and the children to Lord Macsen's care?

"Cecily is well, I hope," Con asked in French, not wanting to arouse his captors' suspicion with too much Welsh talk. "And the young one."

A look of fondness and touching pride softened DeCourtenay's rugged features. "A hardy little rascal, our Master Giles, which is well since he's inherited his mother's insatiable appetite for trouble."

Con chuckled. "I look forward to meeting him someday. Perhaps I can give him archery lessons when he's big enough to hold a bow."

Thoughts of all he had missed with his Bryn, and all he would miss, sobered him. "I have a son, too, you know."

While they had been talking, FitzLaurent's men must have alerted their master to DeCourtenay's arrival. Now, the Marcher lord strode into the bailey toward Con and Rowan.

Rowan only had time to glance at his friend with raised brows. "You always did work fast, but this is a stretch, even for you!"

Con held his tongue while DeCourtenay and FitzLaurent greeted each other with wary courtesy. There would be plenty of time to tell Rowan all about Bryn and Enid on their long ride south...if Rowan succeeded in winning his release.

Chapter Twenty-One

"**M**am," called Myfanwy as she ran into the great hall of Glyneira where Enid had set up her loom, "Idwal sent me to tell you Lord Macsen has come with some of his men. Shall I go bid Auntie Gaynor to ready the water?"

Enid looked up from her weaving. What could have brought Lord Macsen to Glyneira? A shiver ran through her as she recalled him bringing home her mortally wounded husband a year ago at this time.

"Water?" Enid anchored her shuttle in the warp threads as she rose from her loom. "Yes, my pet, that's a good idea."

"May I help wash our guests' feet?"

Enid cast a fond gaze over her daughter, who'd sprouted up far too tall since the spring. A mother couldn't keep her babes small forever. She could only enjoy those sweet fleeting years while they lasted.

"I suppose it's about time you learned the duties of a good hostess. Auntie Gaynor will show you where to find the basins and drying cloths."

Myfanwy rewarded her mother with a bright, eager smile. Hiking up her skirts, she dashed away to fetch the water.

Enid crossed the hall, plucking her cloak from a peg by the door on her way out to the courtyard to greet her guests.

Her breath frosted in the crisp air as she called to them, "Come into the hall and warm yourselves. I hope you had a safe journey."

"We did." Lord Macsen wiped the frost from his dark beard as he and the two younger men followed her indoors. "Even managed to bag some fresh game along the way for your larder."

"That was kind of you." When they reached the hall, Enid pulled a bench nearer the hearth for them to sit on. "I hope you didn't come all this way just to make sure we wouldn't suffer a hungry winter."

Lord Macsen shook his head as he took a seat and began chafing his hands. "Since Falconbridge and Revelstone have been too much occupied attacking one another to bother with Hen Coed, I decided to make a circuit of all the *maenols* under my protection to see how they're faring before winter sets in."

"Indeed?" Enid pretended to believe his excuse. "If the rest are as well-disposed as Glyneira, then you may retire back to Hen Coed a contented man."

"You had a good harvest?"

"The most bountiful I've seen in all my years here," Enid boasted. "Thanks to the peace, some fine weather and the extra acreage Con plowed in the spring."

Though she spoke his name in an offhand tone, deep in her heart a sweet plaintive chord sounded, as though plucked by skilled fingers on a golden harp...with one broken string that would never be mended.

Perhaps Lord Macsen sensed it, too, for he caught and held her gaze in his. "The children are well?"

"Never better." Enid flashed a broad smile that she only

had to force a little. "All growing like weeds. See this one, if you please."

She pointed to Myfanwy, who had entered the hall bearing a ewer with steam rising from it. "You will accept an offer of water I hope. It's too late for you to ride farther on a cold day."

Helydd came in with basins and cloths. Two bright pink spots blossomed in her cheeks as she exchanged a shy smile with Lord Macsen's nephew, Rhys.

Macsen watched the two young people for a moment before he heeded Enid's question. "We would be glad of your hospitality. Warm water feels good on feet chilled from a long ride."

Enid set a basin before Lord Macsen and poured the steaming, herb-sweetened water into it. "Master Bryn finds life here a little dull by times. I promised him he could visit his friends at Hen Coed in the spring if the borders are still quiet."

Though Enid had not expected an answer from Lord Macsen, a twinge of unease stirred within her when none came.

All three of the men pulled off their boots, then let out a communal sigh as they eased their pale blue feet into the water set before them. As Enid, Helydd and Myfanwy washed and dried their guests' feet, they spoke of workaday matters—the weather, the harvest, small doings at Glyneira and Hen Coed.

Once the homely ceremony of welcome was complete, Lord Macsen rose from his seat by the fire and sauntered over to the loom.

Enid followed. "A new cloak for Bryn. I'm in a hurry to finish it before the weather grows colder."

"The color will suit him."

"Aye, if he hasn't outgrown it before I'm done." Enid

glanced toward the fire, where Rhys and Helydd sat talking. "You haven't only come to see how Glyneira is faring, have you?"

"Rhys means to ask for her." Lord Macsen pitched his voice low. "But you didn't hear of it from me."

"Helydd will say yes before he's done asking," Enid whispered back. "But you didn't hear of it from me."

"He's a good lad," Lord Macsen assured her. "I'll give him leave to stay here a few years, to help manage Glyneira until your boys are old enough."

"Gaynor will be delighted to hear it."

With the prospect of new babies at Glyneira, perhaps Gaynor would quit muttering under her breath about Enid's folly in refusing Lord Macsen's proposal.

"It will be good training for Rhys," his uncle said. "Since he'll likely be lord when I am gone."

"May that day be long in coming." Enid crossed herself. "And before it comes, I pray you'll find a wife worthy of you who will bring you many years of happiness and bear you strong sons."

The look on Lord Macsen's face made her wish she had kept quiet. He rallied quickly, though. "I also come bearing news I thought you should hear."

Something in his tone set Enid aquiver. "Con?"

Lord Macsen nodded. "Have you heard from him since we all parted at St. Mynver's?"

"Why should I?" Enid passed a hand over the soft, blue wool strung on her loom. "He's probably roistering around the Holy Land by now, having a fine time."

"He was being held by the Normans at Falconbridge."

Righteous rage blazed through Enid. "What foul dealing was that? Did they fall on him when he rode away from the abbey?"

Lord Macsen swiped his knuckles over his bearded chin. "I reckon Con may have been part of the exchange."

"This is some manner of mistake." Enid fluttered her hand, dismissing the whole preposterous idea. "Con would give up his life sooner than his freedom."

"I find it hard to credit, myself." Lord Macsen shrugged. "I think he did it for the boy. If you doubt me, ask Rhys. He was there for the talks with FitzLaurent—part of them at least. Once Con had struck a bargain to redeem Hen Coed, the Norman announced they had Bryn. After that Con negotiated in private for the boy's release. He would vouch nothing to Rhys about what it had cost."

Enid thought back to their parting at the abbey. If Lord Macsen spoke the truth, it cast all Con's words and actions from that day in a new light.

A light too bright for her to behold without flinching.

"You said Con *was* being held at Falconbridge." Enid held tight to the loom frame and forced herself to ask, "Do you know where he is, now?"

Cheer up, man! a small voice whispered in Conwy ap Ifan's thoughts as he shielded his eyes against the bright glare from a fresh fall of snow that had blanketed the borderlands. *It's Christmas, after all.*

For a fellow who'd relished any form of merriment, those twelve days of feasting and revelry had never failed to brighten the darkest time of year. During his sojourn in the Holy Land, he had celebrated with gusto, perhaps to ward off the gentle ache of homesickness that always afflicted him then. This year no amount of food, wine or music would make up for what was missing from his life.

"Don't complain, now," he chided himself. "You have plenty of plums in your pie to be thankful for."

Chief of which was his liberty. His weeks at Falconbridge had proven to Con that he could still thrive in captivity, and that had given him an additional measure of freedom…from his worst fear. Still, he never rode through the gate of his castle without giving thanks for the simple privilege of being able to come and go at will.

His castle. Just thinking those words made Con dizzier than when he stared out over the battlements at the ground below. What a sight his face must have been when the Empress had offered it to him!

"You have succeeded in your commission beyond any measure I could have hoped, Con ap Ifan." Empress Maud had brushed aside Con's sputtered thanks for ransoming him. "I begin to doubt the wisdom of loaning your services to that upstart who styles himself Prince of Edessa. If you have your heart set on it, I will honor our agreement, but I have another reward in mind that might better suit us both."

When the Empress went on to offer him a Marcher castle in Hereford, left wanting since the death of its childless lord, Rowan had fetched Con a rough nudge and muttered at him to close his mouth.

From the moment he'd lain eyes on Craig Taran, Con had felt a special affinity for the place. Straddling the border as it did, with the wild Welsh Forest of Radnor sprawled to the west and the fertile fruit orchards of Hereford spread to the east, the place reminded Con of himself, with a foot in each of two very different worlds.

It would be no easy feat, balancing between the two in the years to come, but Con warmed to the challenge. There'd be no glory in it. Perhaps he'd end up hated by both sides. Neither of those things mattered to him the way they once might have.

He would be safeguarding this tiny patch of the Marches, doing his best to keep the peace and build bridges between Norman folk and Welsh. That would be enough for him.

Well, almost enough.

"My lord!" The cry dragged Con from his musings. It took him a moment to realize *he* was the lord being hailed.

He crossed the bailey with a wary step, mindful of the treacherous slicks of ice beneath innocent dustings of snow. "What's the trouble?" he asked the guard who had called to him. Besides the Normans and the Welsh, Craig Taran also stood between two warring factions in the struggle for the English throne.

"A party of riders coming from the northwest, my lord." The report added fuel to Con's misgivings.

"Bar the gate," he ordered. "Summon bowmen to the walls."

Entering a guard tower that overlooked the castle's main entrance, Con scrambled up the narrow winding stairs.

"How many?" he demanded of the grizzled veteran on duty. His question discharged a cloud of vapor into the frosty air.

The guard wiped his dribbling nose on the sleeve of his tunic. "Less than ten, sire, and moving too slow for a war party. Do ye reckon they could be guests come for Yuletide, my lord?"

"Guests?" Con gave a mirthless chuckle as he peered in the direction of the riders making their way toward the castle.

Any other words he might have uttered froze in his throat as the party drew close enough to see clearly. The December wind blew one rider's hood back, sending a stream of long golden-brown hair flaring behind her like a proud pennant.

A girl? Myfanwy!

Con squinted so hard, his eyes ached. At the same time

he held his breath. Nearer the party came until he could no longer deny it was Enid, her children and a number of men.

While the sight of them stirred a heady sense of elation in Con's heart, another part of him would have preferred the armed warriors. His only reservation in accepting the lordship of Craig Taran from the Empress had been the fear of seeing Enid's family again.

The family that might have been his.

The watchman snuffled. "You see? It's as I said, my lord, no threat."

"No threat." Con echoed, as if he believed it.

He descended from the guard tower with halting steps. For the first time in his charming life, Con didn't know what he would say.

"Company for Christmas—this is a welcome surprise!"

Enid's heart leaped when she heard Con's voice, only to collapse into the snow at her feet when she got a good look at his face. Contrary to his hearty greeting, she and her children were as welcome here as Con had been when he'd first appeared at Glyneira in the spring.

The children would never guess it though. For that Enid was grateful. Con held his arms open to catch Myfanwy and Davy, who all but threw themselves from the horses and pelted toward him.

"Is this castle really yours, Con?" Davy's eyes grew wide as he stared around a bailey that would have held three of Glyneira's courtyard.

"Are you a Norman now?" Myfanwy asked in a wary voice.

"Yes to the first," Con informed the children. "And no to the second. You'll meet some Normans while you're here, though. Be kind and don't tease them about their teeth.''

Teeth? Enid shook her head over what was clearly a private jest between the three of them.

"What kind of host am I?" Con looked toward Enid and Bryn, his glance shying away without meeting theirs. "You must forgive me, for I've never had a place of my own to receive guests. You'll all be chilled to the bone, and me keeping you standing out in the cold bailey. Come in, warm yourselves and have something to eat."

He called out some orders in the Norman tongue. A horde of guards and servants rapidly descended on the Glyneira party, taking their baggage and leading their mounts away to be tended.

"This way." Con set off toward the main keep with Davy and Myfanwy each clinging to one of his hands.

Enid blushed at her daughter's forwardness when Myfanwy tugged on Con's sleeve, then whispered into the ear he inclined toward her.

"Here's a lady who will school me in the duties of a good host." Con chuckled. "She reminds me I must offer you water for washing your feet. My Norman servants will think it queer, but they have a Welsh master now, so they'll have to get used to Welsh ways."

A Welsh master. Enid swallowed a lump in her throat as she took Bryn's arm and made him follow the others inside. Would a man who had risen so high in the world really want a backward Welsh widow without a word of French—even if she was the love of his youth and the mother of his son?

Suddenly all the bright airy dreams she had spun since Macsen told her Con's whereabouts felt as flimsy and brittle as frozen cobwebs.

Her misgivings must have communicated themselves to

her son, for Bryn hung back. "You see?" he muttered. "I told you we shouldn't have come. Con did mean all the things he said when we parted at the abbey. About not needing the bother of minding a child."

"No." Enid tilted the boy's chin to make him look her in the eye. Con might not want her, but he must want his son. Surely he could not disdain what she prized so highly? "He only said those things because he was being taken hostage by the Normans. In exchange for your freedom. Does that not tell you his true feelings?"

Bryn answered with a wordless grumble that sounded doubtful. Howell had never been a proper father to the lad. Lord Macsen had tried, but he'd been saddled with so many other responsibilities. Con had been ignorant of Bryn's existence until a few months ago. Was it any wonder her son found it easier to believe he'd been spurned than to accept the possibility that Con had made so great a sacrifice on his behalf?

They climbed a broad staircase to an enormous room warmed by not one but two huge stone hearths. When three maidservants scurried in through a back entrance, Con fired off a rapid volley of orders in their language.

Had their new master taken one of them into his bed? As she watched the young women bob their heads and rush off to do Con's bidding, a strange heat coursed through Enid—one that owed nothing to the roaring fires in the hearths.

An old hound rose from his warm spot beside one fireplace and ambled over to Davy, his tail wagging.

"This is Vaurien." Con scratched the beast behind the ears. "He belonged to the man who used to live in this castle. Not much of a hunter anymore, but the old fellow's pleasant enough company."

Enid flinched. She didn't want Con to feel bound to her

out of pity such as he spared the old dog. When he offered
them water, perhaps she should refuse, pretending they had
only stopped here for a little refreshment before continuing
their journey.

"How is Pwyll these days?" Con asked Davy. "I'll
wager he's grown since I saw him last."

Davy gave a vigorous nod as he petted the Norman
hound. "He's almost as tall as this fellow. I wanted to
bring him with us, but Mam bid me leave him back at
Glyneira for now."

"Glyneira?" Con's head snapped up and his eyes
locked on Enid's. "Not Hen Coed?"

Dear heaven, of course! No wonder he hadn't looked
happier to see them. He must have thought...

"Not Hen Coed." Her words came out on a tremor of
frail, newborn hope.

Con left the children and the dog, walking toward her
with the stilted gait of someone abruptly wakened from a
sound sleep. His eyes had a matching vacant stare.

A pace or two from Enid, he halted. "You...didn't wed
Lord Macsen after all I went through to bring it about?"

Was he pleased or distressed by the prospect? Enid
could not tell.

A soft, seductive little voice in the back of her mind
urged her to pretend she and Macsen *had* wed, then con-
coct some story to explain her family's continued presence
at Glyneira. But she'd kept too much from Con in the past.
She would tell him the bald truth now, even if it meant
she might be spurned and humiliated.

"I did not wed Lord Macsen, fine man though he is. It
would not have been fair to him. Nor to myself."

"Stubborn woman." She had never heard Con's carefree voice as it sounded now. Did that bode well...or ill?

"So I am." A golden note of pride rang in Enid's voice.

"Stubborn enough to misbelieve what you told Bryn and me when we parted at the abbey. I have brought him here to be with you. My son needs his father, Con. And whether you will own to it or not, I think you need him even more."

Were those tears in Con's eyes, or the flood tide of an infinite blue ocean of love?

"I do own it." He turned toward Bryn and slowly extended his hand. "With all my heart. Under the same conditions, I would do no different, but I repent any hurt you took from my harsh words. I hope you'll reserve your judgment long enough to let me prove the truth of my feelings."

The boy hung back, scuffing the toe of his boot through the fresh rushes on the floor. He cast a dubious look at Con's outstretched hand, as if fearing it might ball into a fist at any moment. Then he raised a questioning glance to his mother.

And warm smile of encouragement blossomed on Enid's lips. She nodded to her son.

With halting steps, Bryn approached his father. Perhaps what he saw in Con's eyes convinced him, or perhaps he was too young and too much his father's son to have learned caution yet, for he flung himself the last few steps into Con's waiting arms.

Myfanwy and Davy left the dog and ran to their mother. It had not been easy finding the words to tell them Bryn was Con's son, but now Enid was glad she'd made herself do it.

"Will Bryn come back to Glyneira and see us sometimes, Mam?" asked Myfanwy. The child had made no secret of how much she'd enjoyed having her elder brother home from Hen Coed these past months.

Before Enid could reply, Davy piped up. "I like this place. Can I come and live here, too, with Con and Bryn?"

Though Con's arm was around his son, he gazed at young Davy with no less affection. "I would like that, if your mother can spare you."

He raised his eyes and looked deep into Enid's. "But don't you think you might get terribly homesick for her and for Myfanwy?"

The way Con said the words *terribly homesick* told Enid he didn't only mean Davy.

"I know!" Myfanwy jumped up and down. "Mam and Con can get married like Rhys and Auntie Helydd did. Then we can all live here together."

"Aren't you the clever lass." Con treated Myfanwy to a fond smile, before raising his eyes to her mother. "What do you say to your daughter's idea, *cariad?*"

Enid took a deep breath. "I say I've never stopped loving you, Con ap Ifan. I want us to be a family, and if that means following you to the ends of the earth, then I will. Wherever we are together will be home to me."

"What do you say, Con?" Bryn prompted his father.

Con's eyes had never glowed with a greater depth of feeling. "I say, my days of wandering and striving are behind me. What I want to do with my life is here. As long as I have my family with me, no place in the great world can compare with our Welsh home."

Closing the last brief space between himself and Enid, Con swept her into his arms for a kiss so intense it rivaled the heat of the hearth fires.

He stirred from it just long enough to cry, "Now summon the priest before she changes her mind!"

The children joined hands and danced circles around them, hollering "Call the priest! Call the priest!" so loud the bishop in Lichfield might have heard it.

The delicious urgency of Con's lips on hers and the touch of his hands felt as sweetly familiar as homecoming. Yet somehow Enid knew they would never fail to stir her with a sense of fresh adventure.

Only when she feared her knees might buckle beneath the weight of her desire did she part from Con just far enough and long enough to protest, ''No need for haste. We have been a lifetime coming to this, you and I. An hour, a day or a week more will make no difference. You have the best reason in the world to know my mind is not easily changed.''

Catching the end of her long braid, just as he used to do when they were children, Con tickled her cheek. ''Your mind, I know, but what of your heart, *cariad?*''

She lifted his hand to her bosom, so he could feel the joyful rhythm of it.

''For as long as it beats, it will be yours.'' The music of love flowed through her, a blithe bouncing melody wed to a deep constant harmony. ''Perhaps even longer.''

* * * * *

DEBORAH HALE

Since selling her first book to Harlequin Historicals in 1998, Deborah Hale has enjoyed hopscotching through history, from medieval England to nineteenth-century Atlantic Canada, Regency ballrooms to a Montana ranch. With every book, she invites readers to "escape to a romantic past."

Deborah lives in historic, romantic Nova Scotia with her medical physicist husband and four imaginative children. She loves to hear from readers at: P.O. Box 829, Lower Sackville, Nova Scotia B4E 2R0, Canada or through a message on her Web site, www.deborahhale.com.

If you enjoyed what you just read,
then we've got an offer you can't resist!

Take 2 bestselling love stories FREE!

Plus get a FREE surprise gift!

Escape to a land long ago and
far away when you read these thrilling
love stories from Harlequin Historicals

On Sale September 2002

A WARRIOR'S LADY
by Margaret Moore
(England, 1200s)

*A forced marriage between a brave knight and
beautiful heiress blossoms into true love!*

A ROGUE'S HEART
by Debra Lee Brown
(Scotland, 1213)

*Will a carefree rogue sweep a headstrong young lady
off her feet with his tempting business offer?*

On Sale October 2002

MY LADY'S HONOR
by Julia Justiss
(Regency England)

*In the game of disguise a resourceful young
woman falls in love with a dashing aristocrat!*

THE BLANCHLAND SECRET
by Nicola Cornick
(England, 1800s)

*Will a lady's companion risk her reputation by
accepting the help of a well-known rake?*

Harlequin Historicals®
Historical Romantic Adventure!